THE CHANCES WE TAKE

ANNELL ST. CHARLES

For Permission requests, write to:
YBR Publishing, LLC
PO Box 4904
Beaufort SC 29903-4904
contact@ybrpub.com
843-597-0912

ISBN-13: 978-1-7339992-4-3
ISBN: 1-7339992-4-8

Bill Barnier – Senior Editor, YBR Publishing
Cyndi Williams-Barnier – Production Editor, YBR Publishing
Jack Gannon- Production Manager, YBR Publishing

A MESSAGE TO THE READER

Because of my great love for the history of the coastal area of South Carolina, you will find several places in this book where I have inserted dialogue using the Gullah language. The word 'Gullah' refers to a people, their culture and their language thought to have originated in Angola, on the west coast of Africa. From the 1500s to the 1800s, thousands of West Africans were enslaved and brought to the United States to work on plantations and private settlements on the eastern Sea Islands–including Hilton Head Island. Reports indicate that as many as 20,000 enslaved Africans were brought to South Carolina by the mid-1700s. Their descendants can still be found today along what is called the 'Gullah-Geechee Cultural Heritage Corridor' which extends from North Carolina to Florida.

The use of the name 'Geechee' was adopted after many of the African slaves settled along the Ogeechee River in South Georgia. Presently, the word Gullah is used to refer to those who live in South Carolina, while Geechee indicates those who live in Georgia. The Corridor has been designated a Federal National Heritage Area to help preserve and interpret the traditional cultural practices, sites and resources associated with the Gullah-Geechee people. In this book, I refer to their descendants as 'Gullah' because the setting for the story is Hilton Head Island, South Carolina.

I became aware of the Gullah when my husband and I started making regular trips to Hilton Head beginning in the late 1980s, and finally purchased a condo there in the late '90s. The presence of the Gullah tradition on the island is evident everywhere, such as special events that tell the story of their heritage, fairs, festivals, and in shops both on and off the island, where examples of their arts and crafts are on display. Proud descendants of former slaves are often found practicing traditional ways in out-of-the-way spots like the site of Mitchelville (the original village given to freedmen who had been brought to Hilton

Head as slaves and is being restored), as well as in cemeteries such as the one I feature in this book.

My own education about the Gullah people peaked when I took part in one of the tours that are offered on Hilton Head titled the "Gullah Heritage Trail Tours". These two-hour bus tours take visitors through the lesser known parts of the island while the driver gives ongoing narrative of the past and present lives of the Gullah on Hilton Head (Irvin Campbell, whose family are direct descendants of the Gullah, was my driver).

The Gullah/Geechee language technically became known as an English-based creole language in the mid-1700s. Research has uncovered a strong connection between the Gullah language and the Krio language spoken in Sierra Leone, and was adopted by the second generation of African Americans.

Most of the letters used in Gullah have the same sounds as English words. However, there are changes in some sounds, some consonant shifts, and some sounds that are unique to Gullah, but resemble the African-American dialect.

General Rules:

- "v" is always substituted with "b"
- "th" is always substituted with "d"
- the "h" is dropped in most cases
- An apostrophe (') is used to show where a letter, word, or group of words is omitted. It can also show where two words are pronounced as one (mek'um = make them).

I have compiled a Gullah-English dictionary of words used within this novel to assist the reader with understanding the segments where I have incorporated Gullah words and phrases. The dictionary can be found at the end of the book. I encourage readers to take the time to slowly read the words as a way to better understand the uniqueness of the language and the value of the Gullah culture.

I am not a Gullah-Geechee descendent, although a recent DNA test indicated that my relatives were among those who migrated to the South Carolina coast from Ireland in the 1800s in search of a better life. I don't know if they found one, but my life has truly been enriched as a result of my exposure to this fascinating culture. I am grateful to the Gullah-Geechee community for allowing me to dip my literary toes into their history to make it an integral part of this story.

Sources:

Gullah and Mitchelville History: https://www.hiltonheadisland.org/gullah/history/

Emory S. Campbell. Gullah Cultural Legacies. Gullah Heritage Consulting Services. Hilton Head Island, S.C., 3rd edition, 2008.

Virginia Mixson Geraty. Gulluh Fuh Oonuh (Gullah For You). A Guide to the Gullah Language. Sandlapper Publishing Co., Inc. Orangeburg, South Carolina, 2006.

Irvin Campbell. The Gullah Heritage Tours. Hilton Head Island, 2017.

Althea Sumpter. Geechee and Gullah Culture. New Georgia Encyclopedia. 2006. Available at: https://www.georgiaencyclopedia.org/articles/arts-culture/geechee-and-gullah-culture.

Michael N. Danielson. Profits and Politics in Paradise. The Development of Hilton Head Island. The University of South Carolina Press, Columbia, SC. 1995.

Charles Joyner. Down by the Riverside. A South Carolina Slave Community. University of Illinois Press, Urbana and Chicago, 1985.

DEDICATION

To my dear friend and former editor, Donna Clark. Your passing has left a hole in my heart that your kindness and compassion filled. I will never forget you.

ACKNOWLEDGEMENTS

Putting one's thoughts down in writing for the world to see and react to is a daunting experience, to say the least. But it can be made easier when surrounded by love and support. I would like to recognize the following persons who comprised my support team:

Always first and foremost, my husband, Constantine (Costas) Tsinakis. Whether with loving silence or words of praise, you always boost my self-confidence and help construct an environment that allows my creative juices to flow.

My children, Sophia and Andreas. Watching you face the triumphs and tragedies of life as you have grown into adulthood has given me a deeper understanding of the challenge we all face as humans and contributed to my ability to express them through some of the characters in this novel.

My friends and unofficial editors, Mimi Pantelides, Donna Clark, and Carol Percy. I deeply appreciate the time you devoted to reading all or part of my first draft, and providing comments and corrections. I know it is not easy to give tough love to a friend, which makes it all the more special when it is offered.

The team at YBR Publishing, LLC: Bill Barnier, Cyndi Williams-Barnier, and Jack Gannon. You helped lift this previously self-published author up to the next level through your comments, examples, manuscript changes, and blunt honesty (mixed in with a welcome dose of kindness). Joining forces with you all has proven invaluable.

The members of my Nashville Book and Wine Club (in alphabetical order): Trish Blackwell, Donna Clark (now deceased), Becky Dunkley, Jill Hanson (now in Oregon but always a part of us), Joy Marcum, Emily McCluskey, Mimi Pantelides, Kathy Pedigo, Carol Percy, Susan Schipani, Judy Therber, Maureen Turnbull. Listening to your discussion of various written works for more than 20 years has helped me understand that not everyone feels the same about what they read; not everyone loves or even likes the same books; and the only true measure of a worthwhile read is that it stimulates discussion. I am honored to know all of you.

My friends who are lucky enough to spend either part or all of the year on Hilton Head Island (especially my Forest Beach Villa buddies), I hope this story brings you pleasure as it fills your mind with images of our wonderful shared paradise.

Finally, I want to express my deepest appreciation to the Gullah-Geechee descendants from Hilton Head Island and the nearby environs. Learning about your culture has broadened my awareness of how persons from different backgrounds, racial ethnicities, language, and life experiences can still connect on an organic, fundamental level. It is my hope that including parts of your history within this book will help foster a deeper understanding that we are all, ultimately, the same, on a level that matters the most.

"It is my hope that this novel will help preserve and promote the Gullah-Geechee culture on Hilton Head Island."

~Irvin Campbell
Gullah Heritage Trail Tours

CHAPTER ONE

The first time I saw Hilton Head Island I felt at home. I had never been to the coast of South Carolina. In fact, I hadn't been to any coastal town. But sometimes familiarity doesn't come from frequent contact or exposure. Sometimes it's more subtle, like the way a close friendship can shift into a deep love. My response to the island wasn't love at first sight, but something more like; "Oh it's you! I didn't realize I've been looking for you." What I felt was definitely more than just like. It was infatuation, veering in the direction of deep love, with a comforting dose of contentment found along the way.

There wasn't any logical reason for me to feel that way. I didn't grow up near the ocean, so I didn't have some nostalgic childhood memory that was stirred into motion when I arrived on those wooded shores. I hadn't seen pictures of the island that could have fueled my imagination, so Hilton Head Island wasn't even on my wish list. As far as I knew, it was just a chunk of land that lay off the coast of South Carolina and required a longer car ride, from my home in Nashville, than I cared to make. That was one of the reasons I balked at the idea when my best friend Julie suggested that my boyfriend Jon and I accompany her and her husband Harry there for a vacation trip. Well, it was that, and they had only been married for less than a year and never really had what I considered to be a bona fide honeymoon.

"You want us to go on your honeymoon with you? Are you crazy?" I remember asking her. We were sitting outside on the patio of my house in Nashville, enjoying a glass of wine on one of the few rain-free days we had experienced that March. Nashville was notorious for its yo-yo-like weather in the spring. One day the sun could be so harsh people would crank up their air conditioners and dig out their summer clothes, and the next day the clouds would move in as the temperature dropped close to freezing.

When I questioned Julie's sanity at inviting us along on her honeymoon, she just rolled her eyes and took a sip of wine. "Don't you remember we already had our honeymoon a couple of weeks after we were married? We spent a weekend at the Peabody Hotel in Memphis."

The Peabody Hotel is considered one of the south's Grand Hotels, which is one reason people come from near and far to stay there. Its true claim to fame has to do with the March of the Peabody Ducks. Back in the 1930s, the General Manager of the Hotel and one of his hunting friends, decided it would be fun to place some live ducks in the fountain in the hotel lobby. (Rumor has it that this idea came to them after they had sipped a little too much Tennessee whiskey after returning from a weekend hunting trip.) That sparked what became a long-standing tradition whereby a red carpet is unfurled each day at 11 a.m. and 5 p.m. to allow the ducks to waddle their way across the lobby to and from the fountain.

I looked at Julie with surprise. "That was your honeymoon? I thought you went there to see Graceland, since I know how crazy Harry is about all-things-Elvis."

She scrunched up her eyes as she considered what I was saying. "Well, sure. It was part of our motivation for going. But the real reason was; we hadn't had time for a honeymoon, since Harry had to be back at work two days after our wedding. You may recall we booked a cabin in the Smoky Mountains for our honeymoon. But Harry's boss suggested it might be worth his while to stay around town, because there were rumors that one of the VP's might be retiring, and Harry's name was on the short list for the job.

"Unfortunately, it turned out it was nothing more than a rumor. He didn't find out until after we cancelled our cabin in the woods which, by the way, had a hot tub on the deck overlooking the mountains, and two wood-burning fireplaces." Her face took on a wistful look. "Can you imagine sitting in a hot tub and watching the sun set over the mountains, then snuggling up in front of a fire? Let me tell you, the attraction of going to Memphis, even if there was the slightest chance we might meet Elvis, didn't come close to that."

I took a sip from my glass and picked up a piece of cheese to nibble on. "You were so disappointed when you had to cancel that trip. I guess I didn't think you considered your weekend in Memphis as an acceptable replacement." The truth was, for the past several months I had been so preoccupied with trying to figure out where my relationship with my boyfriend, Jon Barnett, was heading, I hadn't been paying much attention to what was going on with anyone else.

I first met Jon when I had been assigned to cover an event held at the Belle Meade Mansion for my job as a fledgling reporter for the Nashville News. The mansion was an impressively restored antebellum house that had been built in the mid-1800s and had originally been part of what was known in the Old South as a Plantation. Plantations at that time, relied on the use of enslaved persons to work the land, which was a practice that made me embarrassed to admit my roots. It wasn't something I wanted to acclaim, and it certainly wasn't something I wanted to write about. But it was my first writing assignment for the News, so I decided to bite the bullet and do my best. And that's what I tried to do, until I butted heads with the man who would become both the love of my life and a thorn in my side.

From the beginning, my interactions with Jon were like oil and water. We always strove to separate into our respective parts until the pot was vigorously stirred. In our case, the spoon that kept our mixture together was attached to the hand of Ida Hood.

Ida was an elderly woman who worked at the Metropolitan Historical Commission in downtown Nashville. I met her when I had gone to the MHC office at the instruction of Don Williams, my boss at the Nashville News. Jon's family was in the newspaper publishing business, and when word came out that Jon had been appointed to the Commission, Don became suspicious that the two facts were somehow connected. What followed was a long and winding road which eventually led to a major scandal that blew the lid off some shady doings involving some pretty powerful players in the local Nashville scene.

My involvement in helping to uncover what was going on had three unexpected side effects: I was fired from the newspaper, Ida Hood became a dear friend, and my relationship with Jon shifted from adversarial to cautiously aligned. That shift occurred, due in great part to the machinations of Ida. When she became aware of the smoldering attraction between Jon and me, she encouraged me to be courageous in exploring what was there. When she suddenly fell ill and died, Jon had been my anchor when I was at risk of floating away into my grief. Our relationship shifted at some point through that ordeal, and we became both lovers and friends. When I discovered she'd not only left me her house, but paid off the mortgage, it just seemed to make sense for Jon to move in with me.

Jon had been renting a small place nearby, which amounted to little more than a bed and bathroom, while he was figuring out how long he would be staying in Nashville. Once his family's publishing company decided that having a representative in Nashville was a good business move, he began to look for more desirable accommodations, prompting me to suggest he move in with me.

He had already been spending a lot of time in my house, so it wasn't too much of a stretch for him to make his stays there more official. My decision to suggest it to him was more than a little influenced by something Ida said to me a few weeks before her death.

Ida and Jon had not had an easy time relating to each other when they first met, due in no small part to the fact that they distrusted each other. Big time! Or at least that's the way things started out. Once Jon understood that Ida had not been involved in the arrangement that caused the demise of the newspaper Jon's family company had hoped to buy, he became something of a champion to her. As a result, Ida softened toward Jon. She advised me to give him another chance, after he had simultaneously stalked me, scorned me, and finally admonished me to figure out what I really wanted, before he would give me another minute of his time.

As those thoughts were swirling around in my brain, I suddenly became aware that Julie had become unusually quiet. I found her peering at me with a knowing look on her face.

"What?" I asked. "Why are you looking at me like that?" She'd always had the uncanny ability to read my thoughts, regardless of how hard I tried to hide them.

"How're things with Jon these days?"

I had confided in Julie that I wasn't totally comfortable living with Jon, or him with me, to be precise. But I hadn't really told her just how much it gnawed on me. "I'm not sure. He seems more distant lately. I think there's something on his mind that he wants to talk about, but I'm not sure what it is."

"Why don't you ask him?"

"I guess I'm afraid of what he'll say. It's like that old saying; 'what you don't know can't hurt you', though I know that's not really true. I'm not sure if it would be better to know what he's thinking, or just to stay in the dark about it."

The firm line of her mouth told me which of the two she thought would be better, but she refrained from stating the obvious. Instead, she finished the last sip of her wine and stood. "Well, maybe this trip is exactly what both of you need; a change of scenery and the chance to relax. It could help you shake free of whatever is holding you both back from saying what's on your mind."

She reached down to rub the tummy of my cat, Ebie. Ebie was stretched out in a patch of sunlight on the patio next to where we were sitting. She had been with me since she was a kitten, and I sometimes stared in disbelief at how big she had grown during the year and a half we had been together.

Julie stood and looked at me pointedly. "Just think about it. That's all I'm asking. The four of us could have a lot of fun."

I followed her into the kitchen, carrying my half empty glass. "Okay. I'll see what Jon thinks about the idea."

We sat the glasses on the kitchen counter and headed up the hallway toward the front door. Julie turned to face me. "You might want to figure out what you think about it first. If I know Jon, if he senses the least bit of hesitation in you, he'll latch on to that as an excuse to say no."

I nodded my agreement. "You're probably right. I'll call you tomorrow."

She gave me a quick hug, then headed down the front walk to where her car was parked. As she opened the car door, she glanced over her shoulder in my direction. "Don't wait too long. I can hear the beach calling!" A grin split her face as she wiggled her fingers at me.

I smiled, waved goodbye, and sat for a few minutes on the front steps before heading back inside. I leaned back and turned my face up to the early evening sun, closing my eyes as its warmth caressed me and brought Julie's offer back into focus. A trip to the beach, I thought. That might be interesting. At least it would be something new to do, and a chance to get away with Jon to maybe find out what was going on in his head.

I glanced at my watch and was surprised to see it was almost five o'clock. Jon would be home soon. I decided I had just enough time to run upstairs for a shower. Maybe I would even put on that new sundress I bought the previous summer and not yet had a chance to wear. When I'd tried it on in the store, I thought it made me look kind of sexy, and sexy was something that always made Jon smile. It certainly couldn't hurt to give him something to smile about when he came home. Nope. Couldn't hurt at all!

CHAPTER TWO

A couple of months later, two months and three days to be precise, the four of us and all of our luggage were comfortably tucked into Julie's dad's sedan on our way to Hilton Head Island. We opted to take his car when it became clear that there was no way four people, a suitcase for each of us, two briefcases carrying work that Harry and Jon felt they couldn't leave behind, a cooler, and a cat carrier could fit into Harry's pickup truck, Jon's convertible, or my VW bug. It was clearly the right choice, which Jon pointed out more than once as he and Harry struggled to fit everything into the trunk of the car. Yet, even with the extra space, it was still a tight fit, only possible because the cooler and the cat carrier were wedged into the back seat between Jon and me.

We decided to leave Nashville as soon as the first signs of daylight began to brighten the sky, which meant we were well on our way before the clock even got close to 7:00 a.m. That was fine with me. I used to love to sleep in whenever possible, but since Jon and I had been living together, I routinely awoke even before sunrise, enjoying the quiet of the early morning to read or just linger over my first cup of coffee before Jon began to stir around the house. He was more of a night owl, preferring to spend his alone-time in the late night or very early morning hours. It was a difference that worked for us, and a pattern that we had quickly fallen into.

"At least the rain held off." Julie said from the front seat. "I hate driving on the interstate in the rain. When those big trucks speed by, it always feels as if they're going to blow us off the road. The rain makes it worse."

We had just passed Murfreesboro and were heading down Interstate 65 toward Chattanooga. "What time do you think we'll make it to Hilton Head?" I asked.

"Let's see. Gran said it takes about five or six hours from Atlanta, and we're at least three and a half or four hours from there." She held up her arm so she could study her watch. "That means we should arrive around four or four-thirty this afternoon."

Jon cleared his throat. "It'll be more like five or after. We enter a new time zone just outside of Chattanooga, so we'll lose an hour." He glanced in my direction. "That depends, of course, on how many times we stop along the way." Jon knew I was not fond of siting for long periods of time, which for me was anything longer than an hour. The idea of being stuck in a moving vehicle for most of the day was not a welcomed prospect.

I shifted in my seat in an effort to get a little more comfortable. "Well, I'm sure we'll stop for lunch, and I'll have to take Ebie out a few times."

Ebie made a sound like a grumble when she heard her name. She wasn't any happier at the prospect of being trapped inside her carrier for long periods of time, than I was being stuck in the car.

Julie looked over her shoulder with a smile. "We don't have to worry about lunch. I made a ton of sandwiches, and there are drinks in the cooler. We can grab something whenever we get hungry."

"Great." I said, although that sentiment was the opposite of what I felt.

Jon winked at me. “Julie, why don’t you tell us what you know about Hilton Head Island? Maybe that’ll help distract Georgia.”

“Sure! Gran said the island is shaped like a foot. The bridge that goes there crosses at the ankle, and the house we’ll be staying in is located in an area called Sea Pines Plantation which covers the entire south end of the island, from the instep to the toe.”

The Belle Meade Mansion came to mind. “Why do they call it a plantation, since there are no longer slaves working there?”

I didn’t think to ask why it’s called that, but once we get there, I’m sure we can find out. Gran has never been to Hilton Head Island, but she said her friends described it as paradise. The name Sea Pines comes from the fact that it’s bordered by water on all sides and covered with lots of tall pine trees. Apparently, the governing bodies on the island have made a real effort to retain as much of the natural beauty as possible.”

Jon grimaced at her description. “So, it’s partly undeveloped?”

“I don’t know. She mentioned there are several restaurants there, and some hotels. There’s also a pretty famous golf course that wraps around an area called Harbour Town. That’s at the toe end.”

Harry’s head swiveled in her direction. “A golf course, huh? Cool. Too bad we didn’t have room for our clubs, Jon. Maybe they’ll have a place we can rent some.”

Jon told me he’d spent a lot of time as a teenager accompanying his dad on golf outings. Apparently, mixing golf and business was a common practice in his line of work, which involved publishing newspapers and pretty much anything else that showed up in print. His dad wanted Jon to learn first-hand how to fit the two together. As a result, Jon had developed a strong dislike for the sport. When Harry had spotted Jon’s clubs tucked into a corner of our laundry room, he convinced him to play a few times, but from the look on Jon’s face, it didn’t seem like his opinion of golf had mellowed any. I decided to try to change the subject.

"I'll bet they have some nice beaches there." I said.

Julie nodded vigorously. "Yeah! Gran said there's a beach just in front of the house where we're staying. Apparently, her friends lucked out and bought the place when the price of an oceanfront lot was still pretty low. I only saw one picture of the house, but from what I could tell, it's pretty amazing."

We all grew quiet at that point. My mind was full of questions about the history of the island, and why anyone would choose to call part of it a plantation. For me, that name had such a negative connotation it was hard to shake the image of slave owners and the people who were forced to work for them. Having grown up in the 1960s when the Civil Rights Movement was in full swing, I was extra sensitive about anything that hinted of racial unfairness. In this case, all I could hope was the use of the word plantation meant something else entirely.

I turned my head to stare out the window, reminding myself that we were going on vacation. Vacations were meant to be relaxing, happy times. Julie had been kind enough to invite us to share this trip with her and Harry. It was the least I could do to set aside my concerns until I could sort out the facts from the fantasies crowding their way into my mind. I vowed to use my experience as a newspaper reporter to eventually figure it all out. But for now, my worries could wait.

Ebie mewed insistently as she stood, and began to stir around in her carrier. "Hey, girl. Do you need a bathroom break? Harry, I think we'd better find a place to stop soon, so I can take Ebie out."

His eyes twinkled as they caught mine in the rear-view mirror. "Sure thing, Georgia. I guess the rest of us could use a stop, too."

He drove a couple more miles down the road to the next exit and pulled into the lot of a gas station. Everyone piled out of the car and headed off in the direction of the shop attached to the station. I grabbed Ebie's carrier and walked toward a grassy strip on the side of the building. Luckily, I trained Ebie to walk with a harness when she was just a kitten so I would be able to take her outside without her sprinting away.

Although most of the time she was what you'd call a "housecat", she quickly learned to associate the harness with the chance to sniff and squat in real grass instead of her litter box. That would be a saving grace on the long trip down, since it meant I could let her "do her business" at road stops instead of stinking up the car. I carefully opened the door of her carrier just wide enough for me to attach a leash to the harness before leading her outside.

"There you go, girl." She sniffed the grass before choosing a spot. "Just between you and me, your timing was perfect. I don't think I could have managed to stay in that car another second without screaming." I walked her around for a few minutes then returned her to the carrier, lifting it so I could place it on the seat of the car. The temperature inside the car was even worse than outside. I wiped my brow as I considered how I was going to take a bathroom break myself without leaving Ebie to roast in the heat. I looked around to see if any of the others were nearby and spotted Jon just emerging from the station. "Hey Jon. Can you stay with Ebie for a minute so I can hit the restroom?"

He nodded and made his way in our direction. "I meant to grab a Snickers bar before I left. Will you get me one?"

I grinned at his unlikely request. Jon didn't have much of a sweet tooth, but he had grown fond of Snickers since I usually kept a bag of them in the kitchen cabinet. "Sure thing. Guess I'll get one for myself too." I made my way across the pavement toward the station, stopping to give him a brief kiss as we passed. Jon had always been something of an enigma to me. There was a part of him that always felt just out of reach, which both frustrated and puzzled me. That was why, when he did something ordinary as asking for a candy bar, it made me feel warm and fuzzy.

I guess that was what Ida meant when she told me once that loving someone didn't mean they always made you happy. It just meant that sometimes you were happy being with them in spite of themselves. It was one of the rare times when I coaxed her to talk about her early life, and she shared that she'd once been deeply in love with a man who'd died in the war. She described their relationship as "a topsy-turvy bundle of emotions that ran the gamut from ecstasy to despair."

I was struggling to sort out my feelings toward Jon at the time, and she shared this tidbit of insight with me as encouragement that things didn't have to be perfect to be good. It made me feel better to hear her say that, though it didn't really take away my concern. Jon was a puzzle, albeit an enticing one. But like all puzzles, I chose to believe that one day, all of the pieces would fall into place.

CHAPTER THREE

The rest of the ride passed uneventfully. It was long, and the last part of the trip seemed to take forever as we made our way down a mostly deserted stretch of Interstate 16 that ran between Macon and Savannah. When we finally turned off I-16 onto I-95 North, I was practically squirming in my seat. "How far is it now?" I asked.

Harry shook his head and smiled. "You've held up pretty well, Georgia. I half expected you to demand that we let you out somewhere along the road so you could walk the rest of the way."

I made a face at his reflection in the rear-view mirror.

"According to the map, we'll be exiting from the interstate in a few miles. Then we travel along a two-lane road for 40 miles or so until we get to a bridge. It shouldn't take much more than an hour to get to that point, and once we cross the bridge, we're on the island."

Another hour! I sighed and looked over at Jon. The lucky man had been sleeping for a large part of the drive, which was something I'd never been able to do in a car. In between naps, he traded driving shifts with Harry. Now, he was looking rested, and there was even a slight grin on his face.

"Harry, you need to understand, for Georgia, an hour sounds like torture. The next time she asks you, just tell her we're almost there." Jon gave me a smug look, prompting me to punch him playfully on the arm.

Julie turned in my direction, and handed me a few brochures. "Take these, Georgia. I picked them up at that last rest stop. I've been looking through them and there's one about the history of Hilton Head Island."

I flipped through them quickly. One seemed to be about the wildlife on the island. Another advertised one of the hotels that was recently completed. A third caught my eye immediately. It was called The Hidden History of Hilton Head. I eagerly began to read.

"It says here that one of the developers of Hilton Head was a man named Charles Fraser who actually created Sea Pines Plantation, where we're going to be staying. Mr. Fraser realized that people from places like Ohio, Pennsylvania, and New York made up a large percentage of the tourists who were looking for beachy vacation spots with easy access from Interstate 95. He even put together what was called the *Ohio Strategy* which involved running a ton of ads in cities like Cincinnati, Columbus, Cleveland, and Toledo in an effort to attract visitors to Hilton Head."

Julie piped up. "You know, my grandparents live in Cincinnati, and some of their friends, like the people who're loaning us their house, visited Hilton Head during that time. They ended up buying lots there because they were well-priced. At least that was true when the island was first being developed. After that, the prices started rising fairly quickly until Hilton Head Island, like most of the rest of the United States, was hit by this recession we're in now."

Harry nodded vigorously from the driver's seat. "We had a meeting at the bank a while back where they brought in some special advisors to explain what we should know about the recession and how the bank may be impacted. Apparently, they call what we're in now a 'stagflation', short for a stagnant inflation. That's where prices are inflated during a recession, and as the interest rates increase, the demand for housing plummets which causes a great real estate collapse. Unfortunately, that combination is causing a lot of people to lose their homes."

Harry was the branch manager at the First National Bank in Nashville where Julie's father worked. It almost resulted in his ruin after he agreed to serve as a pawn in an FBI investigation into the illegal activities of two brothers who had succeeded in committing fraud in several banks in Alabama and were working their way into Tennessee. I grimaced at the memory of those events and at his description of what was currently happening in real estate. I was lucky I was able to live in the house in Nashville that Ida had left me in her will. Yet, even though Ida made sure there was no mortgage for me to worry about, the idea that something could happen to force me to sell it, caused my breath to catch. I leaned forward so I could address Harry. "Why are people losing their houses? Could that happen to me?"

He shook his head. "Not unless you've taken out a second mortgage on your place, which I know you haven't. What's been happening is that many people bought houses they couldn't afford, and as the mortgage rates have risen, they're finding themselves with payments that are above their means. The other thing that's going on is that prices are being slashed on houses that are up for sale, and there are no new houses being built because the demand has gone down. It's what the realtors call neither a buyer nor sellers' market, which means disaster for the industry, and homelessness for a lot of folks."

Julie patted Harry on the shoulder. "Oh, let's don't think about all of that now. Let's leave bank business behind and enjoy this new adventure we're on."

Harry nodded at her and lifted her hand to kiss. "Good idea. I'm ready for a vacation."

Jon glanced sideways at me with a smirk on his face and a small shake of his head. I knew him well enough to know that look meant he found their optimism trying. I smiled back cheerfully, hoping he would keep an open mind to the trip. It had been a bit of a tough sell to convince him to come along. Jon was basically a loner by nature, so the idea of spending a day, much less an entire week, with two other people wasn't something that thrilled him. It was only because he genuinely liked Julie and Harry, and was excited about our being away together, that caused him to reluctantly agree to the trip.

I leaned forward and slapped Harry on the shoulder. "I couldn't agree more, Harry. A vacation is just what we all need." Jon had not stopped staring at me, and his eyes grew darker as the intensity of his gaze deepened. He leaned across the seat so he could whisper in my ear.

"That's not all we need." He pushed my hair aside and kissed my neck. His kiss sent a tingle through my entire body, and made me wish we were already settled into our vacation place.

We finally turned off the interstate and were making our way at what felt like a snail's pace along a two-lane road. The route was scenic, if you liked looking at moss-covered trees, ramshackle houses, and the occasional boiled peanut stand, which I did. But the approach did nothing to dissuade Jon from believing we were heading into the wilds.

Jon had spent most of his life living near Washington, D.C. before he relocated to Nashville. His move to Nashville had been a major change for him, motivated in large part by our budding relationship. Agreeing to a vacation in South Carolina presented an even greater challenge to his notion of what comprised a civilized life.

In Jon's opinion, South Carolina was even more foreign than Tennessee, owing to his experience in the D.C. metropolis. The entire state was sparsely developed and had the reputation for being a hotbed of staunch conservatives, bigots, and evangelical fanatics. At least that's what he made a point of telling the rest of us during the drive from Nashville.

Jon's contention was that at least Tennessee had Nashville to set it apart from the more conservative sectors of the rest of the state, whereas South Carolina had nothing similar to distinguish it from the image of the South that was engrained in his mind. Having never set foot in any part of South Carolina, the rest of us were unprepared to offer any evidence in its defense.

I hoped what I shared about Hilton Head Island from the pamphlet helped reassure Jon that his fears were unwarranted. After all, if the people who took on the task of developing the island had set their sights on attracting visitors from as many Northern states as possible, didn't that mean that Hilton Head was likely to be different from other parts of the South? Having grown up as a Southerner, I wasn't sure if that was a good thing or not, but I hoped it might give Jon a more positive outlook on the place. Unfortunately, the grim look on his face suggested otherwise.

I followed the direction of Jon's stare and noticed that he was watching a man riding in a wooden cart pulled by a mule. The back of the cart was piled high with bushel baskets filled with an assortment of produce. The man wore a battered straw hat that shaded his dark face. He glanced up at us as we passed, lifting one hand in greeting. I returned his wave.

Jon turned to look at me. "If Hilton Head looks anything like this place, it should be interesting." His words implied optimism, but the frown on his face said otherwise.

Julie looked back at us happily. "Yeah. Maybe we'll see an alligator! That wildlife pamphlet I handed you said there are a lot of them around here."

My eyes widened with alarm. "Are you serious? That sounds scary!"

She shrugged her shoulders. "Oh, don't worry. I don't imagine they're any more interested in coming face to face with us than we are with them. But I think it would be fascinating to see one up close."

"Just not too close," I replied.

I settled back against the seat and frowned as the image of a six-foot prehistoric lizard filled my mind. That's what my biology teacher in high school called alligators: 'prehistoric lizards'. Actually, the more I thought of them in that way, the less scary they became. They were just like the little lizards that skittered across the patio behind my house in Nashville and drove Ebie nuts as she tried to catch one. Only these were a lot bigger.

I shook my head to clear the image of giant lizards and began to hum a little tune that had been running through my head for the past several miles.

"What's that song you're humming?" Julie asked.

"I don't know. But I can't get it out of my head."

Harry glanced at me in the rear-view mirror. "It's called 'Under the Boardwalk'. A group called The Drifters recorded it."

"Hunh. Well, I must have heard it somewhere, because it keeps going around and around in my head."

"I can see why. It's all about the beach, the sun, and dancing." He proceeded to launch into a raucous rendition of the song. Pretty soon Julie and I were both swaying to the music and joining him on the chorus. Even Jon, who usually avoided anything that remotely resembled dancing, began to tap his foot to the beat.

I grinned at him, and was pleased to see him return my smile. Things were looking up! I felt hopeful we were about to embark on a great adventure.

CHAPTER FOUR

Harry had been right when he said we had about an hour left before we would reach the island. After exiting the two-lane road that meandered through the town of Bluffton, we drove a few miles along Highway 278 until we arrived at the steel swing bridge that crossed the expanse of water separating us from Hilton Head Island.

A few cars were lined up in front of us, waiting to enter the bridge. The sun was low in the sky, causing the water to sparkle with thousands of little lights. Green shoots of marsh grass protruded from the surface in patches and were undulating gently in the breeze. A few boats were visible in the distance, and several fishermen were standing along the bank with their poles bent in pursuit of the fish swimming unseen below the surface.

"It's beautiful!" I said, and I'm home, I thought. I wasn't ready to say those words out loud. Calling a place I'd never been before "home" made no sense at all, but that was how it felt to me. Home.

Harry ducked his head and looked in the direction of the fishermen. "I wonder what kind of fish are in these waters?"

"I imagine there are sharks. Ever caught a shark, Harry?" Jon caught Harry's eyes in the rear-view mirror.

"Can't say that I have, Jon. They're probably pretty tasty though," Harry replied with a grin. Harry was a good match for Jon's droll sense of humor.

The four of us climbed out of the car to wait for the bridge to open, making sure to roll down the windows before we left, so Ebie would stay comfortable. I walked to the nearest embankment so I could see what was happening. The bridge was made out of some type of metal with rounded spires that rose cylindrically from one side to the other. The middle of the bridge rested on thick concrete supports stuck into the land below the water at the center of the span. It was what was called a swing bridge because it was designed to pivot open by rotating 90 degrees in a clockwise direction whenever a boat needed to pass, then swing back into place to allow cars to cross the expanse. The swing action was controlled by an operator who stood in a control house above the roadway in the middle of the bridge. I was standing on the bank of the river watching the bridge as it swung open when Julie walked up beside me.

"Gran's friends said the swing bridge has made a huge difference to the island. Before it was here, the only way to get to Hilton Head was on a ferry boat that would slowly cover the quarter mile between Buckingham Landing on the Bluffton side, and Jenkins Island on the other. I read in one of those pamphlets I showed you that Jenkins Island is surrounded by marshland that lies between two creeks-Skull and Jarvis. Back then, when cars exited the ferry, they had to travel along a narrow dirt road across the marsh in order to reach Hilton Head Island. The road was prone to being washed out when the tide was especially high, which made the task of getting to Hilton Head iffy at best."

I looked out at the water in front of me and tried to imagine where the ferry would have crossed. From what I could tell, there were actually two bridges that allowed safe passage to

Hilton Head. The first solid span stopped at a small island in the middle of the channel where the control house was located, and the second, which contained the swinging portion, started at the other side of the island and ended on what I guessed was Hilton Head. In the distance, I could just make out a sailboat passing through the opening created when the operator swung the second bridge sideways.

"I can see two bridges," I remarked to Julie.

Jon and Harry joined us. "You're right, Georgia." Jon pointed toward the entrance to the second bridge. "I wonder what that body of land is in the middle."

A woman standing nearby volunteered the answer. "That's Pinckney Island. It used to be a huge plantation for indigo and cotton. It's been pretty neglected recently, but word has it the owners have donated it to the Fish and Wildlife Service. It's supposedly going to be used as a National Wildlife Refuge starting next year."

"Cool. Is it possible to visit?" Julie inquired.

"Not right now. But after they finish setting it up, it will be open to the public. My understanding is there will be picnic facilities, bike paths, and guided tours. I'm really happy it's going to be preserved."

Harry glanced toward the swing bridge, which had begun to move back into place. "Hey everybody, it looks like the bridge is about to open."

After we were settled in the car again, I glanced at Ebie who was standing in her carrier with her nose in the air, sniffing intently. When she saw me, she butted her head against the cage with a grunt.

"Hey, sweet girl. I guess you smell the fish." I poked my fingers in the cage and scratched her head. "Maybe we can find you some for dinner." She made a sound in her throat that was a cross between a groan and a grumble before collapsing in a heap on the towel I had used to cushion the floor of the carrier. "I know. It's been a long day, but we're almost there." She narrowed her eyes at me with what I could only assume was skepticism.

Jon had been watching our exchange with a half-smile. He and Ebie had become best buddies since we began living together. In fact, he was the one who convinced me to bring her along on the trip by pointing out that she would be too lonely without us around for an entire week. He surprised me at times by saying something so sweet it caused a catch in my breath.

The car jerked slightly as Harry shifted into gear in order to keep pace with the others that were now moving across the bridge. The bridge ended on a dirt road leading to a two-lane paved road, which stretched out in what I guessed was an easterly direction, since the setting sun was to our backs. A few simple houses were scattered along the road, interspersed with wide stretches of marshland that allowed a glimpse of the water on either side. The land around the houses had patches of sandy soil that appeared to have been neatly raked. The rest of the yards were covered in a dense layer of dark green grass with broad, flat blades. Tall trees with long, grayish trunks topped with fan-shaped leaves rose from the grass in several spots, and at least every third yard featured a large and sprawling oak tree that dripped silvery gray moss from its branches.

Most of the houses we passed had a prominent front porch where well-worn rocking or ladder-back chairs had been placed haphazardly across sagging expanses. Chickens were roaming freely around the yards pecking at the dirt, and I spotted a couple of dogs dozing in the shade of one of the trees.

A short distance up the paved road I noticed a handmade sign that advertised the availability of local shrimp, tomatoes, and watermelon “up ahead”. Soon, I began to notice the rundown shacks gave way to an assortment of businesses that suggested we had arrived at a more developed part of the island.

Julie pointed at a small market that sat off to the left side of the road. A sign over the door read “Henry’s Store.”

“I’m hungry. Maybe we should stop here and see if they have anything we can use for dinner.”

"Sounds like a good idea," Harry offered. "Maybe they'll have some of those shrimp the signs were advertising." He pulled to a stop.

The four of us eagerly stepped out onto the gravel drive and looked around. Jon took a couple of steps forward and stopped. "I suppose it's too much to expect that they might sell liquor. I wish I had remembered to bring some with me."

I ambled up beside him and looped my arm through his. "Why don't you go find out? I'm going to take Ebie out for a few minutes, then I'll join you." I hooked the harness around her middle and carried her over to a grassy spot nearby. After I returned her to her carrier, I decided to take it with me rather than risk leaving her in the hot car. I sat it on the front porch in a patch of shade and went into the market.

Harry, Jon, and Julie were standing at the checkout counter looking expectantly at a man who sat behind it on an old metal stool. His cap was adorned with an assortment of fishing lures and his coal dark face had a dried and weathered look, like someone who spent a lot of time outdoors.

"Ebenin' folks. Welcome tuh 'enry's sto'. Uh 'enry." His face spread into a wide grin.

Julie took a step forward. "We just arrived, and we're hoping to find something we can have for dinner. Do you have any shrimp?"

He shook his head slowly. "Sol' 'w'ile back. Boy din' ketch 'nuf dis mawnin'. 'E cyas net bruk. Gi'we 'nuf croaker, 'do. Uh kin clean dem fo' oonuh 'speshly."

Julie stood with her jaw slack in complete confusion, trying to decipher the strange speech.

Harry, taking it in stride, nodded eagerly. "That would be great. Eight filets if you can spare that much."

Henry rose slowly from the stool. His back was slightly bent and his feet shuffled a bit when he walked. "Tek leetle mo' time tuh git roun' dan nyuse tuh. Dis ole body jis' luk tuh remin' uh yent 'zackly young as uh wuz." He nodded toward the front of the store. "Some t'ings obuh dey oonuh migh' lukkuh. Fresh maters, snap beans, cawn, few taters." His eyes settled on us for a second before he slapped the top of a large metal box that sat next to the counter. "Hab col' one wile oonuh wait'n'. Uh back tuhreckly."

Jon and Harry immediately pushed open the sliding top. Harry's face broke into a wide grin. "Beer!" He pulled out four bottles, popping off the tops on an opener built into the front of the box.

Jon frowned at his before taking a careful swallow, then shrugged his acceptance. "Better than nothing, I guess." He took another swig and wandered off in the direction of a shelf holding an assortment of tools interspersed with canned goods.

The rest of us spread out to explore what else the store had to offer. It was a small room, but every conceivable space was crammed with an impressive assortment of food and household goods. We each began collecting things that appealed to us before returning to stack them on the check-out counter. Julie chose peanut butter, jelly, bread, and a box of doughnuts that she put on the counter. I placed two bags of potato chips next to her items, adding a roll of bologna and some bacon I fished out of the beer cooler.

I hesitated over a can of tuna with Ebie in mind, but decided she could manage with the bag of dried kibble I brought until I was able to find a store with canned cat food. Plus, there were sure to be some fish scraps left over from our dinner that would suit her just fine.

Harry contributed hotdogs, buns, ketchup, mustard, two lemons, a lime, a half dozen tomatoes, and four ears of corn. Only Jon returned empty handed. I eyed him curiously.

"Couldn't find anything you liked?" I asked.

"Nope. No booze in the entire place, except for this beer." He reached into the metal cooler and pulled out three six packs. "I guess this will have to do for now." I could see his expression had taken on the same wariness I'd noticed as we'd made our way through Bluffton.

Henry returned from the back of the store carrying a brown paper-wrapped bundle tied with string. He eyed the rest of the items we had collected. "Hab sty'foam cooluh fo' col' t'ings. Oonuh kin drap it tuh sto' w'en leabe de i'lun'."

Jon stepped forward and opened his wallet. "Just add the cost of it to whatever else we owe you."

Henry squinted at Jon with a look that was both curious and perplexed, studying his face intently. "Fin' eb'ryt'ing look fuh?"

"I was hoping you might have a bottle of Scotch."

Henry chuckled. "Lukkuh man know wha' 'e wan'! Not 'low tuh sell 'e een de sto'. Fin' ankyhall tuh de ABC sto' uhhead'uh way on de big road. Dey cya' wiskey an odduh t'ings. Hab big boddles, too." When we all looked at him blankly, he continued. "Free-pour ain't lawful een dis stet. Mos' place sell een dem leetle half-ass boddles dat hol' 'bout one tas'e. Cos' tummuch luk dat."

Jon nodded. "Thanks for the advice. How much do we owe you?"

Henry laid the handwritten sales slip on the counter and Jon glanced at it before placing several bills on top. Henry opened the cash register and counted out his change. "Ef don' min' uh ax, weh oonuh stay yuh?"

Julie spoke up. "My grandparents' friends own a house in a place called Sea Pines. They offered us a week's stay there as a belated wedding present." Her eyes sparkled as she glanced at Harry.

Henry's eyes moved from Julie to Harry before turning to Jon and me. "Dat nice fuh true. Mek 'cajun tuh bizzet wid oonuh fren's."

Julie's face flushed slightly. "Well, it's not really our honeymoon. We already had one of those. It's just a nice vacation."

Henry nodded agreeably then pulled out a scrap of paper and a pencil. He jotted something down before handing it to Harry. "Dis de numbuh cuz'n Cha'lee. 'E tek 'e pledjuh fuh fish. Hab boat tuh Broa' Crick.'E bog de maa'sh fuh oshtuh; ketch fish wid 'e pole. Mos' time, 'e pull een big ketch. Ax'um ef wan' mo' fresh fish."

Harry looked at the paper eagerly. "Does he ever take other people out fishing with him?"

Henry bobbed his head up and down. "De boat him'own. 'Spect 'e glad fuh hab de cump'ny."

Harry grinned happily and began collecting the bags. Just before leaving the store, I turned back to Henry.

"I hope you don't mind me asking, but I noticed that you have an unusual accent. Where are you from originally?"

Henry's eyes sparkled as he considered my question. "Wuh oonuh yeddy be de Gullah langwidge. Uh fambly tek f'um Aff'iky een big boat. Dey wu'k as slabes b'fo' de gubmunt leh dem free. Dishyuh i'lun hab fus' freedmun billige. 'Preciate oonuh ax'um. Uh proud weh cum f'um. Proud 'gen weh uh lib. Pa wu'k haa'd fuh mek uh libbin' tuh 'low we hab 'nuf bittle fa'm weh tuh lib. 'E laa'n me fuh do'um luk 'e."

His words were challenging to understand, but I could make out enough of what he was saying to be intrigued. I felt drawn to this strange man. Strange only in the sense of being different from what I was used to. I felt an urge to plop myself down on a stool next to him and learn more about his life, but I knew the others were anxious to leave. I thanked him and made my way out the door.

Once we loaded the car with our purchases, we headed in the direction of the ABC store, stopping to pick up some Johnnie Walker, Gin, Tonic water, and a couple of bottles of white wine. The beer we'd bought at Henry's would do fine for when we were lazing around on a hot afternoon, but once evening came, something more festive was called for.

The atmosphere in the car had lifted considerably after our stop at Henry's store. Perhaps it was the beer that lifted our moods, or the anticipation of what was waiting for us down the road. All I knew was; for the first time since we had left Nashville, Jon looked happy and relaxed, and it was a sight that filled me with optimism. But just as I began to allow happy thoughts to fill my head, my stomach clenched in alarm.

"Ebie! Where's Ebie?"

The mood in the car took a quick downturn as the realization of what had happened sank in.

"We left her at Henry's store! Harry, you have to get back there as fast as you can." We all hopped in the car as Harry turned on the ignition and sped off down the road. No one spoke a word as we stared out the window at the miles that lay between us and the small store where I had left Ebie behind. We were just reaching the last stretch that would take us to our destination when I felt the car slowing down.

"Why are you stopping Harry? We're not there yet."

"There's a police car behind us with its lights on."

The three of us turned to look out the back window as Harry slowly pulled to the side of the road, followed closely by a black and white car with the words "Beaufort County Sheriff's Department" emblazoned on the side and a round blue light flashing from the middle of the roof.

"Oh crap. We must have been speeding." Harry said. "We're in trouble now."

"Everybody just stay calm." Jon instructed.

We watched as the officer got out of his car, hitching up the heavy belt that held his holstered weapon and a radio. He leaned down and peered into the backseat windows, glancing purposefully at the bag sitting between Jon and me. Harry rolled down his window as the officer approached his door.

"I'll need your license and registration."

Harry reached across Julie to open the glove compartment, fishing out a card before retrieving his wallet from his back pocket. "Is there a problem, officer?"

"Not unless you consider driving fifteen miles over the speed limit a problem. Which, I do." His eyes scanned the documents before roaming over the rest of us. "You folks visiting from Tennessee?" Looks like you couldn't wait to load up at our ABC store as soon as you arrived. Guess you were in a big hurry to dig into that bag." He gestured to the one sitting on the floor in the backseat.

I leaned forward so I could see his face. "It's my fault, officer. We stopped at that little store back up the road when we first arrived, and I'm afraid I left my cat sitting on the porch. I was so afraid of what might have happened to her that I pleaded with Harry to hurry back. It's just a short distance up that way." I pointed up the road ahead of us.

I couldn't make out his expression because his eyes were hidden behind a pair of dark sunglasses, but I noticed the edges of his mouth curl slightly. "You must be talking about Henry's store."

I nodded eagerly. "That's the one. We bought some things there and left the cat carrier behind. I'm so worried about her."

He nodded slightly as he stepped back and studied Harry's license before handing it and the registration back to him. "I'm going to have to write you a ticket for speeding. You can stop over at the Sheriff's Department in Bluffton sometime before you leave and take care of it." He pulled a ticket pad out of his rear pocket and scribbled something on it before tearing off a sheet and handing it to Harry. "Just so there's no misunderstanding, we don't take kindly to visitors driving recklessly on our island, especially when they obviously have a fondness for alcohol."

"Thank you officer. I promise we'll be on our best behavior while we're here." Harry tucked away the two cards and waited for the officer to return to his car. A few minutes later both cars were pulling into the parking lot of Henry's.

"It's gone. The carrier was right over there but now it's missing." I pointed to the left side of the porch before yanking open the car door. I ran to the front door and rushed inside. My eyes scanned to the left and right of the small space before settling on Henry who was perched on the stool behind the counter, a black fury ball evident against the white of his shirt.

Henry looked up at me with a gentle smile. "'Spect oonuh tuhreckly. Fin' dis leetle t'ing un de po'ch. T'ink 'e hongry so g'em sum dat croaker. Now us frens." Ebie squinted at me and stretched her legs before settling back against Henry with a purr, cleaning her face with a paw.

I felt a great relief wash over me as I took in the sight of the two of them. "Thank you so much for taking care of her. I can't believe I left her behind."

Henry glanced behind me. "Dat dere Offuhsuh Ben?"

The police officer had entered the store behind me, followed by Jon, Harry and Julie. He removed his hat and twirled it in his hands. "Hey, Henry. What 'cha got there?"

Henry looked at me. "Wha' 'e call?"

"Ebie. Short for Ebony."

He looked down at Ebie as his hand stroked her head and ran down her back. "Suit 'e. Purty gal."

He lifted her up and held her out to me. "Bes' go tuh oonuh mammy."

I took her from Henry and cradled her in my arms, rubbing my chin against the soft warmth of her head.

Henry looked at Officer Ben curiously. "Why oonuh wid dese folks?"

The officer flipped his hat another couple of times before placing it on his head. "'Fraid I had to write them a speeding ticket. They was going 45 in a 30 mph zone." He looked at Ebie with a shake of his head. "My wife would never forgive me for slowing them down if anything had happened to that one. Truth be told, I'm a mite partial to cats, too. It's a good thing you were here to look after her."

Henry seemed to consider what he was saying as he slowly nodded. "Sum'time hab tuh do sum'n' don' seem rite." His eyes turned to mine again. "Dis time, 'e 'low'um see ohnuh 'gen. Seem dat fate wan' 'e be so."

As he spoke, I realized I was also glad we had been forced to return to the store. There was something about Henry that both puzzled me and made me feel happy.

I turned to look at the others. "Well, now that we've gotten this one back, I guess we'd better be heading out. We still have to find the house where we'll be staying."

Officer Ben held open the door for us to leave then followed us to the car, watching until we were all safely tucked inside. He gave a wave of one hand as he headed for the patrol car.

The four of us sat in silence for a minute, each lost in our own thoughts of what had just transpired. Finally, Jon, who had been unusually silent since the officer showed up, let out a sigh. “I’m glad that’s over. It could have gone much worse, you know. We’re just lucky he knew Henry.”

We all nodded our agreement as Harry started the car and began to pull out of the parking lot. I looked down at Ebie, who was curled into a ball in her carrier snoozing away, and wondered how much of what had happened could be chalked up to luck and how much to fate. All I knew for certain was that I wanted to find a way to visit Henry again before we left the island.

CHAPTER FIVE

The entrance to Sea Pines required a Guest Pass that would allow us to go through the guarded gates. Julie said the pass was available at the Sea Pines Welcome Center which sat just outside of the entrance. The long trip, combined with the beer we consumed, made a bathroom break a necessity, so we all piled out of the car and headed inside. When I came out of the restroom, I noticed a display of brochures on a rack in the lobby.

Most of the brochures were of the same type as the ones Julie had picked up at the rest stop along the way. I selected a few others that looked as though they might be interesting, and as I started to walk away, a small stack of paperback books caught my eye. The book was titled "Hilton Head: Then and Now." The title made me think of my conversation with Henry, so I carried one to the check-in counter to purchase. Julie was already there, arranging for the guest pass and a small road map of the gated community. I handed the book to the woman behind the counter along with a five-dollar bill. Julie glanced over at the book.

"What did you find?"

I held it up for her inspection. "Remember what Henry was saying about the Gullah language? It made me curious to learn more about their culture and how things used to be here on Hilton Head."

She nodded enthusiastically. "Sounds interesting." She waved the guest pass at me. "Ready to go? I saw the guys head outside a few minutes ago."

We made our way to the car where Jon and Harry were waiting for us. Jon was glancing at his watch, and he looked up expectantly when we approached. "Harry and I were just saying we're about ready for a real drink. Well, I was saying it, and Harry didn't seem to object. You girls ready to find this house?"

Once we were on our way, I pulled out the book and began scanning the pages in the dim twilight, while glancing at the passing scenery. A mowed grassy patch lined the roadway on either side next to what looked like a paved walkway. Houses were placed at regular intervals to the left of the road with small yards dotted with tall pine trees, an assortment of low-lying bushes, and an occasional sprawling oak of the type I had first seen along the road through Bluffton.

A narrow band of water lay on the other side of the road opposite the houses. The water was the color of moss, which was likely a reflection of the grass that grew next to it, but it gave the impression of one continuous expanse of solid surface. A long-legged, gray bird stood stock-still on the edge of the water, its beak pointed downwards as it stared intently at the surface.

Up ahead, the sky was streaked with bands of pink, dusty purple, and pale gold as the sun began its final descent. The rapidly fading light made it difficult to see where we were, and I squinted to read the street signs we were passing. There were no streetlights in Sea Pines, like the rest of Hilton Head, which made it nearly impossible to see much beyond the reach of our headlights.

From what I could tell, Sea Pines was beautiful, but it looked nothing like my notion of a plantation. The plantations that I was familiar with, mostly by studying about them in school, were large plots of farmland where crops were grown and harvested by workers under the supervision of an owner, known as a "planter". In the earliest accounts of plantation life, the people who did the actual work on the land were usually slaves who had been sold to the planters, then forced into labor.

I thought again about what Henry said about his ancestors, and I wondered if they once worked the land we were driving over. "Julie, do you mind turning on the inside car light so that I can read a little more from this book? I was just getting to the part where it talked about why this is called a plantation."

Julie flipped on the overhead switch. "What does it say?"

From the chapter, 'Plantation Life on Hilton Head', I paraphrased; "Originally, there were around 16 different plantations on Hilton Head Island. Most were located on the North end—the area that we drove through when we first arrived—but there was at least one on the South end. Most of Sea Pines, and parts of the middle of the island, were covered in forest with a predominance of pine trees. In fact, a large part of the middle was used as a hunting camp. At one point, a lot of the trees on the island were harvested and sold for lumber, but Charles Fraser—that developer you mentioned—purchased the area now known as Sea Pines and put a stop to that practice. The book says Mr. Fraser wanted to protect as many of the trees and other natural features as possible by making them part of the total design of Sea Pines."

I started reading from the book. "All of the plantations were originally worked by slaves who were brought here from Africa. When the Union army captured the island in 1861, the white plantation owners fled the island leaving the slaves to fend for themselves. Hilton Head became the Union's Southern headquarters and a military supply depot. The former slaves began showing up at the Union army's camp seeking food and shelter, and as their number grew to several hundred, General Sherman sought help from the U.S. government in Washington to figure out how to accommodate them.

I looked up from the book. "It goes on to say that that led to what became known as The Port Royal Experiment, because

Port Royal was the main sheltered harbor at the time." I continued reading. "Several private Northern charity organizations came to Hilton Head to try to help the former slaves become self-sufficient. In 1862, a military order was issued that freed the blacks on Hilton Head and other Sea Islands. That same year, General Ormsby Mitchel helped the African Americans start their own town, which was called Mitchelville. The town was composed of neatly arranged streets around one-quarter acre lots where houses were constructed. The town had its own rules and governing body. It even had a compulsory education law that required children between the ages of six and fifteen to attend school. That was the first such law established in the South.

"In 1863, President Lincoln issued the Emancipation Proclamation, which freed all slaves in the Confederate states, including South Carolina." I paused to read ahead a few paragraphs. "It says that, for a while, Mitchelville flourished, swelling to around 1,500 residents by 1865. Unfortunately, that was also the same year that President Johnson ended the Port Royal Experiment and returned the land to its previous white owners. The final blow was when the Union army left the island in 1868 taking with it all of the wage jobs that had helped to support the needs of the Mitchelville residents." I resumed reading from the book. "By 1890, Mitchelville was completely abandoned." I frowned at this statement. "So, what caused the experiment to fail? It sounds like the U.S. government screwed up big."

Harry grunted. "It reminds me of the old 'Forty acres and a mule' snafu. It refers to a promise made by the U.S. government to former slaves that promised them the right to own the land they had worked. They were led to believe that after the war they could legally claim 40 acres of the land and a mule to help work it. Unfortunately, that isn't what happened."

Julie turned around to face the back seat. "Getting back to your original question, why is Sea Pines still referred to as a plantation? From what we've seen so far, it doesn't look anything like one."

I closed the paperback book and leafed through the stack of pamphlets I picked up at the visitor's center, opening one titled Sea Pines Plantation. "Give me a second to scan this." I read for a few minutes before responding. "This pamphlet says the developers wanted the name to reflect that the original economy of the island was dependent on growing a variety of crops—mostly rice, cotton, and indigo. Evidently, Sea Pines was the first so-called residential plantation development on the island, but now there are three others: Port Royal, Shipyard, and Hilton Head. All of them are exclusive gated communities that, according to this, strive to provide a safe and secure environment in which to enjoy the natural surroundings and entertainment resources."

I looked up from the pamphlet with a frown. "Obviously, they didn't realize what using the name plantation would suggest. Or, they just chose to ignore it. I wonder why no one thought that maybe calling these developments plantations wasn't such a good idea. I imagine the name doesn't sit well with native islanders like Henry."

Jon shifted slightly in his seat so he could face me. "You don't have to call it a plantation. Just think of it as a private club."

I knew his explanation was intended to make me feel better, but it only reminded me of the exclusive Belle Meade Country Club in Nashville where Julie and Harry first met our new friends, Gloria and Jerome. Jerome had the unfortunate distinction of being the first black employee of the bank where Harry worked. Their attendance at the Belle Meade event had made for a few awkward moments when they, and everyone around them, realized not only were they in the minority, but they were present in a club that made a point of refusing membership to anyone of their race. The evening could have been a complete disaster except for quick action on the part of Julie and Harry who welcomed Jerome and Gloria to their table.

Hilton Head Island didn't impress me as the kind of place that would foster racial exclusivity. But it was in the South, and even though it didn't seem to be very typical of the connotations usually associated with that label, you never knew what was really lurking beneath the cover of civility. After all, we were talking about a part of the Country that took pride in saying "bless your heart" to someone, when what was really meant was, *you are such an idiot!*

Julie gave me a sympathetic look. "I can understand how the use of the name plantation could make you think of racism and all the things you feel strongly against. I do, too. But I have to believe that my grandparents would never have offered us this trip if they believed it was that kind of place. Why don't we just give it a chance? After all, this is our first vacation in forever, and I just want to enjoy it."

Her comment made me realize how selfish I was being. "You're right, Julie. I'm sure it's a great place. It's certainly beautiful, from what I've seen so far."

It was true that Hilton Head Island seemed to be a special place. It was peaceful and gorgeous and I could feel myself falling in love with it from the first moment I had glanced across the water at its wooded shores. But I also knew that looks weren't everything, and what I didn't know about it continued to nag at my comfort level. After all, I reminded myself, I'm a reporter, and there's nothing wrong with doing a little healthy digging while I'm enjoying my vacation. If I had realized at that time what my digging would turn up, I doubt I would have been so quick to don my reporter's cap!

CHAPTER SIX

When we finally arrived at the house where we were to spend the next seven days, darkness had so completely taken over that we could only make out the street names by shining our car lights in their direction. We were looking for Piping Plover Road, and just as we decided we must have missed it, Julie yelled for Harry to stop.

"That's it! Piping Plover Road. Turn left here."

Harry made a sharp left turn and drove to the end of the road where we found ourselves facing a large house. He slowly pulled up to the mailbox and read the name.

"The Landolphs. 15 Piping Plover Road. This must be it."

He pulled the car to a halt at the entrance to a circular driveway. The house was illuminated by floodlights located at both corners and a gas light on the front porch. The warm glow of the lights bathed the house in pale yellow, which made it stand out like a beacon in the surrounding darkness.

Julie rolled down her window and peered out. "Wow! When Gran said it was big, she wasn't kidding. This place is HUGE!"

We all sat in silence for a few seconds staring out at the expanse of the house in front of us. The ground level was occupied by a two-car garage on one side, and a carport with an attached storage room on the other. A wide staircase rose between the garage and carport and led to a covered landing in front of the solid front door. There appeared to be two stories to the rest of the house spanning an equal distance to the right and left.

Harry put the car in gear and slowly made his way around the drive, stopping at the foot of the staircase. He turned off the ignition and clapped his hands together causing both Jon and me to jump in our seats.

"Okay then! Let's get this stuff unpacked and see what's inside."

Jon looked at me wordlessly with a slight smirk as he opened the door on his side and stepped out. Pretty soon we had emptied the car and lugged everything up the stairs to the front door. Jon groaned. "With a place this size, you'd think they could at least have an elevator." He placed a hand on his lower back and stretched from side to side.

"There's a pool! And it's right in back of the house!" Julie had rushed to unlock the door while the rest of us were unloading the car, and she stood grinning at us from just inside. "And I can't be sure, but I think the ocean is really close. I can hear it!"

Her enthusiasm was infectious, and I found myself becoming giddy with excitement as we all trooped in behind her. Once the inside lights had been switched on, we could see the house was even grander than it had appeared at first glance. There was a small foyer just inside the front door. To the right of the foyer was a wood-paneled room that appeared to serve as a study. To the left was a sitting room with an assortment of overstuffed chairs and a loveseat, cozily arranged to face a beautiful large stone fireplace.

A wide staircase rose from the back of the foyer to provide access to the second floor. By walking to either side of the staircase, it was possible to enter a long room made up of a large kitchen and dining area on the right, and a spacious living room on the left. A second fireplace was built into the wall on the left side of the living room. There was also a bathroom tucked under the backside of the staircase.

Tall, French windows lined the entire rear wall of the main floor. Two sets of double doors in the middle of the windows opened onto a full-length balcony overlooking the pool Julie had spotted. The area was lit by gas lamps that flickered warmly and illuminated the circular pool and the paved patio surrounding it. A grassy area was barely visible just beyond the pool and, as Julie had guessed, the white caps of ocean waves could be seen glowing in the moonlight in the distance.

I stepped onto the balcony and breathed in the scent of salt spray and flowering plants. It smelled heavenly, and when I closed my eyes my senses were attuned to the sound of waves rushing onto the shore. Jon walked up behind me and leaned against my back. I opened my eyes and smiled as I settled comfortably against him. "I could live here," I said.

I could feel the deep rumble of his chuckle against my back. "Of course, you could. Who wouldn't be happy living in a million-dollar house on the ocean?"

"Sure. But I meant that I could live here. On this balcony. It smells wonderful."

Jon cleared his throat as if he was about to speak, but the moment was interrupted by Julie and Harry walking up behind us.

"You two want to see the second floor? Harry and I already called dibs on one of the bedrooms, but there are plenty more to choose from."

I turned, somewhat reluctantly, to follow them up the staircase. I was excited to see the rest of the house. But I also wanted to know what Jon had been about to say. Hopefully, I would have a chance to find out later that night.

Julie was right about the number of bedrooms to choose from on the second floor. There were two large suites at either end, each with a private attached bathroom and a walk-in closet. There were two more bedrooms, separated by a shared bath, along the hallway between the suites. They chose the suite to the right of the staircase, so we placed our suitcases in the one at the far left. Frankly, I couldn't see any difference between the two, other than the one they selected was decorated in shades of yellow, whereas, ours was painted a sandy beige. I actually preferred our room. The sand-colored walls and white trim made me think of lying on the beach, which was how I hoped to spend much of the next six days.

Each of the suites also had double doors that opened onto a private balcony jutting out over the top of the lower deck. A wall surrounded the sides of the balcony, but the front facing the ocean was open, except for two railings that ran horizontally across the top and bottom. The arrangement provided some feeling of privacy without blocking the view beyond.

Two thickly cushioned lounge chairs had been placed so they faced the beach, and a round metal and glass-topped table was positioned conveniently between them. Jon sat on one of the chairs and leaned back with his hands behind his head.

"Think anyone would notice if I just stayed here the rest of the night?" I asked.

When he didn't reply, I sat on the other chair and settled back against the cushions. It was surprisingly comfortable. "This is really nice. We're so lucky that Julie and Harry invited us to come along."

His face was barely visible in the darkness, but I could tell his eyes were closed. He had been dozing off and on during most of our drive from Nashville, and I wondered if he was feeling okay. I noticed he'd been unusually quiet for about a week before we left, but I chalked it up to his reluctance at making the trip.

Julie's invitation excited me and I had been eager to accept it, but Jon was less than thrilled at the idea of spending a week in a strange house with two other people, even if they were people he genuinely liked. It had been a bone of contention between us for the rest of that week, which almost made me throw in the towel and give in to his desire for me to tell Julie that we wouldn't be able to join them. It was only because Julie was really counting on our coming with them that kept me from backing down. Plus, the truth was, I was really looking forward to getting away from Nashville for a while.

"Are you asleep?" I whispered. When he didn't answer I decided not to disturb him. I eased my way up from the lounge chair and quietly closed the balcony door behind me.

CHAPTER SEVEN

A couple of days after we settled into our vacation house, I decided to set out by myself on a bicycle I found in the garage. Harry convinced Julie to join him on a fishing trip he had arranged with Henry's cousin, and Jon decided he needed to stay at the house to catch up on some paperwork. I had read about an old Gullah cemetery located in the woods next to a development called Harbour Town, and I was anxious to check it out. My curiosity about the early settlers of the island had not waned a bit since my arrival, and I had been eagerly absorbing every iota of information about them. Luckily, my initial reservations about staying in a place called a plantation had been assuaged. Harry came across a realtor on one of his golf outings who explained that the label was being omitted in favor of the term resort, which was both tourist friendly and unlikely to rankle any of the locals. I knew it was just a change in words, but it implied a change in attitude, or at least an increased awareness of how a word can mean one thing to one person and something completely different to another.

The Gullah cemetery was located a few miles from our rental house in an area known as Braddock's Point, and it was reputed to contain the graves of Gullah slaves, though many of the gravestones were unmarked. I read about the cemetery in one of the brochures I picked up at the Welcome Center, and my curiosity was peaked when I learned that some of the handmade cement gravestones bore round indentations where ceramic plates had been pressed into them. West Africans believed a person is composed of body, soul, and spirit. When the body dies, the soul departs, but the spirit remains. For that reason, Gullah gravestones were often adorned with things designed to placate the spirit of the person buried there, such as a plate suggesting something good to eat would be provided to them after they died, or crossed over, as the Gullah would say.

I made my way along the paved leisure trails that ran alongside most of the roads in Sea Pines until I spotted Harbour Town surrounded by a circular boat basin near the South end of Sea Pines. The basin was home to a large number of impressive yachts. The town itself was composed of shops, restaurants, residential buildings and recreational facilities all decked out in subtle shades of aqua, cream, and salmon.

Harbour Town was also home to a 90-foot tall, red and white striped lighthouse. According to a placard located at the entrance, the lighthouse had been functional when Charles Fraser first had it built in the late 1960s, but now it was only used to house a gift shop and viewing station at the top of its 114 steps. The four of us had climbed those steps one afternoon. In fact, Harry and Julie insisted on counting them one by one as we huffed our way to the top. It was challenging, to say the least, but the view we were rewarded with left me more breathless than the climb.

It hadn't really struck me how completely Hilton Head was surrounded by water until I took in that 360-degree view. Of course, I knew we were on an island, but it was easy to forget that fact when we were on flat land, enfolded by the trees and foliage of Sea Pines.

The view from the top of the lighthouse also made it possible to see a stretch of sand that ran along the water's edge to the East of Harbour Town. According to the 'lighthouse keeper', who was really just a college student making a little extra cash during her break from school, Hilton Head boasted twelve miles of beachfront along the ocean side, starting with the 'toe' of the island, which was the area that I could see, and ending at the 'ankle' where the ocean merged into Port Royal Sound to the North. The mid-section of the island was also marked by bands of water where creeks and streams cut a swath through the marshlands. I guess you could say that Hilton Head Island was a floating paradise, and that realization put me in awe of my surroundings.

The visit to the lighthouse was also the first time I spotted the cemetery I was intent upon exploring on this particular day. It was tucked into a small grassy plot under the watchful eyes of a cluster of condominiums that flanked the 18th hole of the famed Harbour Town Golf Links. It wasn't as easy to locate from the ground, but I eventually spotted the pale gray gravestones surrounded by a makeshift wooden fence fashioned out of the fallen branches of nearby trees.

I leaned my bike against one of the trees, stepping carefully through an opening in the fence. It wasn't a very large cemetery, and it was possible to see most of the gravestones from the fence-line. I carefully made my way between the grave sites and crouched down next to one that sat in the center of the yard. The gravestone bore the hand-carved words IN MEMORY OF WESLEY YOUNG. BORN APR. 20, 1904. DIED SEPT. 26, 1940.

A crack ran through the middle of the stone, though it remained upright. On the bottom half, a blue rimmed, white porcelain plate was embedded in the face. It was chipped slightly at one edge, but appeared to still be firmly secured in the stone.

I glanced around at the other graves and noticed another stone that bore an empty circular indentation I imagined had previously held a similar plate. Some of the graves looked as though they had been recently cared for, with the ground around them bare of any adornment except for neatly swept dirt or carefully trimmed grass. Others were barely visible through the weeds that grew thick and untended around them.

As I was about to leave, my eyes were drawn to a grave-site at the back of the cemetery. It contained a long, rectangular stone that lay flat on the ground with a shell-shaped stone standing upright at its head. Like some of the others, this head-stone also contained a ceramic plate nestled in the center that bore the image of several churches.

"Dat me grum'pa grabe."

I jerked my head in the direction of the sound and noticed an old black woman sitting in a wooden chair under a tree to the right of the grave site. She was almost hidden by the branches of the tree, but as I looked closer, I could see she was wearing a pale blue dress with a white apron tied around her waist, and sturdy black shoes. Her gray hair was pulled up into braids that were tucked close to her head. Her eyes were dark and seemed to bore into mine across the distance, which made me blush with embarrassment, as if I had been caught looking in the door of a private residence.

"Oh, I'm sorry. I didn't mean to intrude."

She lifted her shoulders in a shrug. "Nemmin'. Don' bodduh needuh we." She pointed one crooked finger in the direction of the shell-shaped stone that held the plate with the church images. "Me fambly moobe 'e yuh las' munt. 'Fo' 'dat, one stick maa'k weh 'e is."

I gestured in the direction of the headstone. "I was wondering about that plate. It looks fairly new."

She leaned forward in the chair and nodded. "Cum f'um chu'ch een Chaa'stun. Gib 'e puhtekshun. No chu'ch weh 'e lib. 'E beleeb de woods 'e praise house. Lub spen' time wid de trees fuh' bu'd chune. Folks gib 'e name Bird'." She chuckled to herself and shook her head. "'E uh fine man, an' uh 'e fav'rite. Co'se, all we chillren t'ink dat!"

I smiled at her description of a man who loved to hang out in the woods and listen to the song of birds. "He sounds nice. Did he have a lot of grandchildren?"

"No mo'nuh mos'. Jis' twelb gran chillun f'um 'e nine chillun. Two 'e boys die een de gun-shoot, one de girls f'um de pox. Odduh'res' lib 'roun dese paa't."

"Your family must have been here a long time. Do you know Mr. Palmer who runs the little store just after you come onto the island?"

Her face broke out into a huge grin. "'Enry Junior? Eh, 'e farruh an'uh chillun tuhgedduh. Call 'ese'f, Mr. Tran'po'tation. Run de boat 'tween Broa' Crick an' Sabannah tree time week 'fo de bridge. Folks gib 'enry Senior wuh dey hab fuh sell den say wuh dey wan'. 'E come back, eeduh hab pocket ub money fuh dem, or sump'n' dey be needin'. Nebbuh queschun wuh 'e do.

"Onetime, 'e 'low'um go wid 'e. Oh, dat' 'citin'! Uh nebbuh leabe dis i'lun 'fo'. T'ink uh sump'n'! Til' uh mammy an' farruh fin' weh uh go. Uh growed ooman den. Libe close tuh t'irty yeah. Bodduh dem uh go. Pa yent trus'de boat. Uh nebbuh go wit 'enry 'gen." Her eyes took on a faraway look as she nodded with a smile. "But it sho' bin sump'n'!"

I nodded solemnly as I let her words sink in. Her accent wasn't easy to follow. It reminded me of Henry's, although hers seemed even more foreign. "What's the story about these plates? I heard it has something to do with keeping evil spirits away."

She frowned and narrowed her eyes at me. "Oonuh ben laa'n 'bout de Gullah? Us b'leebe leabe one dem plates on dey grabe, eb'n bruk pieces, hep de sperrit rest. De ole folks b'leebe sperrit walk de nighttime. Some dem' good but restless, odduh no good. Plates hep mek sho' ebil sperrits don' harm de good." She stared at me intently. "Oonuh seen uh blue boddle tree?" I shook my head no. "Dat 'nurruh way we hab keep haants f'um de house. 'Speshly 'portun' if lib near grabe. Sperrits come out at sun-lean, an' de ebil ones stir 'roun' look fo' place tuh hide. Light from de blue boddles draw dem in weh dey be trapped. Oonuh outside ebenin' w'en dis happen, kin yeddy'um moan. W'en sun hit dey boddle, haant light out ub dere."

I looked at her uncertainly. Her story was fascinating, but it was so far removed from what I had been brought up to believe, I was having trouble wrapping my head around it. "Blue bottles, huh." I allowed my eyes to scan the entirety of the area before they rested back on the old woman. "Why aren't there any blue bottle trees around the cemetery?"

"Don' wu'k dat way. Mus'e near tuh house. De plates gib good sperrits sumpin' tuh eat so dey be strong. Kin run bad sperrits 'way den." She patted the seat of the chair. Dis rockuh cheer blan-b'long 'e. Uh luk tuh seddown een 'e 'w'ile. Hep uh feel close tuh 'e."

I noticed that the sun was beginning to drop lower in the sky, and I glanced at my watch. "Oh! I didn't realize how late it is. I'd better be going."

She glanced at the sky and nodded. "Um hum. De sun-lean fuh down now." She stood slowly and crossed the distance between us. "Yuh. Tek dis. It hep you know wha' tuh do." She reached her hand into a pocket on the front of her apron and placed something in my hand, closing my fingers around it.

I opened my hand and gazed down at a small cloth pouch. "What do you mean? Know what to do about what?" Her words caused a chill to run up my spine, and I shivered in spite of the heat of the day.

"Come clear 'ventually. Jis' 'membuh: dog got four foot, but kin't walk but one road. Oonuh know wha' dat mean w'en need tuh." She slowly and smoothed the skirt of her dress. "Be daa'k soon." She turned and began walking in the direction of the golf course.

I looked down at my hand to study the small pouch. It was made from a soft material that appeared to have been dyed a pale red. I ran my thumb over it, and I could feel rough edges where something had been sewn into the top. There also seemed to be things inside the pouch that moved around beneath my touch.

As I continued to rub the soft fabric, I could feel heat moving through my hand and up my arm into my chest, replacing the shivers and warming me from the top of my head to the soles of my feet. My heart began to beat rapidly, but I didn't feel alarmed. In fact, the longer I held the pouch in my hand the more calm I felt.

Since the daylight was rapidly disappearing, I tucked the pouch in the pocket of my shorts and hopped on my bike, turning once more to look in the direction I had last seen the old woman. To my surprise, she was nowhere in sight. "Huh. I guess she must have gone into one of those condominiums." I thought to myself. Although that possibility made little sense to me, I decided it was no stranger than anything else that had just transpired over the past several minutes. I glanced up at the increasing darkness and began to pedal rapidly in the direction of our rental house.

CHAPTER EIGHT

When the last day of our vacation arrived, Julie and I decided to forgo exploring the island anymore, opting instead to spend the day soaking in as much of the beach scene as we could. We grabbed a couple of beach chairs we found in a storage room at the house, and packed sunscreen, towels, water, paperback books, and a few snacks into the canvas totes we'd purchased at a little shop at Harbour Town before heading to the beach.

Jon and Harry drove to the Red and White market, located about a mile outside the Sea Pines gate in Coligny Plaza, to see if they could buy some local shrimp for our dinner. It was shrimping season, and the Red and White was known for selling shrimp that was delivered fresh off the boats every morning. It made my mouth water just thinking about it, and I grabbed a handful of grapes from my bag to lessen my desire for the delicacies that awaited me at the end of the day. Not that it helped any, but at least it gave me something to chew on.

We picked a spot close enough to the water so we could dip our feet to cool off when we wanted, but far enough away so the approaching tide would not force us to relocate anytime soon. We unfolded the chairs and placed the totes between us before settling onto the seats. We only had one more full day on the island before we would have to make the long drive back to Nashville. I was trying to avoid letting my sadness interfere with my enjoyment of the time we had left. Julie must have been feeling something similar because she suddenly released a long sigh. I lifted my sunglasses and looked at her. Her eyes were shut tight and her face looked, as we say in the South, sad as a cucumber. I've never really understood what that meant, but it seemed to fit the moment.

"Want to tell me about it?" I asked.

She opened one eye. "I'm trying to think of a way we can stay longer. I mean, I know that's not possible. We have to go back to work, and besides, they only gave us the house to use for seven days. But I'm feeling sad we have to leave."

I leaned my head back against the chair and closed my eyes. "I know exactly what you mean. I'm having a really hard time accepting that we only have one more day here."

Her voice grew pensive. "Do you think it's the place we'll be missing? Hilton Head, I mean. Or just that life on vacation is completely different from life in the real world?"

I considered her question carefully before answering. "Both, I guess. There's no doubt; being on vacation anywhere is a nice change from having to go to work. But there's something special about Hilton Head. It excites me and relaxes me at the same time. And I have a feeling it would be that way even if I worked here." I glanced in her direction and found her studying me thoughtfully.

"It sounds as if you've given this a lot of thought. Have you been toying with the idea of moving here?"

Her question shook me. I hadn't realized until she asked, but that was exactly what I had been fantasizing about. But a fantasy was all it was, and I knew it. "I can't say I haven't allowed that idea to cross my mind, but I'm sane enough to know how unlikely that would be."

She grew silent for a moment. "Well, I don't see any harm in thinking about it. Maybe you could start by planning a return visit. I'll bet there's someone who would be willing to come back here with you." She looked at me with a sly grin.

"You would? Do you think Harry would be willing to take time off from work again?"

She shook her head. "I doubt it, at least, not for some time. But I was thinking; you and I could come back. That is, if Jon wouldn't mind. I don't expect he would want to join us either. He and Harry have that 'workaholic' thing in common. So, I thought it would be something the two of us could plan to do."

I nodded. "No. I don't think he'd be interested in coming here again any time soon, despite the fact that he's become more relaxed than he was when we first arrived. And, yes, I think the two of us should put on our thinking caps and figure out how we can plan a return visit, sooner rather than later." I leaned back against the chair and smiled to myself.

We grew silent again, each lost in our own thoughts. When I had admitted out loud that I didn't think Jon would want to return to Hilton Head again, at least in the near future, I surprised myself. He and I hadn't really talked about how we felt about Hilton Head since we'd arrived, although I was sure it was pretty obvious I was fascinated with the place. Jon seemed to enjoy himself well enough. He and Harry had gotten in some fishing and scouted out a couple of restaurants for us to try. He'd even agreed to play one round of golf with Harry when he'd heard that Arnold Palmer was supposed to be on the same course that day. Unfortunately, that was just a rumor, but Jon ended up enjoying himself anyway, which seemed to surprise him to no end.

The golf outing turned out to be a bonus for the rest of us too, because one of the men who asked to join their twosome turned out to run a boat service in Harbour Town that took people out into the Caliboque Sound to look for dolphins. Jon and Harry arranged for the four of us to take one of his cruises late one afternoon. It was a glorious, cloudless day, and toward the end of the cruise we were treated to the spectacle of a trio of dolphins who had decided to follow alongside the slow moving boat. Their sleek gray backs rolled along next to us for at least twenty minutes before they suddenly dove under the surface and disappeared.

As we returned to the harbor at the end of that cruise, Jon remarked that the brightly painted buildings and striped lighthouse of Harbour Town reminded him of Cape Cod, which I felt was a good sign. He told me shortly after we met that when he was young, his family spent part of every summer vacationing on the Cape, and it was still one of his favorite places to visit. For him to compare even a little part of Hilton Head to Cape Cod was a big plus in my book.

I was just beginning to doze off when I heard Julie's chair rattle. I glanced over at her and she smiled back apologetically. "Sorry! I hope I didn't disturb you. I thought I'd go to the house and get a glass of wine. You want one?"

I shaded my eyes and looked at my watch. It was nearly five o'clock, which meant the guys had been gone for over two hours. "Sure. I wonder what's keeping Jon and Harry. The store's only a few miles away, at most."

"Remember the other day when they disappeared for a few hours when they went to scout out a restaurant? Turned out they had spotted a hardware store and decided to see what it had to offer. Can you imagine browsing in a hardware store?"

I laughed at the idea. "No, I honestly can't, but I suppose that's as normal for them as it is for us to shop for clothes or shoes."

We heard a shout that caused us to turn in the direction of the house. Harry was standing on the patio surrounding the pool waving in our direction. "We brought the shrimp!" He yelled. "Are you coming up soon?"

We looked at each other with amusement and started gathering our things. "I guess that's our cue to get started on dinner."

"Maybe we should have asked them to pick up hamburger meat instead. That way we could sit back while they fought over the grill. What is it about men and grills anyway?" I asked.

"Must be some throwback to the primitive times." She smiled knowingly.

We climbed the back stairs to the main floor to find Jon and Harry sprawled on the sofa with a drink in hand and a golf game on the television. Harry held out an arm to Julie who snuggled in next to him. "Um. Your skin is warm and you smell like coconut." He dug his nose into her neck, causing her to giggle.

"Georgia and I were just going to ask y'all if you'd like a drink before dinner, but I see you started without us."

"Sorry. We got thirsty while we were out." Harry held his beer in her direction. "Want some?"

She shook her head. "I think I'd prefer a cold glass of white wine. Can I bring you one, Georgia?"

I walked over to where Jon sat with one leg thrown over an arm of the sofa and stood next to him, wishing he would pull me close like Harry had Julie. Instead, he ran one hand up my back and patted me on the butt. Something about his gesture irritated me, and I turned to head toward the kitchen. "I'll bring us both one. You stay put."

While I was collecting our drinks, I heard Harry describing their outing. Apparently, there was no shrimp left at the Red and White market so the owner called around and found some at Henry's–the same place we had stopped when we first arrived on the island. Henry had agreed to put aside two pounds for them.

"When we got there, Henry was out back removing the heads from the shrimp. He handed us a cold beer, and began to tell us stories about the island from when he was a child. Apparently, his dad used to drive a boat back and forth from Hilton Head to Savannah. He said, at the time that was the only way residents of the island were able to get food, clothes, and other household provisions. Folks could also hitch a ride on his boat when there was space.

"His dad ran a store a little way back up the road from where Henry's is now. It's hard to imagine, but when Henry Junior opened the new store it was the largest and best stocked store on the island, until the Red and White opened. Henry said now it's just a stopover for a lot of visitors like us who don't know what else they'll find down the road. Of course, the locals still know to go there for the fresh catch of the day and the things he stocks, just because he knows it's what they might need."

I handed Julie her wine and sat in a chair across from the sofa. "Sounds like his family must have been one of the first on the island."

Harry took another swig from his beer. "They've been here a long time. His family and several others were descendants of some of the freed slaves who remained here after the Civil War. Before the swing bridge was built, there were mostly black folks living on Hilton Head who survived by working the land, fishing the waters, and doing whatever odd jobs they could find. After the bridge was built, Henry's dad switched from operating the ferry to controlling the swing mechanism. According to Henry, white people didn't really start coming to the island, unless it was to hunt and fish, until after the bridge. Up to that time, most of the original islanders lived on the North end and west of the old Mitchelville area in what is called Spanish Wells. When the whites started coming, they built homes along North Forest Beach Drive or Folly Field. Then when Sea Pines was developed, followed by the other plantation communities around the island, excuse me Georgia, resort communities, the housing market began to boom, and the ratio of blacks to whites shifted in the other direction."

I leaned forward in my chair and rested my face in my hands. "Did Henry say how he and the other native islanders felt about the development of Hilton Head? Was it helpful to them or did it have a negative impact on how they lived?"

He thought for a moment then shook his head. "Henry didn't seem to want to talk about that too much. I guess he was being discrete. He did say that when the newcomers started arriving, a lot more attention was paid to creating luxury accommodations and resort-like living environments for them, rather than putting money into improving the lives of the original settlers. I got the impression that things were pretty bleak for the black families during those so-called boom years on Hilton Head Island."

I frowned and took a sip of my wine. What he was describing was a culture of separatism and elitism that favored the newcomers with "deep pockets" and ignored the original inhabitants of the land. That didn't fit with the impression I had of Hilton Head, and I wondered if things had begun to change for the better at some point.

Jon spoke up. "I remember him saying that although the whites and blacks on Hilton Head lived pretty separate lives back then, and still do to a large extent, there were a lot of good things that came along with the redevelopment of the island, like Co-op electricity and better access to the mainland. The increase in employment opportunities also allowed some of their family members, who had been forced to leave the island for financial reasons, to be able to return. Henry's attitude seemed to be that you take the bad with the good and eventually everything will work out."

Harry nodded his agreement. "He didn't seem upset about anything. In fact, I doubt Henry lets very much bother him."

Julie gave Harry a peck on the cheek and stood. "It sounds like you guys had an interesting afternoon. If nobody minds, I'm going to take a shower before starting dinner."

Harry looked up at her with a grin. "I could use a shower too."

They exchanged an undeniable look before heading up the stairs. I glanced at Jon who had returned to staring at the television screen and swirling the ice in his glass of Scotch. I sat down next to him and put my hand on his arm. "How are you doing?"

He turned to look at me. "I'm okay. How about you?"

I hesitated before answering. "I'm feeling a little sad about leaving."

He nodded and gave me a searching look. "I get that. You've really come alive since we've been here. This place seems to suit you."

I was surprised he had been that perceptive of my reaction to the island. "Could you ever see yourself spending more time here?"

He paused for a moment. "I'm not sure. I'm definitely more comfortable in a city. Even one the size of Nashville. But there's something about this place that's been growing on me. Maybe it's the fresh air. Or that everything feels so relaxed. Of course, it could just be because we're on vacation. I haven't had a chance to take too many of those." He took another swallow from his glass.

I looked at him hopefully. "It sounds like you might be willing to come here again."

He wobbled his head from side to side. "Yeah, I think I would. But I don't see that happening for a while." He shifted so he could look directly at me. "But that doesn't mean that you couldn't come back again sometime in the not too distant future. Maybe you and Julie could come together."

My mood made a definite improvement when I heard he might be interested in returning to the island again sometime. It absolutely soared at his suggestion that Julie and I should plan a return trip even sooner. "Really? We actually talked about it a little when we were sitting on the beach earlier. She told me Harry was reluctant to be away from his job very often, kind of like you." I stared at my glass of wine on my lap. "I'm really happy you've had a good time since we've been here. You've seemed distracted a lot lately, and I was beginning to wonder if something was wrong."

Jon cleared his throat. "There's something I've been wanting to talk to you about. Something that's been on my mind for a while."

I looked up at him in alarm. "Something bad?"

He chuckled. "I don't think so. Unless I'm completely off-track in reading this situation." He reached over and took my hand in his. "I think we should get married. Soon. This living together arrangement just isn't cutting it for me. Let's make it official and tie the knot. What do you say?"

What I wanted to say was what a lame proposal that was! "Tie the knot? That makes it sound so romantic."

He squirmed in his seat and squeezed my hand more firmly. "I'm sorry. I'm not very good at this sort of thing, even though I should have remembered from my first go at it that women like things a little more sentimental. What I should have said is; I want to marry you, and I hope you'll do me the honor of becoming my wife." He slipped a hand into the pocket of his shorts and pulled out a small black box. "I've had this with me since we left Nashville. I was just trying to find the right time and, truth be told, the nerve to ask you." He opened the box to reveal a diamond ring. "So will you Georgia? Will you marry me?"

In less than a minute, my heart went from sinking into a dark place to soaring with the clouds, but my gut—that little nagging place below my chest that tended to speak up at the most inopportune moments, told me to tether my urge to jump off this particular emotional cliff until I had some answers to my questions.

I glanced down at the ring then back up at the man who held it. "It's beautiful, Jon. Perfect, in fact. But I don't understand why you're bringing this up now. You've been so distant lately. When you started talking I half expected you to tell me you wanted to break up."

His eyes grew wide as he slowly stood. "Break up? You can't be serious? Why would you even think that?"

I watched his expression change from surprise to frustration. "You don't trust me. I thought we were past all of that. I know I have a hard time expressing my feelings, but haven't I shown you how much I care for you? How much I love you? You've turned my life upside down. And not in a bad way. I'm not the same man I was when we first met; wearing a mask of self-assured cockiness and self-absorption. You stripped that mask away and showed me who I really am; a man who has been trying too hard for too many years to measure up to what others expect me to be, or what my father expects. I don't want to be that person anymore. I want to be the best person I can for you. And if that means showing my vulnerability, I'm willing to do that. And more." He looked down at the box in his hand, then held it out in front of him. "Marry me, Georgia. If you say yes, I promise to continue working on tearing off that mask and allowing you to see the real me, scars and all." He looked at me hopefully.

I looked again at the ring he was holding. It was certainly gorgeous, but its beauty paled in comparison to the love and sincerity I saw shining in Jon's eyes. I held my hand out in front of me. "Yes, of course I'll marry you! You crazy man. All this time, I've been trying to figure out what was on your mind and imagining the worst sort of things. But that's always been one of my problems. I overthink things and doubt myself. But you're right. You're not the same person you were when I first met you, and I'm not the same either. We've grown better since we've been together. I shouldn't have doubted you."

The smile on his face grew as he slipped the ring on my finger and pulled me closer to him. His lips captured mine in a breathtaking kiss that had me rising up on my toes. He looked deep into my eyes and said, "Let's go upstairs. I want to show you just how happy you've made me."

I grinned and took him by the hand, fairly skipping as we ascended the stairs together.

That night, we shared our news with Julie and Harry. We all stuffed ourselves on grilled shrimp and fresh tomatoes. We toasted our engagement, their marriage, our friendship, the beach, the shrimp, Henry, Ebie, and anything else that gave us an excuse to laugh and cheer to our good fortune. Later, I lay in bed thinking over the events of the day. My mind was too full for me to relax enough to go to sleep, and my restlessness was compounded by the fact that my mouth was dry from too much alcohol and not enough water. Plus, I had an urgent need to pee. I pushed myself out of bed and headed into the bathroom, filling a glass full of water from the sink after relieving myself. Unfortunately, by that time I was fully awake.

I pulled on a robe I had hung on the bathroom door and stuck my feet into a pair of slippers. I looked over at Jon to see if he was asleep. It was too dark in the room to be sure, but the sound of his steady breathing told me that he had fared better than I after the events of the night. I quietly closed the bedroom door behind me and headed down the stairs to the main floor.

The living room was dark, except for the light cast by the full moon that shone brightly through the wall of windows. I opened the double doors to the balcony and stepped outside, pulling the door shut behind me so Ebie wouldn't get out. The moon was as big and round as I could ever remember seeing it, and I could make out the marks that I knew to be craters on its surface. The night air was surprisingly cool, even though the temperature had risen to well over 90 degrees during the day. I folded my feet under me and snuggled into one of the lounge chairs lined up along the length of the balcony.

A flash of light caught my eye, and I looked down to see that the source was the moonlight reflecting off the diamond on my finger. I held my hand out and ran the fingers of my other hand around its circumference, admiring how perfectly it fit my finger.

Jon had always been good with details, so it didn't really surprise me he had somehow managed to learn the size of my ring finger, and pick out just the right diamond to suit my taste. It wasn't too large or gaudy, but it wasn't too small either. It was just right. So, why didn't I feel just right? Something was nagging at my gut, but I couldn't figure out what it was. I yawned and realized that whatever was bothering me must have contributed to my being awake at two o'clock in the morning. I snuggled deeper into the cushions of the chair and starred out into the darkness, hoping sleep would eventually find me.

My thoughts returned to my unusual encounter with the old woman in the graveyard. I reached into the pocket of my robe and took out the small pouch she had given me. I had taken to carrying it with me everywhere I went. I rubbed my thumb over the soft fabric and felt heat flowing into my fingers, chasing the chill from my body.

One afternoon, I picked up a paperback book I found in the house and was surprised to find that it contained a detailed description of the Gullah spirituality and beliefs. I read how the belief system of Gullah descendants is derived from Christianity as practiced by white masters or slave owners, but many also hold firm to traditional African beliefs, such as witchcraft, also known as wudu or juju.

Some Gullah believe witches can cast a spell by placing herbs or roots under a person's pillow or at a place where they usually walk. Individuals who have the power to protect against curses and witchcraft are known as "Root Doctors". The book also explained that the Gullah believe in the dual nature of the soul and spirit, and in death, one's soul returns to God, but the spirit remains on earth. In this way, the spirit of one's ancestors can participate in their daily affairs and protect and guide them.

I had searched the book carefully for a description of the small pouch and found that it was called an amulet, although in modern times it is often referred to as a good luck charm. Amulets are often pieces of jewelry, but whatever their form, they are worn to ensure spiritual protection and ward off evil.

I remembered what the old woman told me when she gave it to me; it would help me know what to do when the time came. I had no idea what that meant. But the idea that I was in possession of something that could protect me against evil and somehow guide my decisions was very comforting.

I placed the pouch back inside the pocket of my robe and went into the house.

CHAPTER NINE

Two days later, the four of us were headed off the island in the midst of a full-blown thunderstorm. Luckily, we packed almost everything into the car the night before, but we still got pretty wet carrying the remaining items down the stairs to the garage. I tossed a towel over Ebie's cage to keep her dry. Like most cats, she hated to get even a little wet, and she stood up when I removed the towel and began to furiously work at licking her fur clean of the drops of rain that made it past the towel.

After we had driven a short distance, Julie leaned forward in her seat and peered out the window. "This rain is awful! Harry, can you see where you're going?"

The sky was still dark outside, which would have been the case even without the rainy conditions, because it was just past six o'clock. We decided to get an early start, since it would take us at least nine hours to make it back to Nashville, but I was beginning to think it would have been wiser to wait until daylight.

I couldn't see his expression, but I noticed his hands were wrapped firmly around the steering wheel and he leaned slightly forward in his seat. "It's not easy. Between the rain, and this island has something against street lights, I can barely see the line in the middle of the road."

"Shouldn't we pull over somewhere and wait this out?" I asked.

"There really isn't anywhere to do that right now. Maybe we can find a good place to stop once we get out of Sea Pines." Harry replied.

For the next twenty minutes, the four of us rode in silence as we peered out the windows and hoped for a break in the weather. Finally, Julie sat forward in her seat and pointed to a light visible to our right. "There! I think that's a diner. Why don't we stop and have some breakfast and maybe the rain will be better by the time we finish."

Jon groaned and shifted in his seat. "I thought the whole idea of getting up this early was to make good time. If we stop to eat before we're even off the island it will take us forever to make it home."

Harry turned the wheel in the direction Julie had pointed. "If we eat now we won't have to stop for lunch. We can pick up a few snacks of some kind to have along the way."

He pulled the car to a stop in front of a small building marked by a sign that read Roadside Rest. There were already a few cars in the parking lot, and I could see a handful of people sitting at booths through the wall of windows that made up the front of the building. The inside was illuminated by overhead lights that gave the entire place a welcoming warmth, and I eagerly unhooked my seat belt in anticipation of the food waiting for us inside. "I knew there was some reason why I skipped breakfast this morning. I would love some pancakes and bacon."

Julie nodded her agreement. "Me too. I'm half starved!"

Harry turned to look at her. "When have you NOT been hungry?" He smiled at her knowingly.

I leaned across Ebie's carrier and gave Jon a peck on the cheek. "I'll bet they have cheese omelets, too." He gave me a pointed look and squeezed my leg. A cheese omelet and peanut butter toast was the first breakfast Jon and I shared after he had scrounged around in my barren refrigerator and found little else to eat. He surprised me that day by cooking a meal that was both simple and delicious and very well may have been responsible for helping me tumble headfirst in love with him.

I tickled Ebie under her chin and reassured her that I would return with a treat for her, then followed the others across the rain-drenched lot. Once we were inside, we were ushered into one of the booths by a heavyset, gray-haired woman with a friendly smile, wearing a name badge that read, "Miss Katie".

"How you folks doing? Mighty wet out there today. I'll bet you could use some nice hot coffee. Why don't I bring some over while you look at these menus? We have some fresh cinnamon rolls today, and the pancakes are some of the best you'll ever have." She winked at me before walking away.

"Now, how did she know I was thinking about having pancakes?"

"Just a lucky guess, I imagine." Julie said. "Those cinnamon rolls sound good to me. What do you feel like having Harry?"

Harry was staring intently out the window. "Say, isn't that the ABC store where we stopped when we first got here? You know, the place Henry told us we could buy liquor?"

Jon followed his gaze and nodded. "Yeh, I believe it is. I guess it must be owned by the same people who run this restaurant." He opened his menu.

The waitress returned with a pot of coffee and four mugs, which she placed in front of us. She filled three of them to the brim, stopping over the third one when Julie placed a hand on top.

"I'm not much of a coffee drinker, but some hot tea would be great." She gave Miss Katie an apologetic look.

"No problem. A cup of hot tea coming right up. The rest of you okay for now?" We all nodded and she turned to walk in the direction of the counter, returning quickly with a silver pot which she placed on the table next to Julie.

Harry took a sip of his coffee and smiled. “That’s great coffee.”

Miss Katie’s face lit up with pleasure. “I’m so glad you like it. Can't run a restaurant unless you can make good coffee, and I’ve been working on getting that right for over twenty years.” She took an order pad and pen from the front pocket of her apron. “You folks decide what you want to eat?”

“Do you own this restaurant?” Harry asked her.

She nodded. “My husband, Mack, and I opened it in 1955. Used to be the only game in town. Nowadays, we have a bit more competition, but the locals still come in regularly. Some tourist too, like yourselves.”

“When we arrived a week ago we stopped at the ABC store next door to pick up a few things. I guess that’s yours too? Harry asked.

Kate looked at him in surprise. “That was you? I remember; Scotch, Gin, white wine and tonic water. I’m sorry, I guess I was too tired to pay attention.”

He stood and held his hand out to her. “My name’s Harry, and this is my wife Julie and our friends Georgia and Jon. We just spent a week at a house in Sea Pines, and now we’re heading home to Nashville.”

Miss Katie wiped her hand on her apron and took Harry’s. “I like a young man with manners. Nice to meet you Harry. Why don’t you young people sit back and enjoy your drinks and let me bring you some breakfast. Over the years I’ve grown pretty good at guessing what will please most folks.”

Julie snapped her menu shut. “Sounds good to me, as long as some of those cinnamon rolls are part of the plan.”

Miss Katie laughed with delight. “You bet. Coming up.”

While we were waiting for our food, I glanced around the room at the various photographs on display. Most were black and white images of what I suspected were family members of the owners. There were also a few framed prints of a younger Miss Katie and a man I guessed was her husband, shaking hands with men in suits who gave off an air of importance. There were other photos of dark-skinned men and women who I guessed must have been some of the original islanders. One of the men looked vaguely familiar to me until I suddenly realized where I had seen him before.

"Say! Isn't that Henry in that photograph?" I pointed to the framed print that hung behind the cash register.

The others leaned forward to get a better look. "It sure looks like him, although I suspect that was taken quite a number of years ago." Harry replied. "It makes sense he would know Miss Katie and her husband, since they've all been doing business on the island for some time."

As I looked more closely at the photo, I realized there was someone else in the picture who also looked familiar to me. I pointed at the photograph. "I met that woman in the graveyard the other day. The one standing just behind Henry."

Julie looked at me in amazement. "You were in a graveyard? When? Why didn't you say anything about that?"

"It was the day you and Harry went fishing. I rode my bike to Harbour Town to find this cemetery I read about, which was supposed to contain the graves of some of the original Gullah families on Hilton Head Island. There was this woman sitting in a chair next to one of the graves. We started talking, but I had to leave so I could make it home before dark." I turned to look at Jon. "Remember, Jon? I mentioned it to you that night."

He nodded and shrugged slightly. "You didn't say much about it. I figured it was just some old woman visiting the grave of a relative."

I reached into the pocket of my shorts and pulled out the small red pouch she had given me. "She gave me this before I left."

I ran my fingers over the pouch and felt the same heat begin to flow into my arm that I sensed the first time she handed it to me.

At that moment, Miss Katie arrived with an assortment of plates balanced on her arms. As she sat them down in front of us, her gaze fell on the red pouch I still held in my hand.

A woman gave it to me the other day. I forgot I had it until I saw her picture up on your wall." I pointed to where the photo hung.

Miss Katie turned to look at where I was pointing. Her eyes opened wide as she turned back to stare at me. "Are you talking about Miss Bessie? Bessie Barnhill? Honey, she's been dead close to ten years now. You must have seen someone who just looked like her."

I frowned at what she said, and my insides clenched at the implication. I looked at the photograph again to see if the person really looked like the woman I met. "No, it's her. She was even wearing that same dress, and had her hair braided up around her head like she does in the photo. But that's not possible, is it?" I looked at her in disbelief.

Miss Katie stood staring at the picture and shaking her head. "I've heard stories about her turning up from time to time on the island. Usually at some church service, or when there's a baby being born. She was a midwife, you know. Helped to birth most of the babies on this island before there was any other medical care." She looked back down at the pouch in my hand. "Can I see that amulet?"

I handed it to her and she ran her fingers over the cloth and studied the stitching. "It's one of Miss Bessie's alright. I recognize it from the ones I've seen before, although those were white. Red amulets are supposed to help a person make the right decision when it comes to matters of the heart. It works best if you wear it next to your skin. It's a good luck charm. Sometimes they're called a juju. Same thing." She handed it back to me. "That's a very special gift you were given there, made even more special by the circumstance in which it was given."

I couldn't quite comprehend what she was saying. A DEAD person had given me a good luck, love charm? "But that's not possible. You said she died a long time ago. There must be some other explanation. Like you said, maybe I just met somebody who looked like her."

Miss Katie looked at me sympathetically. "I know it's hard to understand. Harder still to accept. But when you've been around these things as long as I have, you begin to realize that not everything has to make perfect sense to be true. Sometimes you just have to have faith in the unknown." She reached across the table and patted my hand. "Eat your pancakes now, and try not to worry about the rest. It'll all become clear to you in good time." She turned to walk toward the check-out counter where a man stood waiting to pay his bill.

I took a bite of my pancakes and almost groaned out loud at their fluffy, buttery, deliciousness. Suddenly Miss Bessie's words—if that was really who she was—came back to me. She told me the amulet, the juju, would help me decide what to do when the time was right. I also remembered what she said about the dog that had four feet but could only walk on one road. Well, what the heck did that mean? Maybe it was time for me to reconnect with my former therapist, Dr. Blackburn. I hadn't seen her in some time because I didn't feel the need. But perhaps she could help me make some sense of all of this. At the very least, it would be good to talk it over with someone who wouldn't criticize me, even if I told her I'd had a conversation with a dead person.

I shook my head and turned my attention to my breakfast, only to find my appetite had disappeared.

CHAPTER TEN

Jon and I were married four months after we returned to Nashville. Our wedding was far from what could be considered traditional. We had a small public ceremony at the courthouse, officiated by a judge, followed by a reception in the backyard of my parents' house. Their offer of hosting the reception took me completely by surprise, in particular because they never seemed keen on the idea of me being with Jon from the first time they met him. To them, Jon represented everything they most abhorred. He was a Yankee, a protestant, and someone who (in their opinion) led their Catholic daughter to a sinful lifestyle. I could only guess when I told them we were getting married they decided formalizing our union was a lesser crime than our continuing to live together out-of-wedlock.

Jon and I did talk about having a longer engagement. We also discussed the pros and cons of a church wedding versus a civil ceremony. Eventually, we just got tired of talking about it. So, on the appointed day, the two of us, along with Julie and Harry, who served as our witnesses and all-around moral supporters, piled into the limo Jon rented for the occasion and headed downtown to the courthouse.

The judge who was on marriage duty at the time was a bald-headed man whose girth appeared to match his height. He greeted us with an enthusiastic wave and indicated that we should stand in front of the desk where he sat.

"Come on up close here, y'all! Which ones a-you are getting married today?" His face spread into a wide grin as his eyes scanned the four of us.

"We are, your Honor." Jon stepped forward and placed our marriage license on the desk. The judge pushed his glasses up his nose as he leaned forward to study the document.

"Jon Barnett and Georgia Ayres. First time for both of you?" He looked at us quizzically.

Jon and I glanced at each other hesitantly before Jon spoke up. "Second time for me, your Honor." A frown settled on his face.

The judge returned his frown with a reassuring smile. "Well, second time's the charm, so I hear. Or is it the third time?" He laughed loudly, which caused him to break out in an uncontrollable cough. When he finally managed to contain his outburst, he removed his glasses and peered at me with what felt like fatherly concern. "And how about you, young lady. Are you ready to commit yourself to this man knowingly?"

I could feel my mouth grow dry as I sought to answer him. "Yes, your Honor. Yes, I am."

He stared at me a moment longer than seemed necessary before he settled back in his chair with a grunt. "Well isn't that swell!" He clapped his hands together. "Then what do you say we get on with it then? I'm sure there's a herd of hopefuls waiting in the hallway just chomping at the bit to have their turn."

I suppose I must have been more nervous than I realized, because something about what he said caused me to start giggling uncontrollably. Julie looked about ready to set off on a fit of her own until Jon's warning look caused us to choke down our laughter. I cleared my throat and squeaked, "I'm sorry" to the judge, who surprised me by leaning over the bench to hand me a glass of water.

"You have no reason to apologize, my dear. If I could list the number of times I've seen a bride break down in woeful tears before I've been able to pronounce the marriage official, you'd realize what a relief it is to see tears of laughter instead." He sat and shuffled some papers before looking up at me. "Are you ready to continue now, or would you like a few more moments to collect yourself?"

I swallowed the rest of the water and shook my head. "No, your Honor. I mean, thank you, but I don't need any more time."

I could see Jon shift from one foot to the other, which I had come to recognize as a sign of impatience. I reached over and squeezed his hand, and was relieved to feel him return my grip. He looked at me warmly then at the judge. "I believe we're both ready now, your Honor."

When I look back on that day, I have to admit that some of the details of the ceremony are a bit of a blur for me, while others stand out in crystal clarity. I remember the windows of the courtroom were open and the breeze from the outside carried with it the scent of flowers. I remember Jon was wearing his customary black leather jacket, despite the heat of the day, a crisp white shirt and black jeans. He looked incredibly handsome. I wore a short-sleeved, cream colored, gauzy dress with an embroidered trim around the neck and hemline. I don't remember what Julie and Harry wore, but I'm sure they looked great. They had a way of always looking like they'd just walked out of a fashion magazine, even when they were wearing jeans and t-shirts.

I recall the judge said some things about love, and honor, and respect, then asked each of us if we agreed to freely offer these things to each other. When we spoke our consent out loud, he directed us to exchange rings, then seal the pact with a kiss. I can't remember much about what happened after that. I know there was applause from somewhere and music that suddenly burst forth from the back of the courtroom. Before I knew it, we were back in the limousine, heading across the Cumberland River toward my parents' house.

As soon as the four of us were settled into the limo, Harry popped open a bottle of champagne and filled four plastic cups, before raising his in a toast. "Here's to the two of you. May you find love and happiness in your life together." We clicked cups then took sips of the bubbly beverage. The bubbles made my nose itch, which caused me to start giggling again. Comic relief, I guess you could call it.

I was relieved the ceremony was over. I hadn't realized I had been holding my breath until I sat in the limo and felt the tension ooze out of me. Getting married was nerve wracking! But it was also incredibly exciting.

I rubbed my hands along the sides of my face, stopping to massage the place where my cheekbones met my temples. My cheeks felt sore, which I imagined was due to my face being stretched into a permanent grin ever since we left the courthouse. I massaged my temples to ease the soreness as I leaned back against the cool leather of the seat.

I felt something hard rub across my face and I held my left hand out in front of me and smiled again. I was married! It was a feeling that was both good and odd. In a word, I felt happy, which wasn't at all a common experience for me, given that I tended to overthink everything. It was a good feeling, and one that stayed with me the rest of the day and night.

The reception turned out better than I anticipated. My mother went out of her way to make an assortment of canapes that were passed among the guests by a couple of Belmont College students, recruited by our friend and my boss, Thomas. My dad even managed to lift himself out of his usual recalcitrant state to actually appear friendly and hospitable. My mother was flitting about like the proverbial butterfly decked out as a Southern hostess. It was not a scene I ever witnessed before or was likely to see again. If I were to get philosophical about it, I'd have to say, seeing their daughter married off must have shaken them up a bit, but in a good way.

Jon and I left later that afternoon to fly to Washington D.C. That might seem like a strange place for a honeymoon, but it gave Jon the opportunity to see his family and some old friends who missed the chance to watch us get married, and it allowed me to view him in his natural habitat. To be honest, spending my honeymoon touring monuments and museums was not my idea of a romantic adventure. But seeing the happy look on Jon's face made it all worthwhile.

Our time in D.C. was not totally idyllic, to say the least. Most of the people I met were warm and friendly toward me, but his father was the exception. From the first moment he laid eyes on me, it felt as though he was judging me, and I came up short in every aspect. I knew Jon could sense things were off between his father and me. He told me once that communicating with his father was a little like taking a walk with an alligator; you had to watch your step at every moment. That description alone should have warned me what to expect, but I naively imagined he would greet me with open arms. Thankfully, Jon's mother and sister were a different story. They were the antithesis of his father in every way, and their friendly chatter and warm acceptance helped take some of the sting off his father's cold shoulder.

After we returned to Nashville, we settled into our new life together with barely a pause to consider what had changed. We were still living in the house that Ida left me. I still went to work for the Journalism program at Belmont. Jon still spent his days either in the private office he rented in a house in Hillsboro Village, which was only a stone's throw from where we lived, or at the Pancake Pantry where he regularly met with prospective clients over a plate of their melt-in-your mouth buttermilk pancakes. The Pantry had the best pancakes ever, and occasionally I convinced him to go there on the weekend so I could satisfy my craving for them.

Since Jon had made Nashville his home, he had been working hard to establish a branch of his family's publishing company. The scope of that task kept him pretty busy most days and often well into the night. I didn't really mind. We were married now, which meant we were going to be together forever, which would surely allow us to have plenty of time for everything we wanted to do. At least that's what I told myself.

I wasn't sure if I believed in happily ever after. I'd certainly never witnessed it while I was living with my parents. For a while, I even wondered if Jon and I were really meant to be together. Living with him had been a risk, and marrying him was even more of one. I guess you could say at some point along our bumpy road, I just decided to take a chance, not just on Jon and our relationship, but on my ability to trust what I felt.

As I entertained those thoughts, it made me remember something Ida once said to me. On that particular day, I had been tormenting over whether or not I should go out with Jon on an "official" date. We had gone out to lunch once since we had first met, but that had been more about business than pleasure. When Jon asked me to have dinner with him a few days later, I stewed over whether or not I had done the right thing by accepting his invitation, and I expressed my concern repeatedly to Ida. After a while, I guess she just got tired of watching me moan and groan, because she turned me around to face her as I was about to leave her office. "Stop being afraid of what might go wrong and allow yourself to be excited about what could go right". It turned out her advice was right on target, because I went on that date, and it was a turning point in my relationship with Jon.

As the memory of Ida's words filled my mind, I could feel the amulet start to throb noticeably where I had pinned it beneath my bra. Well Ida, I thought, I guess there's no ignoring that.

CHAPTER ELEVEN

Nashville in the springtime was a lovely place. Everywhere you looked, the world seemed to be coming awake from its winter slumber. The trees began to bud new leaves. Flowers poked up from their hiding places and unfurled their colorful blooms. The yellowed, dried grass gave way to fresh new shoots of green. Usually, the arrival of spring filled me with excited anticipation, but for some reason this year, it only made me remember the island paradise left behind.

After Jon and I shared the vacation week on Hilton Head with Julie and Harry, I hoped to be able to return there again in the near future. Julie and I talked about doing just that, which Jon had encouraged wholeheartedly. However, as the months rolled by, I realized that if a repeat visit was going to happen, I was going to have to make it happen, rather than just sit passively by and wait for it to occur. So, when Jon asked me, six months into our marriage, what I wanted for my birthday I quickly replied, "To go back to Hilton Head!"

"Why don't you see if Julie wants to join you?" he suggested. "I can't get away right now, but I'd be happy to give you a week there as a birthday present. I can get my secretary to help book someplace for the two of you to stay." The office Jon rented had barely enough room for his desk and files, but he'd made sure it could accommodate a secretary. It was her job to field his calls, keep his appointment calendar and generally lend an official air to his business transactions.

His offer both surprised and excited me, and I had to keep myself from running to the phone to call Julie. Instead, I walked over to where he stood and looped my arms around his neck. "Have I told you lately how much I love you?" He shook his head with a grin. "Not that I recall. Maybe you'd like to show me now?" His eyes grew dark as he looked deeply into mine.

I could feel the heat grow between us where Jon pressed his body against mine. One thing that hadn't changed from the first moment we met was the instant physical spark whenever we were next to each other. I let my arms drop from his neck to link them around his waist, pulling him even closer to me. "Mmmm. I like that idea. But I thought you said you had a meeting to go to."

His head snapped up as he glanced at the clock on the kitchen wall. "Damn! I forgot about that." He pulled away from me reluctantly with a sigh. "Rain check? I'm sorry, but if I don't leave now, I'll be late."

I smiled sympathetically. "I hate that you have to work on Saturday, but sure, you can cash in on that rain check anytime."

He straightened his jeans and tucked in his shirt. "I'll be back in a couple of hours. Talk to Julie, then give my secretary a call. I'll let her know to expect to hear from you."

After he left, I hurried into the living room and plopped down on the sofa, carrying the phone from the hall table with me. Ebie, who always seemed to have some sort of internal radar for knowing when one of us had an available lap, jumped up on the arm of the sofa and walked her way over me, settling her body along the length of my legs. I rubbed my hand along her back before dialing Julie's number. Luckily, she answered after only two rings.

"Hey, Georgia." Speaking of having an internal radar!

"I won't even ask how you knew it was me. What are you up to?"

"Harry just left to take Sunny and Barkster to Centennial Park so they can run off some of their energy. I was just about to pour a glass of Coke. Want to come over?"

Julie and Harry lived in an apartment on 32nd Avenue a few blocks away from Centennial Park. Harry lived there before they were married, and they opted to live there together afterwards, since Julie's apartment was much smaller than his. Sunny and Barkster were Julie's dad's dogs. Actually, they were supposed to be the responsibility of her brothers, Bill and Mike, but that job had fallen to her father after Bill had moved just outside of Atlanta and Mike was heavily involved in his studies at Peabody College.

Once Harry had become a regular part of the family, he started taking the dogs with him whenever he would go on a fishing trip or head to one of the local parks for an outing. Occasionally, Julie's dad would tag along too, but more often than not, he was glad to have the chance for Harry to take the dogs off his hands for a while. They were both large animals, and the backyard where they spent most of their time had become too limited to contain their enthusiastic antics.

I weighed the idea of driving over to her apartment, which was only a few miles from my house. "No. Jon just left for a meeting and I think I'll just hang out here until he returns. But I have an idea to run by you."

I could hear the familiar sound of squeaking and I imagined her sitting on one of the metal chairs surrounding their kitchen table.

"I'm all ears," she said.

"What would you say about going with me to Hilton Head? Jon offered me a trip as a birthday present."

There was a slight pause on the line. "When?"

"Whenever we can get away. He said he'd ask his secretary to help us find a place to stay."

"Wow! How exciting! And the timing couldn't be better. Harry told me this morning that, beginning next week, he's going to have to start attending classes at the bank in order to learn some new accounting system. The classes are after work, so he'll be away two evenings a week, as well as Saturday afternoons, for a month." There was another pause on the line. "I've got some vacation time built up. I have to give at least a week's notice, but we could try to leave after that, if it works for you."

It was early March, which meant that Belmont College, where I worked in the Journalism department, would be on Spring break in another week. I would have to clear it with Thomas, my boss, but I didn't think there would be any problem for me to be away during the break. Most of the time, I just stayed around campus to catch up on paperwork and some administrative duties on my plate. But Thomas already said I could take the week off, if I wanted.

I could feel the excitement building inside "Let's do it! I'll give his secretary a call now and see if we can find a place. I'll call you back when I know something."

"It's a deal. I'll be here."

I hung up and immediately dialed Jon's secretary. I met Mrs. Hanson on a couple of occasions. She was a "no-nonsense" sort of person, which suited her role perfectly, and she answered the phone with her usual reply. "Mr. Barnett's office."

"Hello Mrs. Hanson. This is Georgia Ayres. I mean, Georgia Barnett." Even after six months of marriage I still hadn't gotten used to the change in my name.

"Yes, Mrs. Barnett. Mr. Barnett told me you might be calling."

"Good. I wonder if you could see if it's possible to find a place to rent on Hilton Head Island for the week of March 15th through the 21st. Just something small. I'll be going there with Julie Simpson."

"Of course. I'll see what I can do and phone you back." Her tone was still business-like, but cordial.

"Thank you, Mrs. Hanson." I hung up the phone and placed it on the cocktail table in front of the sofa. Ebie was still snuggled warmly in my lap and I stroked her soft fur, which elicited a contented purr. She was now a fully grown, adult cat, although on occasion she still exhibited the kitten-like playfulness that I had grown to love about her when she first came to live with me. "What do you think, Ebie? Will you be okay staying home and looking after Daddy while I'm at Hilton Head?"

She mewed quietly and glanced up at me with one eye closed.

"I guess that's a yes."

Two weeks later, Julie and I were on our way to Hilton Head. We borrowed Jon's car for the trip, since I wasn't confidant that Tweedledee, my old VW bug, could get us there without breaking down. Julie wasn't keen on the idea of driving Harry's truck. Jon traded in his rental convertible for a Mercedes sedan shortly after he'd started working to establish the Nashville branch of his family's publishing company. The sedan had more room for him to transport prospective business partners around town, while still providing him with a comfortable ride that was the epitome of luxury and class. That was Jon in a nutshell.

The drive to Hilton Head was just as long as I remembered, but we entertained ourselves by singing along to the radio and catching up on all of the things we missed in each other's lives over the past several months. Even with regular phone calls, there was still so much to talk about. We stopped a few times along the way. Once at a Cracker Barrel, to satisfy our craving for their fried chicken salad, and twice to gas up and use the facilities before continuing on.

When we finally turned off I-95 just north of Savannah Georgia, and made our way onto the tree-lined road that took us through Bluffton, South Carolina, I was flooded with memories of the trip the four of us had taken together the previous summer. The trip had been fun, trying, happy, confusing, and exciting all wrapped up together, and it left me with an unsatisfied thirst for more of the island. The image of the old woman at the cemetery was always near in my mind, and I pressed my hand over the faintly throbbing amulet I still wore. Most of the time it was comforting to feel it next to my skin, but it also reminded me of the unfinished business I had in store for me upon returning to Hilton Head Island.

As we crossed the swing bridge between the mainland and Hilton Head, Julie suddenly sat upright in her seat. "Let's stop and say hello to Henry!" She exclaimed.

I laughed out loud. "Do you think he'll remember us?"

"I don't know, but it'll be fun to find out."

I pulled into the gravel lot in front of Henry's store and was again flooded with memories of the last time we were there. "Poor Ebie got left behind and made a new friend! And do you remember how irritable Jon got when he found out Henry couldn't sell any liquor?

"Yeah, until Henry told him about the ABC store down the road, which reminds me. We should pick up a few things here then make a stop there too."

"Agreed." We climbed out of the car and made our way into the store. A new little bell that hung over the door announced our presence. The store was empty except for a young boy who sat on a tall stool behind the checkout counter. He looked up at the sound and regarded us with a shy smile. Julie stepped forward to greet him.

"Hi there. Is Henry here?"

The boy looked at her curiously. "You know my gran' pa? He out back." He hopped down from the stool. "I go fetch 'em."

While we waited, we glanced around the store. It looked pretty much the same as it had the last time we were here. I noticed a new rack of Lay's snack bags I didn't remember from before, and there was a shelf at the front that held a couple of stacks of pamphlets. I walked over to look at them while Julie made her way to the metal cooler to see what she could find.

I picked up one of the pamphlets and studied the cover. It seemed to be a description of the history of the Gullah people on Hilton Head. A second one was advertising a special event that was to be held at the First African Baptist Church on Beach City Road. I checked the date and realized it would take place during the week we were on the island.

I tucked a copy of both pamphlets in my back pocket and went to join Julie at the check-out counter. She had been methodically collecting an assortment of items from around the store. I glanced over the stack she had accumulated and poked her with my elbow. “Looks like you’ve got all of the essentials.”

Her eyes scanned the counter before she turned to me with a sideways glance. “I guess this is why they say you shouldn’t shop for groceries when you’re hungry.” Her collection included a few items that could pass as real food, along with a wide array of snacks and sweets. My stomach rumbled in response. It had been a long time since our Cracker Barrel stop, and I suddenly realized I was hungry.

“Oooh! Twinkies.” I reached over her shoulder to snag a pack of the spongy, creamy cakes, but her hand caught me midway.

“Not until we pay for them. We don’t want to offend Henry.”

I reluctantly dropped my arm and looked mournfully at the cakes. Luckily, at that moment Henry poked his head in from the back of the store where the young boy had disappeared. His eyes squinted as he looked at us, before opening wide in recognition.

“Look dere! Glad oonuh jis’ happ’n long.” He looked past us to where the car was parked. “Weh odduh’res?”

Julie and I looked at each other. Henry’s words were still sometimes hard to comprehend, and it took us a second to realize he was asking where Jon and Harry were. I smiled at him and held out my hand so he could see my wedding band. “Jon and I got married! This trip is a birthday gift from him. Both Jon and Harry were too busy with work to get away, so they suggested Julie and I come alone." I smiled at Julie. "As you can imagine, it didn't take much to persuade us."

Henry nodded his head with a smile. "Marri'd. Dat beat me time! Uh say tuh Mary, mek um mout' stan'f'um yez tuh yez!" He smiled and shook his head from side to side as he walked over to the checkout counter and began to ring up our purchases. That was another change since our last visit. Instead of writing everything down by hand, Henry typed it into an ancient looking cash register that spit out the total. He glanced at the receipt before laying it on the counter. "Gwine be yuh all dis week? Picnic obuh de chu'ch dis chuesday. All me fambly and frens gedduh tuhgedduh. Wan' tuh eenbite bofe oonuh drap 'roun'."

I reached in my pocket and pulled out the pamphlets. "Is this what you're talking about?" I held up the one that mentioned a celebration at the First Baptist Church.

Henry leaned forward to study it and nodded. "Unh huh. Fambly b'long dat chu'ch since bin bawn. 'Fore dat eben."

At that moment the young boy who had been at the counter when we arrived came rushing in from the back of the store. Henry put his hand out to halt him and caressed his head when the boy leaned against him. "Dishyuh me daa'tuh chile'. 'E hep een de sto'." The boy peeked out at us from where his head was tucked against Henry's leg and gave us a silent wave.

Julie strode forward and held out her hand to the boy. "Hello, young man. My name is Julie and this is my friend Georgia. What's your name?"

The boys' eyes grew big as he stared at Julie's outstretched hand. Henry nudged him with his hip. "Ansuh de lady, Wi'um."

The boy muttered a reply, which sounded like something between combination between Yum and Um.

"'E call Wi'um aftuh 'e farruh. 'E good boy, jis' tetch shy."

Julie dropped her hand and crouched down so she was eye to eye with the boy. “That’s okay, William. I get shy around strangers, too.”

Henry placed our purchases in two paper bags and handed them to William. “’Wi’um, tek dese dey ca’. An shet de do’ behime!” He shook his head with a smile as William rushed out the door, turning around as he left to close it firmly behind him. “Dat boy all-time een hurry. Fo’git sump’n’nurruh eb’ry time. Leabe ‘e ‘ead not on hissef.”

I dropped the pamphlets into one of the sacks and started to follow William out the door. Just before leaving, I turned back to look at Henry. “Hey, Henry. Do you know a woman named Bessie Barnhill?”

Henry squinted his eyes at me and nodded. “Uh bin ‘quaintun’ wid Miss Bessie. ‘E gone-‘cross longtime. Why ax’um?”

I was about to tell Henry the story of how I met a woman who looked like the photograph I had seen of Bessie Barnhill in the Roadside Rest when we were on our way off the island the last time. But something made me swallow my words unspoken. “Oh, nothing. Just something I was wondering about.” I held up my hand to wave in his direction. “Maybe we’ll see you at the church celebration Tuesday.”

He nodded his goodbye.

CHAPTER TWELVE

Mrs. Hanson had been able to rent a place for Julie and me in the Sea Crest Motel. The Sea Crest had the renown of having been one of the first places offering rooms to rent on the entire island. It started with only one unit that was primarily used by mainlanders who had missed the last boat home, as well as short term contractors working in Sea Pines. As demand grew, it was expanded to include ninety rooms spread out over two stories. There was even a small restaurant tucked into the main level of the building that served three meals a day. The real selling point, at least for us, was its location.

The Sea Crest was situated just behind the dunes of Coligny beach, which was at the very end of Pope Avenue. A small sign at the front indicated where the room registration was located, and we pulled into a parking space nearby. The registration area was little more than a hallway with a couple of chairs on one side and a curved counter on the other. A cheery-faced woman with dark brown hair streaked with strands of silver looked up as we entered.

"Welcome to the Sea Crest Motel. You must be Mrs. Barnett and Mrs. Simpson."

"Oh! Yes, that's us. We have reservations for a room for the week." I placed my purse on the counter.

"That's great. I'm Mrs. McKibben. My family owns this place." She reached behind her where a stack of small cubby holes was located and produced two keys. "We're not too busy yet this time of the year, so I took the liberty of giving you one of our two-bedroom, kitchenette units. I figured being two girls on your own you might appreciate having your own space and a stove to heat up some tea or something."

I glanced down at the keys hesitantly. "I'm pretty sure we only arranged for a single room. Will this cost us a lot more?"

Mrs. McKibben laughed heartily. "Not an extra penny! Our busy season doesn't start for another couple of weeks, but we have a large party scheduled to arrive in a few days that booked several of our single rooms. You'd be doing me a favor taking this apartment so my housekeeping staff can have the chance to get into the other units to tidy them up.

"We had a group of men here on a golfing and fishing outing last week who left them in quite a mess. They booked the rooms under the name of a real estate company, so we figured they were here to scout out potential deals on the island. It turned out they were just looking for a chance to get away from their wives and act crazy." She shook her head in disbelief. "It's amazing how grown men can act like little boys when they herd together. I don't imagine we'll be opening our doors to them again anytime soon."

I looked at Julie who shrugged at me with a smile. "Sounds like our good luck!"

I picked up the keys, handing one to Julie.

Mrs. McKibben clapped her hands in approval. "It's unit 202. At the end of the building to your left. There's a set of stairs next to the end that leads almost to your door. If you need any help with your things, I can probably hustle up someone to give you a hand."

"Oh, no thanks. We'll be able to manage fine," I said.

"Well, then, there's an ice machine on the bottom floor near the restaurant. Restaurant's open from 7 to 7 every day except Sunday. Sundays we just open for lunch from Noon until 2pm. There's a grocery store across the street, called the Red and White, which will have pretty much anything else you might need. There are a few restaurants in that area too, in case you get tired of our cooking." She paused to study our expressions. "You girls look tired. Is there anything else I can do for you tonight?"

We shook our heads in unison.

"I'll be here for another hour if you think of anything else. After that, my nephew will be at the desk until we lock up at midnight. Oh! I just remembered that I was supposed to put some extra towels in your unit. If you'll wait just a minute, I'll get them for you." She turned and disappeared through a door behind the registration area.

While we were waiting, I scanned a set of black and white photos tacked up on the wall opposite the registration desk. One of them showed a family standing beside the motel next to a late model Ford. The woman in the photo looked like a younger version of the woman we just met. Other shots were of a single-lane dirt road that ran in front of the motel. An aerial view showed the road ran pretty much along the same route as present day Pope Avenue, starting around the spot where the Roadside Rest stood, and ending at the Sea Crest Motel. The remaining photos were of the motel in its various stages of incarnation, including one that showed the aftermath of a fire, followed by what appeared to be the newly built replacement. The images of several men were evident in the photo of the burned remains of the hotel. When I leaned closer to examine them, I recognized what appeared to be a young Henry standing next to a short black woman. I assumed the woman must be Henry's wife, but something caused me to look at the image again.

"This should do it for you." Mrs. McKibben returned with an armload of freshly laundered towels which she handed to Julie. She turned to me with a curious expression. "I saw you studying that photograph. Did you see someone you recognized?"

I pointed at the image that looked like Henry. "This one looks like the man who runs the market just when you come onto the island. "

She glanced at it and nodded. "Henry. Yep, that's him. He was one of the native islanders who helped us rebuild."

I pointed to the figure standing next to him. "Is that his wife?"

She leaned closer to see who I was pointing at. "No, that's Bessie Barnhill. She and Henry were childhood friends. Bessie passed away a while back." She shook her head from side to side. "Sad story. But you don't need to hear about that. You're here on vacation." She looked at us with a grin. "Is there anything else I can get for you ladies?"

We shook our heads and thanked her before heading out to the car. Julie looked at me curiously. "That was the woman you saw in the cemetery, wasn't it?"

I nodded my agreement. "She seems to keep popping up everywhere I go. It's kind of creepy."

The sky began to grow dark while we were inside and I squinted to see the beach from where we stood. I could just make out the white tips of waves as they washed close to the dunes. Their proximity meant that it must be high tide and I checked my watch to see what time it was.

"Hmm. Six o'clock. That means the tide will still be high when we wake up tomorrow."

Julie raised an eyebrow as she glanced at me. "Not necessarily. It depends on when you plan to get up. I don't imagine I'll be stirring until nine or so."

"Really? Oh yeah, I forgot. You're more of a night owl than me. I guess it's a good thing she gave us two bedrooms. That way you can stay up as late as you want and I can get up when I feel like it, without worrying about waking you."

"Sounds like a plan." She glanced at her watch. "She said the restaurant's open until seven. If we hurry and unpack the car, we can still make it there in time for a little dinner before they close."

I looked at her curiously. “Don’t tell me you’re hungry? I’d have thought those four Twinkies and half a bag of chips you snarfed down since we left Henry’s would have filled you up.”

She grinned and patted her stomach. “Harry says I have a hollow leg.”

“Sounds about right. I’ll unload our stuff while you go to the restaurant and pick up something to go. Just get me a salad or something light. Those Twinkies killed my appetite.”

I unlocked the door to our unit, turning on the overhead lights before heading back for the rest of our things. When I returned the second time, I finally paused to look around the apartment.

The walls were covered in wood panels painted white, and there was a wall-to-wall brown shag carpet on the floor. The bulk of the apartment was made up of a combination kitchen/living/dining room that took up the entire left side. A row of kitchen appliances was laid out along the back wall, and a bar counter with four stools had been built into the area in front of them.

The living area included a sofa and overstuffed chair placed against the wall, and a loveseat that sat parallel to the bar counter facing the front. There was also a small television sitting on a rectangular table located beneath a window to the left of the front door.

A hallway ran the length of the apartment from the front door to the rear of the unit. Two doors opened off the hall on the right side, and there was a third one visible at the very end. I walked down the hall and opened the first two doors to find a small bedroom in each. The third door opened into a bathroom. I flipped the light switch on, revealing a decent sized room with a sink, toilet, and a built-in shower/tub combination. All three of the bathroom appliances were painted pink, which made a nice contrast with the pale gray of the tiles that covered the floor and walls. A plastic shower curtain covered in pink and white flowers hung from a rod that surrounded the tub.

I turned to check out the bedrooms more closely. They were both furnished with a double-sized bed, dresser, and an upholstered chair that sat on top of the same dark brown carpet as the rest of the apartment. The furniture looked old and well-worn, but when I sat on the bed in the first of the two rooms, I was relieved to find it was fairly comfortable. When I confirmed that the mattress in the other room was the same, I chose the room nearest to the front door for myself.

I just started putting my things away when I heard the front door open, followed by a gust of air that carried the scent of fish and cooking oil. "I'm back! Sorry, they didn't have any salad. But I got us two orders of the day's special and since it was almost closing time, they gave them to me two for the price of one!"

I can't say her enthusiasm was contagious. The smell alone was enough to put me off the idea of eating whatever she brought, but the sight of the grease-soaked bags was the finishing touch. "Uh, I think I'll pass. I'll just have some of the wine we bought today and a few cheese and crackers."

She looked at me with surprise. "Are you sure? I got fried Grouper and French fries. There's coleslaw, too."

My stomach did a little flip-flip at the thought of that much grease. "No thanks. You can have mine."

A smile lit up her face as she hurried over to the kitchen and plopped the bags on the counter. "Great!" She yanked open doors of the kitchen cabinets until she spotted a plate, then settled onto one of the stools to eat. "Umm. This is so good!" She waved a limp French fry in my direction. "Sure you don't want some?"

I shook my head and went in search of two glasses. "No thanks. You want some of this wine?" At her vigorous nod I poured some for her, then filled my glass. I tore off a hunk of cheese and grabbed a handful of crackers, wrapping them in a napkin before carrying everything over to the sofa. I stopped to set Julie's glass in front of her as I passed by the counter. Her head turned from side to side scanning the apartment as she munched away happily on the food.

"Any idea of what you want to do tomorrow?"

I settled on the sofa and rested my feet on the coffee table. "Not really. It might be fun to rent some bikes."

"Great idea. I think I saw a bike rental shop over at Coligny Plaza when we passed by. We could go check it out in the morning."

I yawned and glanced at my watch. It was only a little past seven o'clock, but the long drive had tired me out. I took another sip of my wine and stood, tucking the cheese and crackers back into the napkin before picking up my glass. "I think I'll finish this while I soak in the tub, then read for a while before I go to sleep. You wanna use the bathroom first?"

She hopped down from the stool. "Sure. I'll just be a couple of minutes." She trotted off down the hall.

I carried my glass and snack-filled napkin into the bedroom where I could set them on the dresser before walking to the front window to look out at the night. The window was just under the staircase that rose from the first floor of the building, which prevented me from seeing very much outside. I closed the blinds, went to the front door and stepped outside.

I looked down the hallway to the left where I could see several other doors along the way. Each was lit by a single bulb that hung over the entrance and provided a welcome warmth to the darkness that was rapidly enveloping the island.

The air was cool. April was a transition month in the South, when the days could bring the promise of summer, while the nights clung to the memory of winter. It was one of my favorite times of the year, and I was excited to see what it felt like to spend it on the island.

Returning to the apartment, locking the door carefully behind me, and entered the bedroom. I slipped out of the shorts and shirt I had been wearing on the trip and pulled on my robe before grabbing my toilet bag from the suitcase. I picked up my snacks and wine before heading down the hall. Julie had vacated the bathroom by then and was sitting on the loveseat with a second plate of food on her lap watching T.V.

"I'm going to take my bath now," I announced.

Julie nodded eagerly. “All In The Family is on. Archie Bunker just told Meathead he has to get a job or move out. I love this show!”

“Good. I’ll be out in a while.”

“Take your time.”

While filling the tub with warm water I sat on the closed toilet seat sipping my wine slowly and munching on the crackers. I smiled as a thought came to me: I was home. At least that’s how I thought of it. How crazy to think of some place I’d only visited once as home. But the island had wrapped its arms around me and it opened them wide in greeting the moment I returned. I really wasn’t sure what it was about the place that had captured my heart, but it wasn’t something I felt the need to figure out. Some things just defied logic, and I guess this was one of them. All I knew was, I felt at peace.

I slipped out of my robe and sunk down into the luxurious warmth of the tub and leaned my head against the porcelain back, closing my eyes as I felt the heat seep into every inch of my body. Suddenly, a thought came to me that made my eyes fly open again. Jon! I was supposed to call to let him know we had arrived safely. How could I have forgotten to do that? I started to get out of the water but sank back again. There was no need to get out of a warm bath to make a call that was already overdue.

I settled my head against the tub and closed my eyes, but the previous peace I felt was now hindered by the awareness that I allowed myself to get so caught up in the magic of this island paradise, I’d forgotten about Jon. Why did things always have to be so complicated? I finally gave up on the idea I was going to feel any sort of peace until I dealt with the issue at hand, which meant I had to call Jon. I took another sip of wine, then pushed myself up from the tub.

CHAPTER THIRTEEN

I slept later than I had intended the next morning. It took me a few hours to get to sleep after I finally phoned Jon and tried to explain why I hadn't called him earlier. He was irritated with me, and I probably would have felt the same way if our situation was reversed. Still, I didn't appreciate the way his peevish questions niggled their way into my brain and left me agitated.

I quietly opened the door to my bedroom and walked to the front window to open the blinds. The sun streamed in bright and strong and cast streaks of light across the living room. I closed my eyes and stretched in its warmth before turning toward the kitchen. There was a pot on the countertop and I opened one of the cabinets to see if I might be lucky enough to find some coffee left behind by some previous tenants. Unfortunately, all I could rustle up were some dried out tea bags and a packet of hot cocoa mix. I decided to get dressed and walk down to the reception area to see what I could find.

I quickly pulled on some jeans, a flannel shirt, and my sneakers, then grabbed a jacket on my way to the front door. I had no idea what the temperature would be outside, but there was a good chance the damp overnight chill would still be hanging on.

There was a different person at the desk when I entered the reception area. She was a younger version of Mrs. McKibben, with the same stocky build and wavy hair. She looked up when I entered and gave me a friendly smile.

"Good morning. You must be one of our new guests. Mom told me the two of you checked in last night. Is your room alright? There's some fresh brewed coffee over there if you'd like some." She nodded toward the wall to the left of the door where there was a table that held a silver and black pot of coffee, an assortment of mismatched cups, and two bowls with cream and sugar.

"Oh good. We forgot to buy some and I was coming to ask if you had any." I filled one of the cups and added a hearty dose of milk before taking a sip. The coffee was hot and rich, and I closed my eyes as its warmth spread through my chest. "Um. That's wonderful."

She chuckled. "Glad you like it. I can barely function until I've had at least a couple of cups in the morning. We make sure to keep a pot full most of the day. Of course, the restaurant serves it, too. I just like to have a reason for guests to stop by and chat a bit." She walked around the counter and stuck out her hand. "I'm Sarah, by the way."

"Georgia. And thanks for the coffee."

She waved her hand in dismissal. "Don't mention it. As I said, it's kind of my way of luring folks in."

I made my way over to one of the chairs against the wall facing the reception counter and sat, taking another deep swallow of the rich coffee.

Sarah walked back to the counter and took a seat on the stool behind it. "What are your plans for the day? I hear it's going to be a nice one, once it warms up a bit."

"We thought we might rent bikes. My friend Julie said she thought she saw a bike shop over at Coligny."

Sarah nodded. "Across the street from the liquor store. Ask for Billy if you go there. And tell him Sarah said to be sure to give you two good ones. Sometimes the tourists return them so full of sand and grit the chain will hardly move. Billy's usually pretty good about cleaning them up before he rents them again, but every now and then he forgets. Tide'll still be pretty high now. If you're hoping to bike on the beach, I'd wait until around noon. Before that, you won't have enough firm sand to ride on."

I nodded my agreement and finished the last swallow of my coffee before standing to leave. "Well, I guess I'd better be going."

"Why don't you take a refill with you? And a fresh one for your friend." She reached below the counter and handed me a couple of Styrofoam cups with lids.

"I'd love one to go, but my friend prefers Coca-Cola."

Sarah wrinkled her nose. "Well, to each his own, I suppose." She walked behind the counter and disappeared for a moment, reappearing with a bottle of Coke in her hand. "We keep a few of these around, too. My mom likes one with her lunch."

"Thanks. I know Julie will appreciate it." I refilled my cup and took the bottle from her and attempted to open the door.

"Here, let me get that for you." Sarah stepped past me and held the front door open. "Let us know if you need anything else. Mom will be coming in midday, then Jim will be on the desk from 7 p.m. until midnight. There's an emergency number next to the phone in your unit should you ever need to reach anybody after hours."

I smiled at her gratefully. "Thanks again, Sarah." I carefully made my way back up the stairs, setting the bottle on the floor in front of our unit so I could open the door. Julie was just coming out of her bedroom when I entered.

"Is that Coke for me?" Her face lit up with excitement.

I handed her the bottle and went to sit on the sofa.

She rummaged around in a drawer in the kitchen until she found a bottle opener, popping open the top before taking a long swig. “Oh my, that tastes like heaven!” She took another swallow and closed her eyes. “Did you get it from the restaurant?”

“The reception area. Mrs. McKibbens’ daughter, Sarah, was on the desk. She’s really nice, like her mother.”

She sat on the loveseat, cradling the bottle in both hands and folding her legs under her. “Did you sleep well? I was out like a light as soon as my head hit the pillow.”

“Not so good. Jon and I had a little spat. He wasn’t very happy I forgot to call him until we’d been here a couple of hours. He eventually calmed down, but you know how he can get.”

Julie rolled her eyes. “Yeah. He can be such a grouch at times. But at least his other qualities make up for it.” She smiled at me over the top of the Coke bottle. “Did you ask Sarah about the bike shop?”

I nodded. “She said it’s across from the liquor store, and to be sure to tell the owner to give us a couple of good bikes. Apparently, she knows him pretty well.”

“It’s a small community. I imagine everyone knows everyone here, at least those who have been around a while.” She walked into the kitchen and began to rummage around in the cabinets. “Were there any of those Twinkies left?”

“Yuck. You can’t seriously plan on eating Twinkies for breakfast! Especially with that Coke.”

She turned to me wide-eyed. “Why not? They’re soft and sweet and delicious. What’s not to like?”

I shook my head. “You’re welcome to them if you find any. I think I’ll stick with a banana and some peanut butter toast.”

She plopped on the loveseat. “That sounds good, too. I’ll have what you’re having.” She regarded me with a sly smile.

“Okay. I’ll make breakfast. But that means dinner is up to you. And none of that greasy stuff you brought in here last night.”

She pretended to act surprised. “But it was so good! Don’t worry. I’ll find something with more green in it. Maybe the Red and White sells salads.”

I raised my eyebrows in disbelief. “I’m sure they sell the ingredients for a salad, but I think you’ll have to make it yourself.”

I laughed at the anxious look on her face. "Don't worry. We can go to the store together and find something that won't take a lot of work. After all, we're on vacation."

Her face lit up with delight. "Yah! Vacation! We can do anything we want, whenever we want!"

I laughed at her enthusiasm. "Well, right now I want to fix breakfast so I can go to the bike store before all the good ones are gone."

She jumped up from the loveseat. "I'll get dressed so I can go with you. Right after I call Harry, that is."

I looked at her skeptically. "In that case, maybe I should wait to fix breakfast until after I go rent the bikes, while you talk to him. I'll just tell the shop to hold the bikes for us until we can pick them up."

"Thanks, Georgia." She grabbed the phone and stretched the cord as far as it would reach, which just barely made it to the corner of the sofa. The image of her looking so happy about talking to her husband caused a twinge of jealousy. Everything always looked so easy between them that I often wondered what their secret was. With Jon and me, even our good times were tinged with friction. I usually chalked that up to the fact that we were both strong-willed, but I still wished we could be more at ease with each other.

Jon frequently seemed to be fighting some internal struggle with himself, and it tended to make him edgy and difficult to be around. Sometimes he let me in on what he was worrying about, but just as often he kept his thoughts to himself. Whenever we did manage to talk about it, it seemed his tumultuous relationship with his father was at the root of his discomfort. Being subjected to unresolved issues with ones' parent or parents was something I could definitely relate to, but that didn't mean I had any easy answers for resolving them.

I made a conscious decision to table those worrisome thoughts until another time, and grabbed my purse from the kitchen counter before heading out the door in search of the bike shop. Sarah said it was across the street from the liquor store, but

I had no idea where that was. Luckily, I ran into a couple who were crossing the street from Coligny Plaza, and they pointed me in the right direction.

Billy's Bike Shop was tucked into the corner of a building behind a gas station and across the street from Roller's Liquor Store. The shop was fronted by two large glass windows that allowed one to see the entire store from outside. The store consisted of one large room that was brightly lit by several overhead fluorescent lights. I could make out several rows of bicycles on one side of the shop, and the other was crowded by stacks of baskets, helmets, and an assortment of other beach-bike paraphernalia.

I could hear loud music coming from somewhere out of sight, which seemed to fuel the actions of two young men who were energetically cleaning and lubricating two bicycles. I stepped inside the door and stood waiting for them to notice me. When they didn't seem to, I moved closer to where they were working.

"Hello!" My greeting came out a little louder than I intended, causing one of them to drop the can of oil he had been holding. He looked up at me in surprise.

"Oh, hey there. Sorry. We didn't hear you come in." He stood and wiped his hands on his jeans before extending a hand in my direction. "I'm Billy, and this is my brother Pete." He nodded over his shoulder at the other young man.

"I'm Georgia. My friend and I are staying over at the Sea Crest Motel and I mentioned to the receptionist Sarah that we'd like to rent a couple of bicycles. She sent me over here."

He folded his arms across his chest and grinned at me. "Sure thing. I bet she also told you to tell me not to give you any rusty bikes." He shook his head with a smile. "ONE time I let a bike out of here without properly cleaning it and she won't let me live that down. We were just real busy that day, and this girl came in and insisted she had to rent a bike right away. The only one I had available had just come back in from a rental. I told her it might ride a little rough, but she didn't seem to care."

Pete chuckled from behind Billy. "She was a real looker, but I don't think she had a lot going on above the neck, if you know what I mean. The chain came off the ring while she was riding it, and she crashed into a car. That's how Sarah came to find out about it. The car happened to be hers."

Billy shrugged as if to say; "What can you do?"

"Oh, wow. Now I understand. Well, do you have any bikes available to rent today?"

Billy jerked his thumb in the direction of the two bikes he and Pete had been working on. "These'll be ready in about half an hour. Can you wait that long?"

"That's actually perfect. We haven't had breakfast yet, so it will be at least an hour before we come to get them."

He tucked his hands in the back pockets of his jeans. "That works. Do you want them just for the day or longer?"

I considered his question. "We'll be here all week. Can we rent them for that long?"

"Sure. We rent by the hour, the day, or the week. A week's the best deal." He walked over to a desk barely visible under the piles of bike helmets, baskets, chains and greasy rags stacked haphazardly on top. He unearthed a notepad and pen. "Fill this out with your name, and where it says phone, just put Sea Crest Motel."

I did as instructed and handed the pad back to him. "How much do I owe you?"

He tore off the carbon copy of the receipt and offered it to me. "They're seven dollars a week each. Fourteen total."

I rummaged in my purse and pulled out a twenty. After he had given me my change, I turned to leave.

"Oh, I almost forgot." He walked back to the desk and dug through the pile until he came up with two chains. "You'll want to use these. They're combination locks." He pointed to a small scrap of paper taped to each chain. "Just pull that little tab off and make sure you keep the number somewhere handy." I know you might think there wouldn't be any bike thefts on this island but, unfortunately, as the number of tourists has grown, so have the thefts. Just be sure to lock them up anytime you're not on them. You can find bike racks all over the island. The McKibben's have one in front of the entrance to the motel."

"Thanks. We'll be sure to do that. See you later." I left with a wave that was returned by both brothers.

By the time I returned to the apartment, Julie had finished her phone call with Harry and was busily pulling things from the refrigerator. She turned around with a smile when she heard me come in.

"Hey. I thought I'd get everything ready for breakfast." She had placed a loaf of bread on the counter next to the jar of peanut butter and a couple of bananas. "You want some milk? I don't think I can swallow peanut butter without some."

"Sure. Just let me put my purse in the other room and I'll be right back."

"No problem. I know I'm not much of a cook, but I can toast bread with the best of them."

I quickly dropped my purse on my bed and went to wash up. The sight of all the sand, grease and debris that covered every conceivable surface in Billy's bike shop left me feeling gritty.

When I returned to the kitchen, Julie had set two places at the counter with plates, utensils and glasses, and was waiting for the toaster to pop up. I went to the refrigerator for the milk. "The bikes will be ready for us whenever we decide to pick them up."

"Great! We can go get them after we eat. Do you want to ride on the beach?"

I filled the glasses with milk. "Sarah said the tide will be too high for biking until around noon or so. Why don't we take the bike trail into Sea Pines?"

She placed a slice of toast on each of our plates and sat the jar of peanut butter between them. "Only problem is, we don't know the gate code."

When we were here last year we were given a pass that allowed us to enter the Sea Pines gates either by car or bike. I frowned at her reminder. "I forgot about that." I spread peanut butter on my toast and peeled a banana, adding slices to the top.

"I guess we could bike as far as we can on the path, then cut onto the beach for a little way before we head back into Sea Pines."

Julie gave me a wide-eyed look. "Why, Georgia Barnett! Are you suggesting we do something illegal?"

I flushed slightly at her reminder. It was true that going by the book had been my modus operandi for most of my life, but I had been trying to loosen up a bit over the past year or so. Living with Jon was proof I had been fairly successful in that effort, but the suggestion that I would willingly break the law still caused me to blush with embarrassment.

"Yeah, I guess I am. I just can't think of any other way we can get in."

She took a hefty bite of her peanut butter toast and wagged her head from side to side. "It's fine with me. It's not like we're planning to cause any trouble or anything. I don't know why they have to make it so hard to get in."

"I imagine that's what the thieves say, too."

She turned to me with a look of alarm. "Do you really think anyone would steal from someone here? It seems so safe!"

"Billy at the bike shop warned me to lock our bikes when we're not using them, or someone could steal them. So yeah, I think it's something to at least be careful about."

Julie finished eating before me, which was no surprise. She had been a big eater when I first met her in high school. Despite her petite size, that trend continued into her twenties. She rose from the stool and began to collect her dishes. "I'll put these things in the sink and get changed. What's the temperature like outside?"

"It's warmer than it was when I first went out. I guess I'll change into shorts. Do you want some water for the ride? I can fill up a few of those screw cap bottles we brought.

"Sure thing. I'll be ready in a few." She disappeared down the hallway.

By the time we were both ready, the sun was fairly high in the sky, and a warm breeze wafted over me when I stepped outside. It was a gorgeous day, and I could feel the tension that had lodged in my back and shoulders after the long car ride begi2n to dissolve.

I paused to gaze out at the beach, which was now clearly visible beyond the line of dunes. A trio of bike riders caught my eye as they made their way southward. The sight of them stirred my memory of where we were headed, and I turned to look for Julie. She was leaning on the railing nearby with a dreamy look on her face.

"What are you thinking?" I asked.

She turned to me with a start. "Oh! I guess I was daydreaming. I was remembering when we were here before with Harry and Jon. One evening, Harry and I slipped out to the beach while you and Jon were doing something upstairs. I remember how nice it was to be outside. There was no light except from the stars, and we just walked arm and arm for about an hour, talking about everything and nothing. I guess I was missing him a little."

Her words made me think of Jon, and I realized again how infrequently he had been on my mind since our arrival. I reassured myself that the only reason was because I had been so busy getting settled in. But it worried me enough, I vowed to call him as soon as we returned from our bike ride.

I stepped away from the railing and turned toward the stairs. "Let's go get those bikes."

I could see Julie frown at me out of the corner of my eye, but luckily she decided not to pursue whatever she was thinking. She followed me down the stairs and looped her arm through mine. "Can I talk you into stopping at the bakery on our way to the bike store?"

I looked at her to see if she was kidding. "You can't be hungry."

"What's hunger got to do with it? Hot baked goods trumps fullness anytime."

I sighed with a shake of my head. "You'll have to tell me sometime how you manage to eat so much and weigh so little. All I have to do is look at a doughnut and I can feel it settling around my waist."

She jabbed me in the side with her elbow. “You’re crazy. You haven’t gained an ounce since we were in high school.”

“That’s not quite true, but the only reason I don’t weigh a ton is that I don’t allow myself to give in to eating those kinds of things. At least not very often.”

“Oh, come on. We’re on vacation! Besides, we’ll bike off whatever we eat.”

I had to admit she had a point. “Okay. Maybe just one.”

“Yay! At-a-girl!” She quickened her pace as she herded me in the direction of the bakery.

CHAPTER FOURTEEN

Riding a bicycle became one of my favorite things to do on Hilton Head. I rarely ventured out on a bike in Nashville, since that usually meant competing with automobile drivers who had little regard for someone on a bike. But on the island, when the tide was low and the winds were blowing in the right direction, it was possible to bike for miles on the firmly packed sand. When that wasn't feasible, there were paved pathways alongside most of the main streets in Sea Pines.

The paved trails were also used by people walking, jogging, or pushing carts loaded down with beach paraphernalia, which made for some scary near-misses at times. But in general, it was possible to spend hours biking without any major difficulty. This was especially the case when it wasn't the peak of tourist season. The previous time we visited the island, I was surprised at how crowded the trails were, but in April, there were far fewer people to worry about.

Lucky for us, there was also a paved bike trail that ran from Coligny Plaza to the Sea Pines gate along one side of South

Forest Beach Drive. As planned, Julie and I cut off the trail just before we reached the gate and followed a dirt path to the beach. The tide was still fairly high, but there was enough flat sand to allow us to bike south far enough to be certain we had passed the east gate, then turn into Sea Pines using one of the paved paths that ran perpendicular to the beach.

A brown and white sign at the entrance to the path stated it was only accessible to owners and guests of Sea Pines, and anyone else who dared to enter could be shot on sight, or at least that's the impression it gave! That meant we had broken two rules so far: entering the Resort without a pass, and venturing onto a private walkway.

We pushed our bikes along the paved entrance, deciding not to risk strike three by disobeying the sign that said the pathway was for pedestrians only, and bikes must be pushed. The path was long and lined on both side by houses and the stately pine trees that gave Sea Pines half of its name. When we finally reached the end of the walkway, I pushed down the kickstand on my bike and reached into the basket that rested on the handlebars for some water, handing one to Julie in the process.

"That was scary!" she said around a mouthful of water. "I kept imagining any minute some police officer was going to jump out of the trees and arrest us at gunpoint."

I downed half of my bottle and put the rest back in the basket. "Me too. There has to be a better way to enjoy biking here, rather than run the risk of getting caught sneaking in."

"Well, we're in now. Which way should we go?"

The path intersected with South Sea Pines Drive, and I could see the bike trail on the far side of the street. That meant the gate to the plantation was to our right. "If I remember correctly, if we go to the left we'll come to a fork where we can either keep going straight and head down to the south end, or cut off to the right to go to Harbour Town."

Julie scrunched up her face in deep concentration. "I vote for going to Harbour Town. Maybe you can show me that cemetery you mentioned. You know, the one where you saw an old woman who looked like that photo we saw in the Roadside Rest."

Her mention of my odd encounter in the cemetery caused the amulet I wore to throb noticeably. I wasn't sure I wanted to return there, but at the same time, I was curious to find out whether the woman I saw before would be there again.

"Okay, then. We'll bike to the left a little ways, then follow the signs to Harbour Town. Once we get there, we'll take the sidewalk around the harbor to the cemetery. It sits in front of some condominiums behind the golf course."

"Lead the way. I'll just follow you."

It was a beautiful day for a bike ride. The sun had warmed things considerably, and the sky was a cloudless blue. All along the route to Harbour Town we were rewarded with sightings of snowy white egrets, great blue herons, and alligators basking in the sun on the banks of lagoons. The first time I spotted one of the alligators that Hilton Head was famous for, I was shocked by its size and the ferocity of its large head and spiked body. Since then, I witnessed several more of the prehistoric lizards in various sizes and states of repose, including a few only about a foot long. I much preferred to see those, since their small size tricked me into thinking of them as cute. However, my opinion quickly changed whenever I encountered one of the six or seven foot monsters, which made me remember what the little ones would grow into.

The ride to Harbour Town only took about twenty minutes from where we first entered Sea Pines. We looped around the harbor basin, stopping once to admire the view of the lighthouse and the impressive yachts docked there, then made our way to the cemetery. I stopped my bike just outside of the surrounding fence and leaned it against a nearby tree.

Julie pulled up next to me and dismounted. "Do you think we should lock our bikes?" She asked.

I looked around the area. There was no one else in sight. Not even the old woman I had seen before, which made me feel both relieved and disappointed. "I don't think so. We won't go far, so we'll be able to keep an eye on them."

I made my way through an opening in the fence and stopped to look at the grave markers, noting again the unique display of hand-carved gravestones, some of which were decorated with the ceramic plates, or at least the imprint of where they had been.

Julie walked up next to me. "Wow! I've never seen a cemetery like this. Not that I've spent much time in any cemetery. But this one feels different." She crouched down and studied the one in front of us. "What's this plate doing here?" She reached out her hand as if to touch it.

"Don't!" I put a hand on her shoulder, almost causing her to topple over. "Sorry. It's just that this place is sacred to the Gullah people, and I don't know how they'd feel about someone touching the gravestones.

She stood and jammed her hands in the pockets of her shorts. "Sorry. I wasn't thinking. I was just so surprised to see these plates stuck onto some of the gravestones. What do you think they mean?"

"It's apparently a Gullah custom. They believe putting a plate on the grave will comfort the deceased and reassure them there will be good things waiting for them in the afterlife. At least, that's what I think it means."

Julie looked at the plate. "Huh. Makes sense, sort of. I wonder what type of food they liked to eat."

I looked at her with a smile. "You would wonder something like that. I don't know what the Gullah ate. Or still eat. But I'll bet Henry could tell us."

She turned to me with wide eyes. "Say! Maybe we'll find out if we go to that church party he told us about. Wouldn't that be fun?"

Would it? I wasn't sure how I felt about digging further into the mystery of the woman in the cemetery, and that's surely what would happen if I went to a gathering of Gullah descendants. "Maybe. I'm not sure if I want to go."

She looked at me with disbelief. "You're kidding? I thought this whole thing was one of the reasons you wanted to come back to Hilton Head; to find out more about that woman you met. Are you telling me you've lost interest?"

"No. I'm just saying I don't know if I want to go to that church party. It could end up getting me deeper into this issue than I'll be comfortable with." I started walking in the direction where I saw the old woman. "This is where I spoke with her. She was sitting in that chair over there. Her hair was braided on top of her head, and she was wearing a blue dress with an apron over it. Before I left, she was walking in the direction of that building. I turned away for a second and she disappeared from sight. I thought maybe she went inside. Maybe she worked there. But that didn't really make sense. What I remember most is that she gave me this amulet and told me it would help me know what to do when the time was right."

I placed my hand over the area where I had pinned the little red pouch inside my bra. I wasn't really comfortable having it there. It tended to poke into my skin and make me want to scratch in the most inopportune moments. But that's where the owner of the Roadside Rest said I was supposed to wear it, and I was determined to see if it would help me understand what the old woman meant when she said it would help me know what to do when the time was right. Right for what? I had no idea.

I unhooked the pouch and handed it to Julie who held it gingerly in the palm of her hand. "What's in it?"

"I don't know. I've been afraid to open it."

"Don't you want to?" She started to finger the strings on the pouch.

I plucked it from her hand and pinned it back inside my bra. "Not really. I guess I'm afraid if I open it, whatever it's supposed to help me understand will be lost, not that I believe in that sort of stuff. I'm just curious to see if anything will come out of what she said."

Julie wandered over toward the rocking chair and started to sit. As she began to lower herself into the seat it suddenly fell over sideways, causing her to jerk into an upright position to avoid falling. “Woah! What just happened? That chair just fell over by itself.”

I hurried over and gazed down at the chair. “You must have hit it without realizing.” I reached down and lifted the chair so it was upright again.

“Maybe, although I’m pretty sure I didn’t touch it.” She shivered and crossed her arms over her chest. “Can we go now? This place gives me the creeps.”

I nodded and we walked back toward our bikes. Julie hopped on and pushed off in the direction of the harbour basin, quickly putting distance between herself and the cemetery. I started to follow her, but stopped and glanced once more at the chair. When I lifted it back into place, I was sure I had set it so it faced the gravestone next to it. Now, it was turned in the opposite direction so it faced the harbour. As I stared at it a second more, I could detect the faint wispy image of the woman I had seen before. She seemed to be nodding at me with a smile. I nodded back, then hurried to catch up with Julie.

CHAPTER FIFTEEN

We biked back to the motel along the beach to take advantage of the low tide, cutting into the paved leisure trail before we reached the gate. Exiting by the gate allowed us to see the code we would need if we wanted to re-enter Sea Pines again during our stay.

By the time we returned from our ride, the sun was low and bands of color had already begun to herald the approaching sunset. We locked our bikes in the rack on the side of the motel, and headed up the steps to our apartment. Julie immediately went inside, but I decided to linger outdoors a while longer. The day had been wonderful, despite the eerie experience at the cemetery. After leaving there, we stopped at Harbour Town, leisurely walking along the gravel path that ringed the yacht basin, then browsed some of the shops located along the south side of the basin. Eventually, we picked up a couple of ice cream cones and settled on two of the red wooden rocking chairs lined up to face the basin and the docked ships.

I leaned against the railing to scan the expanse of beach in the distance. A young man was tossing a Frisbee to a dog, angling the arc so it sailed into the water. The dog took off after each throw, happily jumping over the waves before retrieving the disc and returning it to the man, then waiting eagerly for a repeat of the pattern. Two couples were walking hand in hand as their eyes scanned the ground, stopping from time to time to pick up a treasure from the sea. Several people were sitting or lying on beach towels turned toward the changing colors of the sky.

To my right, I could hear the faint sound of music coming from the Tiki Hut, which sat on the beach side of the Holiday Inn Hotel, less than a block south. The Tiki Hut was the only beachfront bar in the area. It was located outside the gated communities, so it drew a constant crowd of beachgoers eager to quaff down a few cold beverages while listening to live music, or just relax after a day on the beach. There was also a makeshift volleyball court marked off in the sand in front of the bar, and there was usually an energetic game going on to add to the entertainment.

I heard the door open behind me and turned to see Julie step out of our apartment.

"Whatcha' doin', Georgia?" She leaned on the railing next to me and regarded me with a smile.

I looked at her quizzically. "Are you always this cheery when you're on vacation?"

Her mouth twisted into a semi-frown. "I don't know. This is the only vacation I can remember ever being on, except for my honeymoon, and the trip the four of us took here last summer. I guess what I mean is, it's the only vacation I've been on by myself. Except you're here, of course." The smile on her face reminded me of the fable of the Cheshire Cat.

I nudged her with my arm. "Yep. I'm here. But I know what you mean. I feel as if I'm on vacation by myself, even though we're together. It's a good feeling to have someone to share this with, and yet still feel like my time is my own." I stared back at the beach and considered what I was saying. "You know, I think there must be something about this place that breeds happiness. I can't remember when I've felt more content than I do right now."

Julie turned to look at me with a huge smile. "Yay! Happy Georgia! I'd say that's cause for a celebration. What should we do for dinner?"

I rolled my eyes and shook my head. "I guess you're hungry again?" When she started to protest, I stopped her with one hand extended. "Don't worry. I'm hungry too. Why don't I go over to the Red and White and see what I can find?"

"No, I should go. You arranged for the bikes, and I said I'd get us something for dinner."

"True, but I sort of feel like taking a little stroll. Why don't you take advantage of me being gone to call that husband of yours?"

Her face lit up with a grin. "You must have read my mind. Okay. I'll phone him, and take a shower while you're gone. When you return, I can get everything ready while you're cleaning up. I'll even take care of washing the dishes after dinner."

"Deal. Just let me freshen up a little and I'll be on my way."

When I finished in the apartment, I headed down the stairs to meander my way through the walkways that fronted the shops of Coligny Plaza. I had only spent a little time exploring the Plaza during our last visit, and I was curious to see what it had to offer.

The bakery we visited in the morning anchored one end of the shops on the East side of Coligny. A hardware store, hair salon, fast food restaurant called The Fin and Feather, and a laundromat were lined up to its left. There was even a small movie theater—appropriately called the Island Theater—in the middle of the Plaza, and around the corner from the Red and White Market. On the West side were a couple of gift shops, Roller's Liquor store, and Billy's Bike Shop. Coligny Plaza had the distinction of having more shops than the rest of the island in total, which is likely why the locals regarded it as Hilton Head's downtown.

Someday I hoped to make a thorough investigation of what these various businesses had to offer, but since the daylight was growing faint, I knew I'd better make a beeline to the grocery store. The Red and White was a small, family owned grocery store that carried the basic essentials local residents and visitors might need. It was homey, and quirky at the same time, and I developed a fondness for the place during our first visit to the island.

I noticed the parking lot across from the market was almost empty, which meant the store must be closing soon. I quickened my steps and slipped in the front door, grabbing a shopping cart at the entrance. Since we still had several things from Henry's, I was mostly looking for something suitable for dinner.

I made my way through the produce section, selecting a couple of ripe tomatoes and a head of lettuce, then tossed in a wedge of cheddar cheese and a jar of Thousand Island dressing before pushing my basket toward the back of the store. I remembered from our previous trip that there was a counter where you could find pre-cooked chicken, pork chops, and ribs, as well as a generous selection of fresh seafood, much of it caught that morning by local fishermen.

I stood in front of the counter and surveyed the offerings, finally deciding on a roasted whole chicken and a dozen steamed shrimp. A teenage boy popped his head up from behind the display case and smiled at me eagerly.

"Hey there! Welcome back! What can I get for you today?"

His friendly greeting and his indication that he somehow remembered me from before made me blush. I ducked my head and peered into the case. "Can I have a dozen of the large shrimp? Steamed please."

"Sure thing. It'll just take a few minutes for me to steam them. Why don't you finish your shopping and stop back by? I'll have them ready for you. I'm David, by the way. My dad owns the store, but I help out whenever I can." He pulled a plastic bag from behind the counter and began to fill it with shrimp. "These beauties just came in this morning from Florida. Our season doesn't get underway until May. That's when they start harvesting the brown shrimp. Come September, we'll have the large white shrimp. They're the tastiest, in my opinion. But they're all good." He smiled across the counter at me.

"I didn't realize there was a shrimp season. I just thought they were available all of the time around here."

He looked at me curiously. "Where are you from? I'm guessing somewhere inland."

I nodded. "Nashville, Tennessee. We don't get much shrimp there. Or seafood of any kind for that matter, unless you count fish sticks."

He grimaced. "Sure don't. I remember you from last summer. You here on vacation?"

"For the week. My friend Julie and I are staying over at the Sea Crest Motel."

He smiled and nodded. "Good spot. The owners are friends of my family." He emptied the contents of the plastic bag into the steamer and set the timer. "They should be ready in 5 minutes."

I walked away with a wave of my hand and wove through the rest of the store, adding to the shopping cart a couple of cans of beans, a six pack of Coke, a pound of coffee, and a small carton of half and half. When I returned to the seafood counter, David had disappeared, but a woman whose brown hair was covered by a hairnet peered at me from behind the case. She pushed a bag wrapped in brown paper in my direction. "This must be yours. David said to tell you to be sure and pick up some fresh lemon to go with them."

"Thanks for the reminder." I placed the bag in the shopping cart and headed back toward the produce section to grab a plump, yellow lemon, then pushed the cart in the direction of the check-out lines. A woman stood behind one of the counters looking vaguely bored. She waved me into her line.

"Do you have an account with us, or do you want to pay cash?"

"Cash please. I'm just here for the week."

After she rang up the total, she squinted at me curiously. "I think I've seen you in here before. You were here last year, weren't you?"

I nodded in surprise. I guess that's how it was living in a small town, or on an island, for that matter. Everyone who lived there got to know each other, and strangers stood out in contrast, making them easy to recognize the second time around. "Last May. My friend, Julie, and I were here for the week. I wish it could be longer, but that's as much time as I could get off work. I hope to be back for a longer stay in the summer." She nodded as if she had heard that story many times before. "When are you going to give in and just move here?"

Her question took me by surprise. "I'm not sure I'm brave enough to take that step."

She pushed my items to the end of the counter so a young man standing there could transfer them into paper bags. "People start coming here regularly, and they get the bug to buy something permanent. A lot of times, they don't think it through very carefully. Worst case scenario, they end up renting their place out until they can make a permanent move. Or else they just give up on the idea completely. Either way, it's not a bad investment. Rentals here bring in a tidy chunk of change."

I frowned as I mulled over what she was saying. "I hadn't thought of that. It's definitely something to consider."

She glanced at the total on the cash register. "That'll be seventeen dollars and thirty-two cents." I laid a twenty-dollar bill on the counter and she counted out my change. "If you ever decide to do more than just think about it, my cousin is a realtor." She fished into the pocket of her jeans and handed me a small business card. "Give him a call. Be sure to tell him Jody said hi."

I glanced at the card before tucking it into the side pocket of my purse. "Thanks. I appreciate it." Once I was outside, the full impact of what she said hit me. Move to the island? That was something that never crossed my mind. Well, okay, it HAD crossed my mind, but not seriously.

I couldn't deny there was just something about the place that made me want to come back as often as possible. But live here? How could that actually work? I shook my head and began to pick up my pace as I headed back to the motel. The sun would be setting soon, and I was eager to catch the last vestiges of color that were certain to light up the sky. And after that, I wanted to call Jon. I was anxious to tell him about my day, and more than anything, I wanted to let him know that I was thinking of him. I also wondered what he would say about Jody's comments, though I had a feeling I already knew.

CHAPTER SIXTEEN

I awoke early the next day. My sleep had been more restful than the first night, mostly due to my conversation with Jon having been peaceful and loving and absent of anything remotely stress inducing. He even surprised me by saying that maybe we should think about Jody's suggestion. Not that we should do anything about it, just that it deserved some thought.

I glanced at the clock and calculated what time the sunrise should occur, bolting upright as I realized it would be soon. I stepped barefoot onto the floor and moved quietly to where I had tossed my clothes the night before, hurriedly pulling on shorts, a t-shirt, and a hooded sweatshirt, and stepped into my sandals.

I made my way down the stairs leading to a boardwalk that extended from the front of the property to the beach. By that time, the sky had begun to grow lighter, and it was possible to see the images of other early risers moving along the sandy shore. I estimated it must be close to high tide since there was very little beach to walk on without stepping around the sudden rush of water as it licked the sand. I kicked off my sandals and decided to carry them in my hand. The water still held a chill from the night, and I shivered as it bathed my bare feet.

I glanced up at the sky with a smile as I caught sight of the rosy hue that hinted at what was to come. I had made this early morning trek to the beach a few times during my last visit. I could say with confidence that it was worth getting up early to see. On one of those mornings, the round globe never fully appeared, its presence only evident from the color that seeped out around the edges of the clouds. But on the other days, it stood-out golden and bright in the middle of a cloudless sky. The sunrises had each been different, and had never failed to amaze me and leave me longing for more.

On this particular morning, the sun appeared gradually, first as a rosy sliver that seemed to flicker just above the horizon, then revealing more and more of itself until it hung suspended above the water. The sky above the globe was a pale orange, taking on more of a reddish cast as it surrounded the sun and blended into the water. A lone seagull stood with its back to the spectacle, its backlit image cast into shadow. The water shimmered with red-orange light as the waves rolled softly toward the shoreline.

There were a few other people visible along the beach. Some strode purposefully along, intent on completing their morning walk. Others stood quietly, silent sentries to the display unfolding in front of them. Occasionally, a bicyclist passed by, throwing up a spray of water as their wheels pushed through the surf. There was barely enough exposed sand to walk on, much less ride a bike. At low tide, the uncovered beach grew by dozens of feet in width, which made biking a breeze. Unless, the actual breeze that stirred along the coast forced one to shove against it.

I remembered with a smile how Jon and I biked South on the beach one day. Delighting in the easiness of the ride, we turned around and realized the wind that seemed so light when it was at our backs, was suddenly forcing us to push hard on the pedals in order to retrace our route. When we'd finally made it back to the beach house, we were ready to collapse from the effort.

A flight of pelicans caught my eye as they flew just inches above the water, their beaks tilted downwards as they searched for breakfast. The thought of food made my stomach rumble. I reversed my route and set my sights on a sandy path that cut through to the street next to the Sea Crest Motel, which I knew would lead me in the direction of the bakery at Coligny Plaza. The bakery was one of the few places that opened early in the Plaza, and my mouth began to water in anticipation of the treats offered.

A few people were in the bakery ahead of me, and I stood back and scanned the pastry display case until it was my turn to order. I settled for two apple fritters, two strawberry and cheese Danish, and—because it seemed like the right thing to do—a couple of bananas from a basket on the counter.

The smell of coffee greeted me as I walked in the door of the rental unit. Even though Julie didn't drink the stuff, she knew how much I loved a fresh cup as soon as I got up in the morning, so it was an extra treat that she thoughtfully brewed a pot for me. She was sitting at the kitchen counter pouring Coca Cola into a glass filled with ice.

"Morning, early bird. How was it out there?"

"Beautiful! Did you see the sunrise from the window?"

Her mouth twisted into a grimace. "I forgot to look. I guess I was too intent on remembering how to make coffee."

I set the bags down on the kitchen counter and headed for the coffee pot, pouring a cup and adding a dollop of cream. "Thanks for making the coffee. I brought some breakfast."

"You went to the bakery?" She thrust her hand into the bag and pulled out a Danish, taking a huge bite before sitting on the sofa. "Yum. These are great." Her eyes closed in contentment.

I fished out an apple fritter and laid the bananas on the counter, before handing the rest of the contents over to Julie. Her eyes lit up eagerly as she dove in for the second fritter. "These are so good." She held the bag out to me.

"It's all yours."

I sat at the kitchen counter and dunked my fritter into my coffee. "What do you feel like doing today?"

Her eyebrows scrunched up as she munched thoughtfully. "We could browse the shops over at Coligny. Or just hang out on the beach."

"Maybe we could do both." I glanced at the clock on the kitchen wall. "We could spend a couple of hours on the beach this morning, then get cleaned up and walk over to Coligny for lunch. We can get something from the Fin 'N Feather and carry it over to one of the picnic tables in front of the motel to eat. Afterward, we can check out the shops."

She jumped up from the sofa. "Sounds like a plan! I'll put on my suit and some sunscreen. Where did you put the beach towels?"

"They're on the top shelf of the hall closet. Our beach bags and sand chairs are in there, too."

"Cool. I'll meet you back out here in a few." She scurried happily down the hall in the direction of her bedroom.

I peeled one of the bananas and added a little more coffee to my cup. The two pamphlets I found at Henry's were lying on the end of the counter. I picked up the one that mentioned the celebration at the church, taking note the date was two days away.

The thought of attending the event caused my stomach to clench. I wasn't sure why the idea of going to the celebration at the church made me anxious. After all, it would be my chance to find out more about the woman I met in the cemetery. I shook my head and laughed at myself. Oh, is that all, Georgia? You just want to ask a bunch of strangers to tell you about the dead woman you met? I'm sure that will go over well!

I stood and headed toward my bedroom so I could get ready for the beach. Maybe a little time in the sun would help me sort out my feelings and decide once and for all whether I really wanted to dig deeper into the mystery of the cemetery lady.

That's how I thought of her; "the cemetery lady". But she had a name. What had the woman at the Roadside Rest called her? Oh, yeah. Bessie Barnhill. Well, Miss Bessie, you've chosen to show yourself to me for some unknown reason. I guess now it's up to me to figure out what that is. It also dawned on me that this whole affair was not what one would consider normal. Yet, I wasn't afraid or creepy about it. I simply accepted what I saw and heard. And the amulet was certainly real!

CHAPTER SEVENTEEN

I decided to go to the celebration at the First African Church. It wasn't really that I decided I would go, as much as I just got tired of thinking about it one way or another. Eventually, I realized that trying to avoid digging deeper into the mystery of Bessie Barnhill wasn't going to work. My inclination as a journalist was to find out everything I could about intriguing stories. Not to mention the amulet had begun to throb consistently since I again spotted the faint image of Bessie at the cemetery. The nagging questions it provoked started to rankle my mind.

As we drove close to the church grounds at the heel of the island, we could see a large crowd had already gathered. Cars were parked on every conceivable spot along the road and in the grassy median, so we continued driving until we spotted a young man waving cars into a vacant lot. He pointed us in the direction of the far back corner where we could see there was still space for a few vehicles. I turned the car into the nearest one, and we set out for the church on foot, following along behind several other people who were headed in the same direction.

As we came close to the building, I noticed a sign out front indicating the church was founded in 1862. I pointed it out to Julie. "Look at that. If my math is correct, this church is at least 112 years old."

Julie scrunched up her face and gazed at the sign and the building behind it. "Sure doesn't look that old. I wonder if this is the original building."

The front of the church had a small porch covered by a pointed overhang that matched the peaked roof of the building. I could just barely make out the tip of a wooden cross that rose above the roof. The front of the church was constructed out of what looked like rough concrete on the bottom painted a pale cream, and the top half was lined with white wooden shingles.

I walked around to the side of the church and was surprised to see it was actually much larger than it first appeared. Six columns lined the wall along the side of the building with windows tucked into the spaces between the columns.

Tents were set up in the yard at the side of the church, and the air was pungent with the smell of roasting meat, boiled greens, and freshly baked sweets. My mouth began to water at the aroma, and I turned to look for Julie, certain she must be having a similar reaction.

"Oonuh fren obuh dere een de ten'. Nebbuh shum gal 'joy bittle luk dat!"

The voice startled me, and I jerked around to find Henry standing next to me. His eyes were studying me curiously and a grin lit up his face. He was dressed in a sharp looking navy-blue suit with a starched white shirt and a striped tie. His head was covered with a brown felt hat, which he took off as we stood looking at each other. He lifted it to point at the church and nodded. "Dis chu'ch not de firs' one. Not firs' name eeduh. Call de Goodwill Ba'tis' Chu'ch, den Cross Roads Ba'tis' Chu'ch. Moobe dis place 1800s, den 'ventually call 'e First African Ba'tis' Chu'ch. Not only de FIRST African Ba'tis' chu'ch on dis i'lun, also de murruh chu'ch fibe odduh, all een Beaufor' Coundee.

Rebil' 1966. Fus' one not mo' dan shack. Call dem praise houses." He looked at me expectantly.

I was so distracted by his accent and the proud manner in which he held himself it took me a second to realize he was waiting for me to say something. I shook my head to collect my wits. "It's nice. Really nice. And larger than I expected. How many people are members of the church?"

He twirled his hat in his hands and looked down at his feet. "Tink mebe hund'ud. 'Nuff tuh spill out de do' wen wusshup meet'n'." He nodded in the direction of one of the tents. "'Dat 'ooman een yalluh dress lawfully lady, Mary. 'E shum oonuh come 'long de road, ax kin meet bofe oonuh."

I glanced in the direction he was looking and spotted a rather robust woman in a bright yellow dress that was belted around the middle with a red sash. A straw hat with a similarly colored sash sat atop her head so that it dipped to one side. She must have felt our eyes on her because just at that moment she looked in our direction and gave a slight wave.

"Bes' mek'ace obuh dey." He started walking toward the woman, which left me no choice but to follow. When we reached the spot where she stood, Henry stepped aside and indicated that I should approach her. I had only taken a couple of steps when I found myself engulfed in a bosomy hug.

"Blessit chile! 'E good fo' see oonuh." She pushed me back from her embrace and studied me up and down. "'Enry, 'e purty gal, enty? Uh t'ink could use sum meat on dese bones. Oonuh hongry?" She looked at Henry and burst into loud laughter. "'Spect 'enry say kin gib sum ub min'."

Her laughter continued until Henry gave her a loving but stern look. "Hush, ole woman. Le'm'lone." He looked back at me again. "Leh we go obuh weh oonuh fren' be. 'Spect 'e look fuhr'um."

Mary shook her head at him. "'E ain' worry nutt'n'. 'E playin' jump de rope 'wid de gran'chillun." She turned her attention back to me. "Yeddy oonuh hab bis'tor tuh de haa'buh.

Miss Bessie 'pear dere time tuh time. Debble ub uh t'ing happen 'e grum' pa."

Her words took me by surprise. I glanced at Henry and he looked back at me sheepishly. "Wu'd git 'roun' 'bout um. Oonuh fus' w'ite folk shum 'e."

I looked at him uncertainly. "But, how did you know? I don't remember telling you about it."

He shook his head. "Oonuh ent crack 'e teet'. Hea' f'um Miss Katie obuh Roadside Rest. Stop een dey eb'ry few mawnin' jis' tuh taste 'e sweet rolls. Uh yeddy um talk 'bout dis."

I felt like my heart had stopped when Mary, then Henry, mentioned my encounter with Miss Bessie. I was having trouble concentrating on anything other than trying to make my breath flow again. Mary must have noticed my odd behavior because she looped her arm through mine and pulled me close. "Tummuch talk. No need say mo' bout' dis now."

I allowed myself to be pressed against her warmth. "I appreciate that. I'm still trying to understand what I saw and heard, and it makes me uncomfortable to think people are discussing it behind my back." I looked at her hesitantly. "Maybe you and Henry could help me make some sense of what happened. I could stop by the store sometime so we could talk privately."

Henry raised his eyebrows as he looked at Mary and she nodded in reply. "Eb'n bettuh, us hab bofe oonuh obuh home. Mary good cook. Cum tuh dinnuh 'morrow 'roun candl'light'n'. Us lib Spanish Wells on Brams Point. T'ird house on de right f'um big road. Navuh know we. Git los', jis' ax'um."

At that moment Julie reappeared. "Hi Henry! Man, your grandchildren have a LOT of energy. They practically wore me out." She looked from Henry to me, then back again. "I'm sorry. Did I interrupt something? I can go away and come back later."

I grabbed her arm to stop her from leaving. "No, don't go. Henry was just inviting us to join him and his wife Mary for dinner at their house tomorrow night."

I could see her visibly perk up at the mention of food. "Well, if she can cook HALF as good as what I've eaten here today, count me in!"

Henry chuckled and put his hat back on his head, straightening the brim with a twist of his hand. He laid a hand on Mary's arm and she smiled warmly at Julie. "'Spect oonuh roun' fibe. We eat early cos' 'enry got tuh git tuh de sto' by seben een de mawnin'." They started to walk away but Mary stopped and turned back to face me. "Nutt'n' happen Gawd don' t'ink be rite. Jis' need hab faith 'e so." Henry nodded his agreement and took his wife's hand as they resumed their departure, fading quickly into the crowd gathered around the tent where the food was being served.

Her advice shook me in the same way as seeing Miss Bessie. There were certainly some strange things going on, and on one level it made me want to pack up and head back to Nashville as fast as I could. Yet, at the same time, something was pulling at me to stay. Even though we had just met, I felt a true trust in Mary, the same as I felt with Henry the first time we stopped in his store. They were hard not to like. Meeting them was like saying hello again to old friends who I hadn't seen in a while but whose presence was firmly engrained in my heart. It was odd to feel that way about people who came from such different backgrounds as mine. But I was used to discovering that the way things really were, and the way we expected them to be, were often worlds apart.

I was reminded of my special but unexpected friendship with Ida Hood, and my eyes filled with tears. There had been at least five decades separating us in age, and cultural differences that stemmed from her Northern versus my Southern heritage. Still, that hadn't kept us from becoming fast friends, and I missed her terribly.

Julie placed her hand on my shoulder and squeezed gently. "You okay?"

I nodded. "I guess so. I just wish I understood what's going on. I feel like I'm balancing on the edge of two worlds. I sense there's a deep mystery surrounding the death of Bessie's grandfather, and it's somehow connected to the Gullah culture on the island. My hope is that talking more with Henry and Mary can help me figure some things out, although I'll admit that I'm more than a little reluctant to get in any deeper than I already am."

"Ha! Well isn't that the whole point of a mystery? It keeps you guessing until the end finally reveals itself. I'm sure it's scary. It freaked me out the one time I went to the cemetery with you. But don't you realize how special it is that this person, this spirit, has chosen you to help bring the truth to light? I mean, come on girl, that can't be an everyday occurrence!"

Her bluntness was something I always appreciated about her. "I guess you're right. And Henry and Mary have been great. Let's just see how things go tomorrow night. At the very least, we'll get a good meal out of it."

She laughed and looped her arm through mine. "Speaking of which, what are we going to do for dinner?"

I smiled and shook my head, but then realized I hadn't had anything to eat since breakfast. "With everything that's been going on I guess I forgot to eat lunch. What do you say we try that place over on Skull Creek? Hudson's, I think it's called. I overheard someone in the Red and White say they serve really great seafood dinners, and they have a dining room that overlooks the water."

"That sounds perfect. I can't think of anything I'd rather do than eat fresh fish and look at a great view. Well, except maybe eat hush puppies and slaw along with that fish. OH, and some FRIES! I'll bet they have good fries."

At least there was one thing I could be certain of in the midst of all of the uncertainty surrounding the events I had been occupied with since our arrival on the island: Julie's appetite would never fail me. Nor would her friendship. She'd always been there for me since the first time we met in high school, and I could still count on her just as much seven years later.

I squeezed her arm where it was still looped through mine. "Yep. I'll bet they do too. And if not, we'll ask them to make some." We shared a boisterous laugh as we made our way to the car.

CHAPTER EIGHTEEN

Spanish Wells was located on the west side of the island, not far from Henry's store. At first glance, it appeared to be a nondescript neighborhood of modest homes tucked amidst sprawling oak and pine trees. It was very quiet; sleepy was the word that came to my mind. There were no businesses to draw a crowd, only an occasional roadside stand displaying the local harvest of vegetables and fruit. Children could be seen playing freely in their yards, and older folks sat in the shade of a porch overhang or under one of the majestic oaks that were scattered plentifully over the island.

As we drove down Spanish Wells Drive, I noticed it was possible to catch a glimpse of water through the trees on either side of the road. At one point, Julie pointed out the window on my side of the car toward one particularly wide opening that revealed a long wooden pier jutting out from the bank. The weathered gray of the wood made a soft contrast to the bluish water and the bright green shoots of reeds that poked up from its surface. The pier looked to be at least twenty-five yards long. There was a roofed area at the very end, and I could just make out the images of two fishermen standing in the shade it provided, their poles dipping down toward the water below.

"Is that the ocean?" She asked.

"Not exactly. I looked this area up on a map in one of those pamphlets I picked up at the Welcome Center. That's Broad Creek we're looking at, and MacKay's Creek is on the right. MacKay's is an extension of the inter-coastal waterway that we crossed when we took the bridge onto the island. Sailing ships used these deep-water creeks as protected harbors to escape storms and to stock fresh water and food. That makes this area only a stone's throw away from the mainland. I read that its location was one of the key reasons native islanders gravitated to Spanish Wells to make their homes." I looked out the windows on either side of the car. "From the looks of it, it doesn't seem like the developers have dug into this area yet, like they have other parts of the island. I guess that's a good thing for folks like Henry and his family."

Henry said we were to turn onto Spanish Wells from the big road and his house would be the third one on the right. Unfortunately, there was no sign indicating the Spanish Wells community, except for a small sign that marked one of the streets from the main road onto the island. I guessed the main road was the big road Henry had referred to and I made a left turn at that corner.

Spanish Wells Drive was barely two lanes in width with no separation to indicate which side to drive on. It also seemed to be shared by more than just automobiles, as indicated by the people we spotted walking or riding rusty old bicycles along the sides, and the unfortunate presence of a mule-drawn wagon that took up most of the road and forced us to slow to a crawl.

Henry also said that the neighbors knew him and would be able to help us if we got lost. So, when we spotted an old woman and a young boy walking on the side of the road, I pulled up close and asked Julie to roll down her window. They were both carrying paper sacks loaded with what appeared to be groceries, and they looked up in alarm as Julie spoke to them.

"Hi, there. Can you please help us find Henry Palmer's house? He said it was somewhere around here."

The boy looked at the woman questioningly and she gave him a slight nod. "Dey house down 'dere." He shifted his bags to one side so he could point down the road ahead of us. "It dat green one wid' da black truck out front. Old dog in the yard migh' bark at ya, but don' min' him. He jis' make noise but don' bite none."

We looked up the road where he was pointing and could just make out a green house on the right side. "Oh, great. I see it now. Can we offer the two of you a ride somewhere?" I asked.

The boy looked eagerly at the old woman but she shook her head. "We close by. 'Preciate yo' offuh, 'do." She nudged the boy ahead of her and started walking in the same direction we were heading.

Julie rolled up her window as she watched them leave. "Hunh. I wonder why they wouldn't let us give them a ride."

I began driving toward the house they had indicated. "I'm not sure I would have accepted a ride from us either. From what I've seen, we appear to be the only white faces around here."

It was true. Spanish Wells seemed to be the first primarily black neighborhood we had seen since we'd first visited Hilton Head, other than the few houses we spotted along the road leading up to Henry's store. I looked at the homes on either side of the road and noticed; although many were of lesser quality and often made of repurposed materials, they were as neatly kept as the others.

There was a curved, dirt drive in front of the green house, and I pulled into it carefully. A tan dog stood up slowly from its spot under the bumper of a black pickup truck and lumbered its way toward us. I remembered the boy said the dog was harmless, and I hoped he was right as I opened the door to get out.

"Hey, boy. Who's a good boy?" I regarded him cautiously. The dog wagged his tail and walked closer to where I stood, bumping his head against my leg when he reached me.

"I think he wants you to pet him," Julie said from behind me. "That's what Sunny does when she wants attention." I bent down and patted the dog on his head which caused him to turn his nose and give my hand a sloppy lick. "Ugh." I wiped my hand on my shorts. "You didn't warn me he'd do that."

Julie laughed at my discomfort. "He's a dog, Georgia. That's what dogs do."

I rolled my eyes at her. "Well, since I'm a cat person, how would I know that?"

I looked up at the sound of a door slamming to see a young girl running down the steps of the front porch in our direction.

"Grammy say ta' come fetch ya."

She grabbed one of my hands and turned to latch hold of Julie's with the other. Julie looked down at her with a smile. "I remember you. We played jump rope at the church picnic." She scrunched up her forehead. "Your name's Neesie, isn't it?"

The little girl ducked her head with a smile and nodded vigorously.

The front door opened again and Henry stepped onto the porch.

"Push dat ole dog 'way, Neesie, an bring dese gals tuh de po'ch weh it shady. Den fin' out weh grumma be."

Neesie led us to where he stood and released our hands reluctantly.

Henry regarded us with a welcoming grin. "Miss Maisie cawd tuh say oonuh come tuhreckly. Say offuhr'um ride. Dey lib jis' obuh dere." He pointed to the opposite side of the road.

"Wow. Word travels fast!" I said with a shake of my head.

He chuckled deep in his throat. "'E stan' so. 'Cep' w'en wait'n' on good news. Den kin tek fo'eber." He pointed at the chairs on either side of where he stood. "Uh yent hab time fuh seddown much. Set een dese rockuh cheer wid we. Mary cum' tuhreckly wid some sweet tea. 'E still hot dis time a day, tho' summuh not full on we yet. Hab dinnuh attuhw'ile when 'e sun lean down."

I eased myself into a chair. The rocker was a weathered gray, and looked like it had been well used over its lifetime. I was surprised at how comfortable it was. I leaned back against it and allowed it to rock slowly. I was just settling in when I felt something wet press against my leg. I bolted upright and looked down to find the same dog that greeted us when we arrived resting his head on my lap. Henry snapped his fingers, and the dog reluctantly moved away from me and lay on the porch with a grunt.

"Don' min' dat dog. 'E jis' ole an' lonesum'. Chillun don' play wid 'e anymo' cos' 'e don' get 'round like 'e ustuh." The dog raised his head slightly and looked at Henry. "Dat rite. Oonuh know warruh say. Wan' tuh run but jis' hab tuh walk. B'leebe us mo' luk den us t'ink." He softly snapped his fingers again and the dog pushed itself up and lumbered over to Henry, laying at his feet with a sigh. Henry leaned over and scratched the dog on its head before turning to regard us again.

"Oonuh been 'joyin' de bizzit tuh de i'lun dis time?" His gaze turned directly to me. " Fin' wha' oonuh look fo'?"

His question puzzled me and I hesitated before answering. "I'm not sure what you mean. We're just here on vacation."

His eyes peered into mine briefly before he looked away. "Sum'time, it not summuch wha' try tuh fin', but wha' fin' oonuh."

The image of the old woman at the cemetery crossed my mind just as I heard the screen door slam shut. Henry's wife, Mary, emerged from the house loaded down with a tray that held a pitcher of iced tea and four glasses, and what appeared to be a frame tucked under one arm.

"Yuh uh is! Whew! 'E sho' wawm tuh'day." She placed the tray on a table next to the door and handed me the framed photograph she'd been holding. "Disyuh fo' oonuh tuh see."

I studied the photograph curiously. It contained the black and white images of a group of people gathered around what appeared to be a gravesite. I recognized a much younger Henry in the photo and a woman who looked like a thinner version of Mary.

The rest of the group contained a mixture of dark and light faces, none of whom I recognized. Mary leaned over the picture and pointed to the woman on the far right.

"Dat Miss Bessie w'en 'e 'bout uh age. Us 'ten' de fun'real ub 'e grum'pa. 'E git 'e de't 'bout fi'teen yeah, still yet 'e duh grebe fuhr'um. 'E haa't hebby an' 'e haa'dly'kin nyam 'e bittle. Attuhw'ile, bex tek'um. Don' onduhstan' 'e de't. B'leebe 'e fin' de ansuh ef 'e wuk haa'd fuh 'e. Miss Bessie lose 'e strengk 'fo' den." She shook her head and tut-tutted before taking a seat in the rocker next to Julie.

I studied the picture more carefully. The longer I looked at it, the more I began to recognize a little bit of the old woman I met at the cemetery in the image Mary pointed out.

"What did her grandfather die from?" I asked.

She pursed her lips and shook her head. "Uh sho'ent know ansuh tuh dat. Miss Bessie study 'bout'um long time. De doctuh 'zammine 'e but not fin' ansuh. G'em med'sin, don' wu'k. Tell de trute, mos' folk's tink 'e die f'um ebil cast on 'e."

I waited for her to explain, but she just took a long drink from her glass of tea and looked as though her mind had drifted somewhere else. I glanced at Henry, who returned my look with a slight nod. "Haa'd fuh Mary talk 'bout. Bessie 'mos' luk murruh tuh 'e. Go roun' Miss Bessie house aftuh school an' mos' all de summuh. Bessie hab no chillun huh'own, an' Mary's fambly hab summuch not nuff 'tention tuh go 'roun. Wu'k fo' all two dem."

Mary seemed to snap back into the present at his explanation. "'E 'paw'tun' tuh uh. Tell 'um, Miss Bessie, uh lub you luk you me own ma. 'E jis' smile an' hug me tuh huh. Attuh 'e gwine, uh dat deestrus' uh eye duh leak." She shook her head sadly. "Mos' folks say 'e de't from bad haa't. Miss Bessie weak w'en was bed chile, an' haa't jis' give out 'ventually. Uh tink it mo' luk 'e gib up on huh haa't."

Her words confused me. She seemed to imply that Miss Bessie's grandfather's death was due to some suspicious circumstances that left Miss Bessie devastated in a way she couldn't get over. Was that why she'd been hanging around his grave? Was she trying to tell me something about the way he died? And if she was, why me?

Her parting words came back to me. You'll know what to do when the time is right. I had thought she'd intended to tell me something about love and my relationship with Jon, but what if all along she was trying to hint that I was supposed to do something about what happened to her grandfather?

The idea that I had actually seen a dead person was far-fetched enough, but to think that same person had also been trying to send me a message from the grave was way more than I could comprehend.

Julie must have sensed my discomfort because she chose that moment to speak up. "Y'all sure do have a nice place here. How long has your family lived in this area?"

Henry and Mary exchanged a look before he replied. "Dis faa'm een de fam'bly since fo' uh bawn. Grum'pa gib 'e attuh de Union ah'my light out fuh de mainlan' an' leabe wuh cawd de contraban' behine. Haa'd fo' dem lib till Gen'rl Mitchel 'stablish freedmun billage. Attuh dat, folks staa't tuh look out fo' demse'f mo'. Uh grum'pa and few odduh come tuh dis part ob de i'lun tuh look 'roun'. No mo'nuh swamp an' trees den, but dey hab notion wuh 'e could be. Fus' house wey us sittin'. No mo'nuh shed. 'Ventually, me Grum'pa laa'n tuh burn up oshtuh shell an' mix wid watuh, san', 'n ash tuh mek wha' call tabby. Dat 'low de house be strong 'gen de wedduh. Mo' strong den wen mek wid jis' boa'd.

"Next ting 'e do, laa'n mo' folks tuh mek tabby. Nyuse bofe timbuh wood an' tabby tuh mek house cool fuh summuh an' wawm fuh wintuh. 'E an' me farruh an' odduh chillun lib yuh long yeahs. House stan' strong. Mary 'n me only moobe 'cos don' hab 'nuff room." He stood and pointed to his far left. "Dat house obuh dere bin dee 'riginal home. Nyuse tuh smoke meat an' fish one side, dry cawn and beans an' 'tings on todduh. Mek sho' us hab 'nuf bittle all yeah."

"W'en 'e do 'e rite!" Mary stood up and folded her arms across her ample bosom. "Got tuh hab de tem'chuh jisso or meat spoil an' cawn dry up."

Henry's right eye twitched as he looked at his wife. "Tink uh don' know dat, ole ooman? Been curin' an' dryin' 'tings since uh binnuh leetle chile. Yo' ain't go hongry dat uh see." They stared at each other for a long moment before breaking out in spontaneous laughter.

Their frivolity was a welcome relief from the tension that had been building in me while I was listening to Mary and Henry talk, and I smiled and shook my head at them. "You two had me going for a minute. I thought sure you were mad at each other."

Mary picked up the pitcher and refilled our glasses. "Can' be marri'd dis long an' 'low leetle 'tings bodduh we. Mos' tings not worth frettin' obuh." She sat back and unfolded a fan she had removed from the pocket of her apron, waving it quickly in front of her face. "'Enry shum oonuh bofe marri'd. Huccome oonuh juntlemun not wid oonuh?"

Julie leaned forward in her chair. "They work a lot. Harry, that's my husband, works for a bank in Nashville, and Georgia's husband Jon is in the publishing business. It was actually Jon's idea that we make this trip. He gave it to Georgia as a birthday present."

Mary's cheeks rose to reveal a toothy grin. "Dat nice! Mos' juntlemun not cumfuh'ble 'nuff tuh 'low'um oomen go off 'lone." She continued fanning herself as she seemed to contemplate the idea. "Enry, wha' oonuh tink 'bout I do dat?"

Henry gave a side-ways glance at the three of us and pushed himself up from his chair. "Uh t'ink uh best be checkin' de ribs fo' dey bu'n." He opened the screen door and disappeared into the house.

Mary watched him leave as she stifled a laugh. "'E not cumfuh'ble talk 'bout dis. Men 'roun heah like tuh b'leebe dey in charge ub dem oomen. Trute be, dat ain't so. Nemmin'. Don' min' dem t'ink 'e. Mek dem happy." She looked at each of us in turn. "'Spect you gals know sump'n'nurruh 'bout dat."

Julie and I looked at each other uncertainly. I wasn't sure how we were supposed to respond to her comment, and I was even less certain if I understood exactly what she meant. After a long pause, Julie spoke up.

"We haven't been married that long. I'm sure we have a lot to learn about how husbands' minds work. But Harry is so sweet. He's always looking out for me and trying to find little ways to let me know how much he loves me. He spoils me, really."

Mary seemed to like her comment because she nodded happily. "Dat nice. B'leebe oonuh hab good man." She gave me a questioning look.

I reached for my glass of tea and took a long swallow. "Sometimes I think Jon and I are complete opposites. He'll say or do something that confuses the heck out of me. But then he'll turn around the next day, or even the next minute, and do something so sweet it makes my head spin. He certainly keeps me on my toes."

Mary nodded slightly. "Nuttin' wrong wid dat. Git too cumfuh'ble, fuhgit tuh 'preciate wha' oonuh hab. Nuttin' wrong wid dat 't'all."

Neesie, who had been sitting quietly on the porch the entire time we'd been talking, stood and spun around in a circle. "I wan'tuh git married someday! I wan' me a hansum man who'll take care of me and buy me pretty t'ings!"

Mary shook her head at her granddaughter. "Chile, 'e bes' be uh long time 'fore oonuh eben t'ink 'bout marri'n. Mo' den 'nuf time fuh dat. Got tuh travel own paat' fus'. No need tuh mek'ace."

Neesie hopped off the porch and ran off in the direction of the wood and tabby house.

"Don' go too far, chile, an' fetch one dem watuhmelyun f'um de shed." Mary watched her go then turned back to us. "'E so quiet sum'time fo'git 'e dere. Got tuh be careful wuh say 'roun chillun. Leetle pi'chuh got big yeah. Nebbuh know wuh dey hol' on tuh."

The rest of the visit was a lot less intense. There were no more discussions of death or dead people, husbands' idiosyncrasies or how wives were supposed to act. If anything, it seemed Henry and Mary were purposefully trying to keep controversial topics out of the conversation. Instead, we talked about food and fishing and things that couldn't threaten anyone. In retrospect, it was a little boring, compared to our earlier exchanges, but at that point, boring suited me just fine.

Dinner was delicious. Henry slow cooked pork ribs over a wood fire. They were basted in some type of sauce that was smoky sweet and the meat was fall-off-the-bone tender. Mary pulled out all the stops on completing the meal, loading the table with cornbread cooked in an iron skillet which made the outside crispy and the inside soft. There was a plate of corn on the cob fresh from their garden and dripping with melted butter, a bowl of baked beans in a bacon tomato sauce, another with tender collard greens cooked with a ham hock, and a large platter that held thick slices of garden fresh ruby red tomatoes.

Everything tasted so good I found myself eagerly accepting second helpings, which I only began to regret when Mary brought out two homemade pies at the end of the meal; one topped with pecans and the other brimming with fresh peaches that oozed out the sides of a golden-brown crust. I leaned back in my chair with my hand over my distended stomach and groaned.

"I ate so much I'm miserable!" I looked mournfully at the pies.

Mary smiled and proceeded to place a slice of each on my plate. "Time 'nuf tuh wurry 'bout bein' full w'en dere no mo' bittle." She filled everyone else's plate with an equal serving of both pies. I noticed she didn't serve herself any, and I wondered why.

Henry glanced in my direction before stabbing a large forkful of pie. "Mary hab de shuguh di'betes. Wuss' day huh life w'en dey tol' e can' hab no mo' sweets. 'Fo' dat, 'e hab hebby belly fuh sweet t'ings."

I looked at her to see how she would respond, but she just nodded sagely. "Dat uh fact. Dat tea uh drinkin' hab no sweetness een 'e. Haa'd tuh swallow at fus', but get ustuh 'e. Redduh hab watuhmelyun anyway. Nuss obuh de hawspittle say 'e sweet but don' hab shuguh." She went back in the kitchen and returned with a plate brimming with slices of the melon Neesie had brought from the shed. "Jis' sweet f'um de sun, lukkuh uh gran'chile." She patted Neesie on both cheeks.

We all dug into the pies. They were both wonderful, and I was surprised to find myself scraping up the last crumbs of each from my plate, as if I hadn't already eaten enough to last me a week. I looked across the table at Julie who was eyeing the last piece of peach pie in the dish as if she was willing it to find its way onto her plate.

Mary looked at Julie with a grin as she pushed herself up from the table. "Uh hab mo' pie so kin gib sum tek wid oonuh." She walked toward the screen door into the house. As she passed her grandchild she remarked, "Neesie, star' clearin' dem dishes 'fo' oonuh run off tuh play." Neesie rolled her eyes, but began collecting the plates and silverware.

Henry pushed his chair back from the table and folded his hands across his belly. "Mary bes' cook on dis i'lun. Always hab tummuch. Dat why keep habin' tuh mek mo' room." He laughed as he adjusted his belt a notch.

He gave us each a discrete glance before looking out across the yard in the direction of the rapidly setting sun.

"'De sun lean fuh down."

I remembered Henry saying he had to be at work very early, so I folded my napkin and pushed back my chair. "Yes, we should be going. Can we help take some of these things into the kitchen first?"

Henry placed his hands on either arm of his chair and pushed himself upright. "Nice ub oonah tuh ax, but Mary an' Neesie tek care ub 'e." He stood with his hands hanging loose by his side and regarded each of us. "Din' mean oonuh hab tuh cut-out hasty, but 'e true dat uh got tuh be at wu'k by dayclean. Uh glad oonuh drap 'roun' dis ebenin'. Hab uh nice cumpuhsayshun. Berry nice."

Mary came out of the house carrying a foil wrapped pie in each hand. "Why 'e go 'n' chase dese gals off, 'enry?"

I accepted the pies from her and turned to hand one to Julie. "We've stayed too long already. Thank you so much for everything. Dinner was great, and we really appreciate you having us over to your home."

Mary responded with a wave of one hand. "Glad fuh hab dey cump'ny. Didn' talk 'bout eb'ryt'ing oonuh wan' know 'bout Miss Bessie, but t'ink 'e 'nuf fuh dis day. Come 'roun dey chu'ch dis Sunday. Meet de pastuh. 'E bes' one talk wid bout' dis. 'E one ub we people."

I frowned at her words. "Unfortunately, we'll be leaving the island before then. We're only here for the week, and our rental ends on Saturday."

Mary fanned herself rapidly. "Dat rite? Dere one mo' t'ing mus' tell oonuh den." She eased herself into her rocking chair and motioned for us to sit.

Julie and I glanced at each other as we sat down. I could feel my stomach clench in anticipation of what she might say.

"Miss Bessie's grum'pa wu'k fuh Maussuh Pinckney. 'E hab de largest crop indigo on dis i'lun. Flower f'um 'e plant mek blue dye, an' Bessie's grum'pa bes' fo' coaxin' dye out de plant. Back den, dye utuh mek color fo' aa'my coat, 'do' dese day use tuh paint dey windo' an' do'. Blue 'trac' good sperrit so dey stay behime an' watch obuh fambly ub dem d'et'. Bad sperrit—us call dem Boo Hags—turn way by de blue. Boo hags berry ebil sperrits. Tek dey skin off de body w'ile sleep an' wear lukkuh clothes cum' dayclean. Sun-lean, shed dey clothes an' fin' someone tuh ride. Suck de breeze out dem. Leabe dem weak.

"Back den, use urine tuh bring blue out de plant. Folks' tink dis gib bad luck. Turn 'way good sperrits an' 'tract boo hag. Man cum 'roun, say 'e pastuh ub chu'ch obuh Chaa'stun. Wan' pit spell on de groun' weh Miss Bessie's grum'pa workin'. S'posed hep gib puhtekshun tuh 'e. Attuh dat, Miss Bessie grum'pa hab berry po' he'lt. 'Ventually, bring 'e d'et'. Eb'rybody ax did Pastuh wu'k good spell or ebil, but don' hab ansuh."

She slumped back against the chair and shook her head slowly. "Miss Bessie beside 'se'f wid wurry attuh 'e d'et'. Say can' 'splain wuh happ'n. Wan' tuh fin' ansuh.

"Sheriff, he a buckruh—dat wha' we call white man. 'E listen to huh but don' b'leebe. Say 'e gon hep, but do nutt'n'. Attuhw'ile, ebry one jis' b'leebe 'e obuh. Not Miss Bessie. Keep tryin'. Still trying day 'e die. Gone huh grabe dat way."

Her story boggled my mind. I had never heard of Boo Hags, but what she described sounded a lot like the ghost stories one of my camp counselors used to scare us with when I was in elementary school.

I began to sense a growing heat where the amulet was pressing against the skin of my chest. At first, I tried to blame it on the lingering warmth of the day, but I also felt myself shiver as a cold chill ran up my spine. The contrast between hot and cold made me feel lightheaded and I leaned forward so that I could rest my chin on my hands.

Mary reached out and put her hand on my shoulder. "Oonuh feel'n poorly, chile? Kin gib sum watuh?"

I shook my head and tried to smile reassuringly. "I'm fine. I just felt a little woozy all of a sudden."

I glanced at Henry, and found his face mirrored the same worried look as his wife's. I straightened my back and rubbed the chill from my arms. "Really. I'm okay. I guess that story just spooked me a little." I looked apologetically at Mary.

"'Magine 'e could'uh. Dat' why hol' back f'um tellin' fo' now. Hard tuh tek in. 'Spect mite 'splain why Miss Bessie repeah tuh oonuh. 'E sperrit hang roun' waitin' fo' ansuh."

Maybe so, I thought, but that still didn't explain what any of it had to do with me. I stood and glanced at Julie, willing her with my mind to do the same.

Julie nodded at me imperceptibly and stood too. "Well, that was certainly a special story Mary, and I appreciate you sharing it with us. Thank you both again for a wonderful evening." She smiled warmly at the two of them.

Mary pushed herself up from her chair and moved so she could embrace first Julie then me. "'E fuh sho' good hab bofe heah. Could drap 'roun 'gen w'en 'e less wawm. Bring oonuh juntlemun wid oonuh." She held me at arm's length and allowed her smile to embrace me as warmly as her hug a moment earlier. "Miss Bessie mus' tuh see sump'n special een oonuh. Mek huh wan' tell huh story. Oonuh jes need tuh b'leebe een own 'se'f. Trute cum clear 'ventually."

Julie and I made our way to the car, placing our pies carefully on the back seat before getting in. Just before we drove away, I looked across the field at the streaks of beautiful evening color that now lit the sky. It made me think about something Ida once said; there was always a ray of light in the midst of any darkness, just waiting to help us find our way. The thought of Ida brought tears to my eyes, and I brushed them away as I turned to look back at Mary and Henry. They were both such sweet people, and I felt privileged that they allowed me to share their home and a little bit about their lives. I liked Henry from the first moment I met him, and meeting Mary was an extra bonus. There was something almost familiar about her, though we shared very little in common.

It suddenly occurred to me I had been thinking the same thing about Ida earlier in the week. We hadn't shared much in common, but our bond was based upon a recognition that began in the heart. That pretty much described my experiences at the cemetery, too. None of it was logical. Not my encounters with Miss Bessie's spirit, my developing friendship with Henry and Mary, or the way the island itself opened my heart.

I smiled to myself as I began maneuvering the car up the dirt drive. Whatever was happening was bound to be interesting, to say the least. And I couldn't help but feel excited anticipation, mixed with a healthy dose of anxiety, about whatever lay ahead.

CHAPTER NINETEEN

By the time we returned to Nashville, spring had fully arrived. The winter's cold had disappeared, leaving behind only a trace of cool air that settled in overnight and disappeared shortly after sunrise. The rain that had been a regular visitor to the city in March and early April, had given rise to a multitude of colorful blooms, and coaxed green life out of the trees and lawns. It was a picture-perfect example of the old saying; "April showers bring May flowers", except it wasn't quite May yet.

We were rapidly approaching the end of the final semester of the year at Belmont College, which meant there was a never-ending stack of papers to grade and reports to finish. Plus, it seemed every one of my students wanted to meet with me privately to see if they could convince me that just adding one more point to their grade would make the difference between life and death, which was the same as passing or failing in the academic environment.

Jon's work gained momentum too, causing him to be up earlier and out later than usual most days of the week. Even the weekends seemed full to the brim with a never-ending to-do list, which kept each of us occupied from dawn to dusk. The schedule left a lot to be desired.

A morning came in mid-May, when we found ourselves eating breakfast at the same time, and we hardly knew how to act. It was almost like I remembered it had been when we first started dating, or more to the point, when he first started staying overnight. We just smiled at each other awkwardly, took surreptitious glances to gauge the others' mood, and generally avoided eye contact. It was weird, to say the least.

Luckily, Ebie wasn't affected at all by our odd behavior. She sauntered in from the patio where we had left the door open to capture the breeze, and sat on the floor between us with a look that seemed to say "I'm here and I'm adorable, so you'd better pay me some attention SOON." Jon, who was always a sucker for her coquettish looks, reached down and scooped her onto his lap.

"What do you say, Ebie girl? Are you in the mood for tuna or turkey today? I'm thinking turkey."

We had this ongoing joke about how we each tended to feed her whichever flavor of cat food appealed to us the most on a particular day.

She responded to his query with an unblinking stare and a steady thump of her tail.

"I don't think she's interested in food right now. It looks like she's trying to tell you that she's not happy being forced to perch on your lap." Ebie was famous for her propensity to stretch the full-length of her body along the top of anyone who happened to lie still long enough for her to claim space.

He scratched under her chin. "Is that right? Are you trying to tell me you think I should lay back down so you can snuggle with me?" He was speaking to Ebie, but he was looking directly at me. "I think that's a great idea. It's been a long time since your mom and I had time for a morning nap."

I looked at him questioningly. "Don't you have to be at work?"

The grin on his face answered my question before he spoke. "Nope, took the day off. I told Mrs. Hanson not to call me unless there was a flat-out emergency, and even then to think twice before she picked up the phone."

My eyebrows lifted in surprise. "But last night you said that you had that meeting today. When did that change?"

"After I heard you didn't have to go in to work. I called the office after you went to bed and left a message telling her to cancel the meeting and anything else that came up." His mouth twisted into a smirk. "I hoped that would be a nice surprise. Is it?"

I hesitated for only a second, but unfortunately it was long enough for Jon to notice. His frown told me that he wasn't pleased at my reaction. "It's not. Is that what you're trying to tell me?"

"No! I was just caught off guard. Of course, I'm thrilled to have some time alone with you. I just wasn't expecting it, and you know how hard it is for me to shift gears suddenly."

His scowl told me he wasn't happy at all with my explanation. "That's not one of your more attractive traits, but I usually try to be patient, because I know you'll eventually come around."

His comment had me bristling with irritation. "Oh really. And all this time I thought you liked that I had a mind of my own. Now you're telling me you've just been tolerating me until I come around to doing things your way?"

We stared at each other for a long moment, each waiting for the other to back down and end the discussion, but there was something about the way he stated things that made me want to dig in my heels. Finally, he released a deep sigh and shook his head.

"Look. I didn't mean what I said. I was just hurt that you didn't seem to want to spend time with me." He reached over and took my hand. "You know how much I love you." His thumb stroked the top of the hand he was holding.

I leaned back against the chair and tried to relax. "I know. But sometimes it seems that isn't enough. Why do we have to argue about everything? Sometimes I wish we could be more like Julie and Harry. They always seem to have such fun together, and even when they disagree, they do it respectfully."

Jon grew quiet as he stared at our joined hands. "I don't know. I guess I'm not very good at compromise. Or maybe I just don't know how to express myself in a way that doesn't sound critical." He stared at the top of Ebie's head while his hand stroked the length of her body. "I guess there's a lot I could learn from a cat, at least THIS cat. She doesn't seem to have any problem letting me know what she wants and doing it in a way that doesn't seem like a demand. Well, that's not quite true. She's very demanding, but in a way that makes it impossible to refuse her." His eyes looked directly into mine. "Can we start again? At least, from a few minutes ago? All I really wanted to say was that I miss you and want to spend some time with you. But only if that would please you, too."

His sudden shift from belligerent to apologetic made my heart flutter and I could feel the amulet heating up. Tears began to pool in my eyes, and I sniffed and swiped at them before they could cascade down my cheeks.

"I'd like nothing better than to spend some time with you. Now, later, and forever. And I'm sorry too, for letting my insecurity get the best of me. Sometimes I just don't know how to react when you get upset with me. It seems no matter how much I try to change, my kneejerk reaction is to get defensive." I reached to reclaim his hand in mine. "Yes. Let's absolutely start over. And I can think of the exact place where I'd like to start." I stood and tugged on his arm.

He gently pushed Ebie off his lap with one hand while keeping a firm grip on mine with the other, pulling me onto his now vacant lap with a firm tug.

"Oh! That was unexpected." I smiled into his eyes.

"I just couldn't wait another second to do this." He placed one hand behind my head and gently pulled my lips against his. The kiss started slowly, but quickly sparked into a flame so intense it felt as if my lips were burning. Jon pulled back to look at me questioningly, his eyes dark with passion. I nodded my consent as he lifted me into his arms and carried me over to the kitchen table. The hard wood pressed against my rear and I shifted in an effort to get more comfortable. Soon, any thought of discomfort was replaced by the extreme pleasure I was feeling as our bodies melded together.

There's something to be said for make-up sex. Actually, I never really liked that expression, but it does get right to the heart of things. The same passion that inflames an argument can carry forward into a passionate igniting of lust and love in the aftermath. What happened in the wake of our own private storm was tumultuous, hot, and totally satisfying.

Afterward, as we collapsed on the sofa luxuriating in the sweet inertia that comes from an intense physical connection, I couldn't remember what we had been fighting about. Well, actually I could, but it didn't seem important anymore.

I rolled onto my side and raised up on my elbow so I could see Jon's face. The sunlight was streaming over his features, bathing the scruffiness of his whiskers and tanned complexion in gold tones, made more impressive by the contrast to his black hair. Jon was one of those people who could tan by just walking through the sunlight, whereas I had to slather on sunscreen even on a cloudy day or risk getting burned.

I pushed a lock of hair off his face where it had fallen across his forehead and he opened one eye to look at me. "Hey there." His eye crinkled at me before closing again.

"Hey yourself. I'm going to get a glass of water. Do you want anything?"

He shook his head. "I think I'll take a little nap, if it's okay with you." Before I could answer, I heard his breath shift into the sound that told me he was already asleep.

I eased myself up from the sofa and quietly made my way across the kitchen, pulling on the clothes I had discarded earlier.

Ebie was sitting in a pool of sunlight in front of the doors to the patio staring at something in the distance. When she heard me walk up, she stood expectantly and began to mew and hop in place. I opened the door to the outside and she quickly scampered in the direction of a squirrel that had been munching on one of the hickory nuts fallen from a nearby tree. The shell of the nut was still green, but the squirrel seemed intent upon coaxing it open.

The air was warm, and I closed the door again to try to prevent the heat from entering the house. I surveyed the room and noticed our breakfast dishes were still sitting on the table. Usually, we were both sticklers for cleaning up after meals before doing anything else, so the fact that we'd left the kitchen in such a state meant we felt being together was more important than tidying up. I smiled as I remembered how urgently we had come together. I picked up the dishes, washing and stacking them to dry while I watched Ebie out the kitchen window.

The squirrel had apparently eluded Ebie's attempt at capture, and she was sitting in a pool of sunlight washing herself and occasionally gazing off into the bushes surrounding the patio. I noticed the bushes had grown thick with leaves while I was out of town, and I vowed to trim them back a little. Right now, all I wanted was to see if I could entice Jon to move into the bedroom so we could continue what we started in the kitchen. I tossed the dish towel on the counter and headed for the sofa.

CHAPTER TWENTY

When I left Hilton Head the last time, I never expected to be able to return again so soon. But when Jon was asked to speak at a conference in Atlanta, just a little over a month after Julie and I returned from our trip, he suggested we drive together then continue on to the island once the conference was over. The fact he willingly added a return trip to Hilton Head to his other plans took me completely by surprise, but I knew better than to look a gift horse in the mouth. So, I happily accepted without subjecting him to my usual barrage of questions designed to ferret out the "hows and whys" of his suggestion. It was safer that way.

The conference was held on a Wednesday and Thursday, which meant we were on the road to Hilton Head Island by Friday morning. The plan was for us to stay on the island until the following Wednesday, which gave us five nights and four full days there. Classes at Belmont had ended for me in mid-May, so it wasn't a problem for me to take as much time off as I wanted. Since Jon was basically his own boss, he also had the flexibility to be out of town whenever he chose.

Since he was so passionate about his work, which is a nice way of saying he was a bona fide workaholic, the idea of him taking a vacation intentionally was a rare phenomenon. I wondered if our trip the previous June had spurred his appetite for the island, or if he was just going there because he knew how much I liked it. Whatever the reason, I was thrilled to be going back.

We arrived on Hilton Head in the midst of a heavy thunderstorm. At one point, the visibility was so bad we had to pull into the parking lot of a gas station to wait for the rain to ease up. Jon hadn't said much during the drive. Whenever I tried to engage him in conversation, he gave me a distant look and asked me to repeat what I'd said. I assumed that whatever had gone on at the conference was on his mind, but it would have been nice if he'd chosen to include me in his thoughts.

While we were waiting out the storm, I scooted over next to him so that I could link my arm with his. "Hey there. Penny for your thoughts." I gave him what I hoped was a reassuring smile.

He had been staring out the window, and he turned to me with a jerk of his head. "What? Did you say something?"

I pulled my arm back and frowned at him. "Do you realize you've barely spoken to me since we left Atlanta? At least you can tell me what's on your mind."

His eyes seemed to focus on me for the first time, and he let out a slow breath. "It looks like my family's publishing company has been sold."

I looked at him closely to see if he was joking. "Sold? But I thought you told me a while back the company was stronger than ever. Why would they want to sell it?"

His gaze turned back to the rain. "My dad wants out of the business. He said he's ready to retire, and he told me last fall that he wanted me to take over for him. That would have meant I'd have to move back to D.C. so I told him no, but I'd like to keep our involvement in Nashville viable by making it an independent operation.

"While I was at the conference, I had a meeting with the representatives of a publishing company based in Atlanta.

Apparently, they've been talking with my dad over the past few months to try to reach an agreement for them to purchase our company. I guess when I told him I wasn't interested in taking over for him, he relented and agreed to their terms. Too bad he didn't bother to let me in on what he was thinking, not that I could have changed his mind, unless I was willing to change mine.

"When I met with the new owners, they informed me the documents had already been drawn up that would make their acquisition of my family's company final by the end of the month. They also said they had decided to terminate the Nashville branch because they didn't feel it was showing enough profit. They offered me the chance to come work for them, but I turned them down."

It took a couple of minutes for his words to sink in. What he was describing was life-changing, for both of us. It meant he would soon be out of a job, and life as we knew it would be irreparably altered. Suddenly the idea of taking a vacation took on new meaning.

"Is that why you suggested that we come to Hilton Head? Because you knew things were about to change dramatically and you wanted to soften the blow by telling me about it in a place I love?"

His eyes widened in surprise as he shook his head vehemently. "Not at all. In fact, I hoped to be able to surprise you with the news that I was going to be able to permanently settle in Nashville, since I thought my business there would be secure. I imagined the Nashville branch would really take off, once the rest of the company was disbanded, and I thought we could celebrate with a few days of vacation together before things got too hectic." He shook his head slowly. "I've been blindsided before in my life, like what happened with *The Daily Courier*, but this is one I definitely didn't see coming." He resumed staring morosely out of the window.

The Daily Courier had been the competitive newspaper to *The Nashville News* until a political move caused it to shut down. Jon and his family had planned to save the *Courier* and take over its publication, but he was taken completely off-guard by the underhanded actions of a few political figures in Nashville who had more to gain from its demise. It was only the quick work of Jon, Ida, Thomas Bookman and myself that enabled it to be relocated to Belmont College as a student-run paper.

I found myself struggling to find words in response to his announcement. I wasn't used to Jon looking so defeated. He was usually the one who was able to bolster my self-confidence whenever things didn't go quite the way I expected, but it seemed the tables had turned on us. Now I was the one who needed to find the strength to boost his morale. The only problem was, I had no idea how to do that. Suddenly an idea occurred to me. "Maybe there's a silver lining to this whole thing."

He looked at me skeptically. "I can't see how that could possibly be true, but go on."

"Well, remember when I got fired from *The Nashville News*, then Ida died? I felt like my world had ended and there wasn't possibly any way things could ever be okay again. But Thomas offered me the chance to work with the journalism program at Belmont. I found out Ida had left me her house and paid off the mortgage, and you and I got closer and moved in together. I never would have predicted any of those things would have happened, but they did, and they gave me the chance to make my life better. Maybe there's some opportunity out there waiting that you've never dreamed of. Something that could turn your life around in a fantastic way."

He frowned. "And what exactly would that be? If you have some sort of crystal ball that predicts the future, I'd sure like to see it."

I squirmed in my seat. I had no idea what I was talking about, and I sure didn't know what might be lurking out there in the future that would make everything okay.

"I don't know what I mean. But I do believe things will work out, somehow. You just have to keep your eyes and ears open and believe that everything is going to be okay."

"Humph. I wish I had your confidence. Right now, the only things I know for sure are that I'm about to be out of a job, and I might have to move back to D.C., since that's the only place I have any contacts."

His words caused my stomach to clench. "But you told your dad you didn't want to run the family business because you didn't want to move back there. Why would you change your mind at this point?"

He ran his hand through his hair. "I don't know. I don't know anything right now. I just need some time to think things through."

I recognized the frantic tone and realized the best thing I could do was to stay calm and reassure him that things would be all right. The problem was I had already tried that, which hadn't gone over very well. Plus, I was having trouble believing it myself. "Well, I think this trip couldn't have come at a better time. We can take a few days to let things sink in, then put our heads together to see what we can come up with." I reached over and took his hand in mine. "Whatever happens, we're in this together."

He looked into my eyes. "I'm glad. This is tough enough without having to worry that I'm disappointing you."

His revelation surprised me. It hadn't occurred to me that part of his misery might stem from his concern over how his announcement would affect me. Despite the dire circumstances, that realization lifted my spirits.

I reached to squeeze his hand. "We're a team, and whatever happens won't change that." I glanced out the front window and noticed the rainstorm had reduced to barely a sprinkle. "Looks like the rain has stopped."

He followed my gaze and nodded. "Yep, so it has." He turned to smile at me. "Thanks. I feel like a load has been lifted off my shoulders. I was really worried how I would break the news to you."

I scooted back across the seat and fastened my seatbelt. "I could tell something was bothering you. I'd rather know what's going on, than just wonder what you're keeping from me. That's when I start imagining the worst."

His mouth turned up in a grin as he started the car. "I know. You shoot holes all over that saying about 'what we don't know can't hurt us'. In your case, I guess it's better to know the truth than to allow your imagination to run wild." He pulled the car out of the parking lot and headed down route 278 which would eventually end at Pope Avenue and lead us to the beach. "Let's get to our rental unit. I could use a hot shower and a cold drink."

I settled back against the seat. That he shared his worries with me should make me feel better. At least now I knew what had been eating at him since we left Atlanta. Still, I couldn't ignore the idea of his pending unemployment, and the precarious situation that worried me to death.

I slowly released the breath I hadn't even realized I'd been holding and promised myself I was going to do everything I could to stay positive while we searched for an answer to this dilemma.

CHAPTER TWENTY-ONE

When Jon first mentioned the idea of taking a short trip to Hilton Head, I assumed he asked Mrs. Hanson to book us in the same motel where Julie and I had stayed during our visit the previous April. Instead, he drove right past the Sea Crest Motel and continued down North Forest Beach Drive before making a right turn onto Dove Street. He drove two blocks before turning left on Dune Street, pulling to a stop in front of a small house.

The house was all on one floor and hugged the ground from side to side. A small porch framed the front door, its roof held up by two wooden beams in the front and secured to the wall in the back. The door to the house was painted dark green with a stack of vertical white-trimmed glass panes embedded into the frame on either side. A set of double windows was located midway along the walls to the left and right of the door, and a row of straggly and unkempt bushes grew beneath the windows. The roof of the house was nearly flat with dark brown shingles that gave a slight contrast to the khaki colored wood siding of the house itself. A large tree flanked the left side of the house. Its low-hanging branches threw shade over two rusty metal chairs sitting on a small patch of grass.

I looked at Jon for an explanation of why we had stopped in front of this old and dismal looking place. "What's this?" I asked.

"This is where we're staying. Mrs. Hanson couldn't get us a room at the Sea Crest Motel because of the short notice. The lady who runs the motel told her the owners of this house had just decided to make it available for short-term rentals. I have no idea what it looks like inside, but I knew you'd love the location."

I swallowed my retort as I stepped out of the car. The house was bordered on the right by a sandy path and I walked slowly in that direction. As I rounded the corner, my pulse quickened as I spotted the expanse of ocean visible through the sea oats atop the sand dunes just beyond the rear of the house.

"Oh! The ocean is so close!"

Jon laughed as he walked up beside me. "I thought you'd like that. I know the house isn't much to look at, but Mrs. Hanson said the owners assured her that it has everything we'll need for a short stay, and you can't beat the proximity to the beach."

I eagerly turned and started walking back to the car. "Let's unpack the car and look inside." Jon stopped me with a hand on my shoulder.

"I'll bring everything in. Why don't you unlock the door and look around?" He reached in his pocket and produced a key ring. "The larger one opens the front door and the other one is for the door that leads out back."

I took the keys from him and eagerly made my way to the front of the house. The door opened easily and I pushed it aside. I scrunched up my nose as I was greeted by a damp, musky smell and squinted as I looked around. The curtains were closed across the front windows so I hurriedly pushed them open, which brought a welcome wash of sunlight over the dim interior. A hand crank beside each window allowed me to let in the outside breeze. By the time I made the rounds of the small interior space, I could already feel a change in the atmosphere.

The house was quite a contrast to the home where the four of us stayed on our first visit to the island. All of the rooms were on one level and were divided by a hallway that cut a swath through the middle from the front to the back. The two front rooms were open areas that housed a kitchen on one side and a living room on the other.

I made my way down the hall and opened a door to the right that revealed a small bedroom. I crossed the hall to open a second door to the left and found another bedroom somewhat larger than the first. I entered that room and discovered a door just inside that opened into a decent sized bathroom. A door in the hall just past the first bedroom also revealed another small bathroom.

I walked to the rear of the hallway where it ended at another door. I tried the doorknob and found it locked, causing me to remember what Jon said about the second key.

I pushed the key into the lock. The door seemed to be stuck, so I gave it a firm push causing it to swing out of my hands and slam against the wall behind it.

I checked the door and was relieved to find it was still in one piece. The door opened onto a screened-in porch that stretched all the way across the back of the house. A second door led out from the porch onto a small back lawn. I discovered a row of stepping stones that led to the sandy path I spotted earlier. The air was full of the scent of fish and salt. I closed my eyes and allowed myself to drink it in.

"Nice, huh?"

I turned at the sound of Jon's voice and smiled at him happily.

"Yeah, it is. The house isn't much to look at, but as you said, the location is fantastic."

He walked up behind me and wrapped me in his arms, pulling me snugly against his chest and pressing his chin against the top of my head.

"Um, you smell good. Kind of like a mixture of flowers and…fish."

I laughed at his description. "I'm glad you think so, but I could really use a shower about now." I swiveled in his embrace and looked past him to where he'd placed the luggage along one side of the hallway. "One of the bedrooms is bigger than the other and has a private bathroom. Why don't I unpack our stuff in there while you make us both a drink? I imagine you could use one about now."

"That sounds great. I'll just put my work stuff in the second bedroom then dig out the drink fixings. You want a gin and tonic?"

"Oh yeah. With extra lime, please."

He smiled knowingly. "How could I forget?"

I knew he was remembering the first time he and I had gone out on a real date. It was to a restaurant in Nashville called Ireland's, and Jon had ordered me a gin and tonic with extra lime. I never had one before, and I swore it was the extra lime that made it special. That, or maybe because I was with Jon.

I picked up our two suitcases and stepped inside the larger bedroom. The floor of the bedroom was covered in a dark brown shag carpet, which reminded me of the apartment where Julie and I had stayed at the Sea Crest. I peeked into the bathroom and found it also had a similar style of linoleum on the floor and a shower curtain with the same nautical design as the motel. "Humph. Must have been a sale on these things," I said out loud.

I quickly set about unpacking the suitcases and arranging our toiletries in the bathroom, then shoved the bags into the bottom of the closet. I headed back up the hall toward the kitchen, pausing to scan the contents of the living room. There was a lumpy looking brown tweed sofa against one wall with a matching love seat and chair placed diagonally so that they all faced the front of the house where a small television sat on top of a metal tray table. A bookshelf was placed on the back wall with what appeared to be a decent assortment of novels and brochures about the island. There was also a small wooden cabinet next to the bookshelf.

I walked over to where it sat and opened two doors on the front. To my delight, it revealed a record player and a stack of LPs.

I lifted the record player and placed it on top of the cabinet and plugged it into a socket on the wall. I leafed through the albums and came up with one I thought Jon would like and placed it on the phonograph. Soon, the sounds of "If You Could Read My Mind" filled the room.

"Is that Gordon Lightfoot? Where'd you find the music?" He walked toward me carrying two drinks and handed me one, clinking my glass with his. "Cheers." We both took a hearty swallow from our drinks.

"Umm, that's good. There was a record player and some LPs in that cabinet. There's a pretty decent selection of music, from what I could tell."

Jon looked around the room and crossed over to where the loveseat was located. He sat and patted the seat next to him. "Join me?

I settled myself carefully to avoid spilling my drink.

Jon's eyes scanned the room while he sipped from his glass. "I have to say the décor is pretty shabby." He shifted around on his cushion. "And this loveseat has seen better days."

I nodded my agreement. "It's definitely not much to look at, but like you said, the location is great, and it has the essential stuff we'll need.

He looked at me tiredly. "Like a bed, you mean? I hope the mattress isn't as lumpy as this loveseat."

I took his hand and squeezed it. "Let's think positive. It's only for a few days, and if we have to, we can use the bed in the other room too."

His eyes darkened. "Sleep in separate rooms you mean? Not even a few lumps could make me want to do that." He turned his head away and sipped quietly on his drink. After a couple of minutes of silence, I was about to ask him what was on his mind when he surprised me by blurting out a solemn "Thank you".

"For what?"

"For listening, and not getting upset that I'm about to be out of a job. I've been dreading having to tell you ever since I heard the news." He shook his head and frowned. "I never expected this to happen. Not in a million years. Pretty naïve on my part. Especially given the precarious nature of the publishing industry. I should have guessed my dad would consider selling after I told him I didn't want to run the company." He turned purposefully to look at me. "Do you think I made a mistake?"

I thought for a minute before answering. "It seems to me you made a decision based on what you felt was right for you and for me, so I can't see how that could possibly have been a mistake. Maybe this is your chance to decide what you want to do with the rest of your life. Didn't you tell me once that you always felt your path had been paved for you by your dad's expectations of what you should do? Well, maybe it's time for you to choose your own path, based on what you WANT to do."

"He sighed. "But my decision put us in a risky situation. I just hope I don't end up regretting it."

I remembered something I once read. "In the end, the only things we'll regret are the chances we didn't take."

His mouth twisted into a cross between a smile and a grimace. "That sounds like something Ida would have said."

"It does, doesn't it? Sometimes I feel her presence so strongly I half expect her to walk through the door."

He sat his glass on the floor and pulled me close to him, wrapping his arms around me. "I miss her too. She frustrated the hell out of me sometimes, but there was no denying she had a way of cutting through all of the B.S. to get to the truth, regardless of whether or not anyone else wanted to hear it." He grew silent for a moment. "I wonder what she'd say about this predicament."

I thought long and hard about his question. It was true that Ida had been a no-nonsense kind of person. In her words, she hadn't been one to "suffer fools gladly". She didn't have the patience to listen to annoying or ignorant people without telling them exactly what she thought of them, although she always managed to do so in a way that was kind and straight-forward.

I tried to imagine what she would say about Jon's current situation, and suddenly her words came into my head as clearly as if she had spoken them out loud. "I remember one time when I was struggling over a tough decision I asked her advice about. She said; "Be wise enough not to waste your time, patient enough not to settle, and strong enough not to force it. Whatever is meant to be, will be.'"

Jon gave me a look that was somewhere between doubt and surprise. "That sounds just like her."

"Yeah. I know." What I hadn't told him was the decision I sought her advice over was whether or not to allow myself to get involved with Jon. So far, acting on my gut instinct about that had proven to be the right thing to do, although at times I had to admit I still had doubts about our relationship. Remembering her words now was reassuring. I realized I had not settled for less than what I wanted in the relationship, and was definitely not wasting my time being with him. What I still had to learn was how to not force things, but just allow them to happen, and not just with respect to my relationship with Jon, but in almost every aspect of my life. That was something I had been working on for a long time.

I turned to Jon with what I hoped was an encouraging look. "Maybe this shift in your career plans will end up being a blessing in disguise."

He looked at me skeptically. "That's hard to imagine, but I'm willing to try to be open to any opportunities that come along." He let his head drop back against the headrest of the loveseat. "I've done what was expected of me by my dad my entire life, at least when it came to my career. It might be interesting to see where things take me if I allow myself to take control of that decision for a change."

His thoughts stirred something in me. What if I allowed myself to also consider whether I was doing what I really wanted to do in my career? Were there other options I hadn't allowed myself to think about? I certainly didn't have any answers to those questions, but I vowed to give more thought to them in the days ahead. Maybe Jon wasn't the only one who needed to be open to change.

CHAPTER TWENTY-TWO

The next morning, I woke to the smell of coffee and the sound of a thunderstorm rattling the windows. I rubbed my hands across my face and opened my eyes to find Jon sitting on the edge of the bed holding a steaming cup.

"'Morning, sleepy head. I thought you could use this."

I regarded the cup he was holding eagerly, and pushed myself up so I could lean against the pillow. "That smells so good! What time is it?" I took a small sip of the hot brew, then a deeper one when I realized it wasn't going to burn my mouth.

He settled himself more snugly on the mattress. "It's around eight o'clock. There are some pretty dark clouds outside, which makes it seem like it's later. I watched the Savannah news, and they're predicting rain for most of the day."

I shifted to more of a sitting position. "I don't usually sleep this late."

He nodded. "Don't forget that we're on Eastern Standard Time now, so it's really seven, according to your body clock."

"Yeah, but we've been in that time zone since we arrived in Atlanta. You'd think I would have adjusted to it by now."

"Don't worry. There's a lot of daylight left. Although, with the weather the way it is, I'm not sure how much we can get out."

I narrowed my eyes at him. "Are you suggesting we might have to find something indoors to occupy our time?"

He sat his cup on the bedside table and placed mine next to it. "Well, now that you mention it…"

Two hours later, I had finished my shower, dressed, and was scrounging around the kitchen trying to find a few things to tide us over until we could get to the Red and White market. Henry hadn't been in the store when we'd stopped by, but his grandson told us he'd let him know we were visiting for a few days.

I was disappointed not to see him, but also a little relieved I could delay a little longer any conversation that might force me to think about the strange events that had transpired during my previous two visits, and the questions that Henry and his wife, Mary, had planted in my mind.

Everyone I spoke to seemed convinced the ghost of Bessie Barnhill had appeared to me more than once. I still had trouble making sense of what happened, but I began to gain a greater understanding when I happened across a television special called "Ghosts, Haints, and the Spirit World." According to the documentary, when a Spirit crosses over from life to death they lose their physical body but may still be sensed by a living human being when they choose to make us aware of them. Some religions believe our human-sensing ability is always with us and is not lost when the human spirit has no physical body. The Spirit may reveal itself to us by linking with our energy and using our physical body as a vehicle of communication. Or, the Spirit may collect their now-free energy molecules into a human shape that can be seen.

Either of these descriptions of how the dead might communicate with the living was foreign to me, but my experience in the cemetery also defied logic. Then there was the issue of the amulet. Did Miss Bessie bring it with her from the afterlife, or collect it from the present? I remembered reading in one of the pamphlets I had picked up on the island how, in the Gullah culture, amulets were often worn as protection against dangerous spirits entering a person and enslaving them against their will. The television special explained that having a good spirit link with our energy could leave the door open for evil spirits to also merge with us. If that was true, then perhaps Miss Bessie was able to take an amulet from those that remained on the island to provide me both protection and guidance.

I shivered at these thoughts and the recollection of what Mary said about the odd circumstances behind Bessie's grandfather's death; that Bessie seemed to have tormented herself to her own death in its aftermath. I rubbed the goosebumps on my arms and filled a kettle with water so I could brew a cup of tea. I usually preferred coffee, but I developed a fondness for tea once I started spending time around Ida. She introduced me to a particular brand called *Constant Comment*. It became a fast favorite, and I reached in the kitchen cabinet to take one from the box I purchased at the store.

I heard the padding sound of Jon's sock-covered feet behind me and I turned to him with a smile. "Want something to eat? I was just about to see what we have."

He walked over to the refrigerator and opened the door. "We have some of the pizza left from last night and there's a little bit of salad, although the lettuce looks a little the worse for wear."

I frowned at the thought of limp, soggy lettuce. "Pizza sounds good. Let's warm it up a bit so the crust is crunchy."

He placed four slices of pizza onto an aluminum pan and slid it into the oven. "Want some juice?" He lifted a carton of orange juice out of the refrigerator and poured some into a glass, pausing over a second one while he waited for my reply.

"No thanks. Just some water will be fine.

Mary and Henry mentioned a preacher who might be able to tell me more about what happened to Bessie Barnhill's grandfather. I was thinking about asking them how I could get in touch with him."

He squinted at me over his glass of juice. "I was hoping you might have lost interest in that particular subject by now."

I looked at him with surprise. "How could I? I have a feeling Bessie is counting on me to help her find some sort of resolution to her torment."

He concentrated on his glass before answering. "But Bessie isn't real. I know you believe she's been communicating with you, but isn't it possible that you conjured up her image yourself because you were hanging out in that cemetery?"

I knew Jon didn't believe in ghosts, or in anything that couldn't be factually proven. That was his nature. As a reporter, you would think it would be mine too; relying on facts to tell a story. Yet, another sign of a good reporter was to keep digging until the entire story was revealed, however that might turn out. "I have to find out what happened to her grandfather before Bessie can rest. At least, I believe that's the case. I know that's hard for you to appreciate."

He shook his head slowly as he regarded me with a smile. "You need to find out so you can rest, too. I know that about you. But are you sure you want to dig deeper into that particular issue? You might end up finding more than you bargained for."

I shrugged my shoulders. "I know. But there's something about the whole thing that nags at me. I don't think I'll be able to let it go until I get some answers to my questions."

He gave me a long look. "Are you sure that's all you want? Answers?"

"I just can't help but think there's a good reason why she appeared to me. Bessie, I mean. She must think there's something I can do to help. I have no idea why, but I think it's only fair for me to see what I can find out."

He regarded me with concern. "Be careful what you wish for."

Because you just might get what you want. That was another Ida-ism, as I tended to think of them. But in this case, all I really wanted was for the niggling sensation that someone or something was waiting for me to take action to disappear. "I know you're right. But I feel there's something I'm supposed to do. I'm just hoping talking to the preacher might shed some light on what that may be."

He grabbed a dish cloth and pulled the tray of pizza out of the oven and plopped a couple of slices on a plate, handing it to me before taking two for himself. "Well, in that case, why don't I call Henry when we finish eating and see if I can arrange a visit? I think it would be better to give him some advance notice of what you're wanting, rather than just spring it on him out of the blue."

I lifted one of the slices. "Sure. Although I bet he won't be surprised. When Julie and I were at his house for dinner, I kept getting the feeling both he and his wife were just waiting for me to quit dragging my feet on figuring things out."

He finished his first slice and reached for the second. "I can't say your description of any of this gives me a great deal of comfort. But there's no way I'm letting you go on this witch hunt on your own." He stuffed the rest of the pizza in his mouth and pushed his chair back, chewing energetically as he walked to where the telephone lay on a table in the living room.

He reached into his pocket and removed his wallet, pulling out a folded slip of paper before beginning to dial the number. After a minute, I heard him talking to someone before he hung up the phone. "Okay. I spoke to Henry, and he suggested we meet him and his wife at the church at 5 o'clock today. He said you'd know where it is."

His announcement caused the amulet to begin to throb noticeably against my chest. "Yeah. Julie and I went there the last time we were here. That's where we met Mary, his wife. Did he mention whether the preacher would be joining us?"

"That's the impression I got, although you know how difficult it is to understand exactly what Henry's saying sometimes. Let's just go and hope for the best."

The idea that I would soon be closer to understanding what my mysterious sightings of Bessie Barnhill meant filled me with a mixed sense of dread and excitement. But more than anything, I was relieved I wouldn't have to take this next step by myself. “It means a lot that you’re willing to do this with me. The idea of going there by myself is a little unnerving.”

He sat at the kitchen table. “I’m still not sure why you want to get involved in this, but I realized a while back, you weren’t likely to let it go without coming to some resolution.” He took my hand in his. “I’m glad I can be here for you. Like you told me about the change in my job situation; we’re a team, and whatever it is, we’ll face it together.” He gave my hand a squeeze. “Now, why don’t we see what we can find to do on this island? Even if it does appear it’s going to rain all day.”

I walked to the kitchen window, pushing aside the curtains. “It looks like it has eased up a bit. How about a walk on the beach? I noticed a couple of umbrellas in the hall closet.”

He carried our dishes to the sink. “Sure. Just give me a few minutes to make a phone call. There’s something I need to check on before we go.”

I looked at him curiously, wondering if his call had something to do with what had happened in Atlanta, or if he was just checking in with Mrs. Hanson. Whatever it was, I decided the best thing I could do was wait until he told me whatever I needed to know.

My past therapy sessions with Dr. Blackburn had helped me understand that sometimes the best course of action was to do nothing. That wasn’t an easy thing for me to do. I was determined to give him enough space to figure out his next move without crowding him into a corner that might make him feel trapped into doing something that both of us would regret. Not that I knew how things could get any more disconcerting than they were already.

It seemed to me things were as topsy-turvy as they could possibly be for us. At least when it came to his job, and the unfolding mystery of Bessie Barnhill that, for some reason, I was smack in the middle of.

I walked to the sink “I’ll just put away our breakfast things and get ready. Take your time.”

He nodded, but his mind looked far away. “I won’t be long.” He turned on his heel and walked quickly out of the kitchen.

CHAPTER TWENTY-THREE

We arrived at the church a few minutes before 5 o'clock and parked on the street in front of the building. Jon hopped out and strode around to open my door, surprising me by offering me his hand. I glanced up at the sky as we walked toward the front of the church. There were still a few dark clouds lingering around, although the rain had stopped mid-day, and there were patches of blue visible across the sky.

Jon pushed open the front door, stepping aside so I could enter first. A whiff of candle-smoke filled my nose, and I squinted to see my way inside the dimly lit room. Rows of dark wooden benches were lined up on either side of the room facing a raised, wooden altar. A painting of Jesus on the cross hung on the wall behind the altar. The rest of the room was nondescript except for the multitude of stained-glass windows that lined the walls and allowed a welcome splash of light to enter the room. An assortment of glass candle holders was neatly arranged on a table just behind the last row of benches, and a stack of well-thumbed bibles sat beside them.

I felt a sense of familiarity that had nothing to do with having visited once before. It reminded me of the chapel in my high school where we were required to attend mass several times a week. The 'have to do' part of that always annoyed me, but I had eagerly sought out the quiet peacefulness of the space, very much like the one I stood in now.

As my eyes began to adjust further to the dim light, I became aware of a man standing in the middle of the room. The whiteness of his shirt stood out in stark contrast to the darkness of his face. He was wearing a pair of faded blue denim jeans held up by suspenders. His hands clutched a straw hat in front of his chest. The sight of him caused me to remain frozen in place and I became acutely aware of the nervousness that had steadily intensified since we began our drive from the rental house. The amulet remained warm ever since Jon announced he had set up the meeting at the church, but now it began to throb rhythmically like a small heartbeat which seemed to match my own.

I could feel Jon walk up beside me and place a hand on the small of my back. He nodded to the man who stood before us and extended his hand. "Hello. I'm Jon Barnett and this is my wife, Georgia. We're supposed to meet Henry and Mary Palmer here."

The man accepted Jon's offered hand. "They told me to expect you. I'm Reverend Henderson. They'll be along shortly." He glanced down at his clothes. "Please forgive how I'm dressed. I stopped over at the home of some parishioners on the way here. Needed a hand moving their tractor out of a ditch, so I figured I'd better dress for the job." He turned and gestured with his hat to a bench on his right. "Why don't we sit and you can tell me a little bit about yourselves. Henry mentioned he met the two of you and your friends a while back?"

Jon pressed his hand firmly against my back, indicating I should take a seat on one end of the bench, then sat beside me. The reverend pulled a chair up from where it sat at the end of one of the rows and turned it so it faced us.

I cleared my throat and addressed the preacher. “That’s right. We first came here about a year ago with our friends Julie and Harry. That would have been in the spring of 1974. Jon and I were married about four months later, after we returned to Nashville. I was able to come to Hilton Head once since then, when Jon gave me a surprise birthday gift of a week here with Julie. This is the first time Jon and I have been back together since that first trip.” *Come on, Georgia,* I thought. *He didn’t ask for your life story!* I glanced at Jon to see if he wanted to add anything, but he was just staring at the Preacher.

Reverend Henderson regarded us both with squinted eyes and a pleasant smile. “If you were here in the spring of ’74, you must ‘a just missed all the excitement. That summer, the bridge was hit by a barge that got out of control when the driver was headin’ down to Savannah. Knocked the swing bridge right out of commission. Nobody could get on or off the island for a couple of weeks ‘till they rigged up a pontoon bridge. Took another month after that for the swing bridge to be fixed.”

He shook his head with a chuckle. “You would ‘a thought we was back at war the way folks panicked. Reminded me of the days when there wasn’t any way to get across the water ‘cept by ferry. I guess most of us take for granted what we have ‘till it’s gone.” He looked at me directly. “Mary told me about your conversation over dinner. I ‘spect you’ve got some questions built up in you by now.”

The throbbing of the amulet intensified, and I placed my hand over it without thinking. “I do, but I’m not sure where to start.”

Jon shifted on the bench so he was facing the Reverend. “Tell us what you know about Bessie Barnhill’s grandfather’s death.”

“Get right to the point, you mean. I thought I’d ease into it so the young lady would have a chance to catch her breath.” His eyes sought mine. “Are you ready to talk about all of this?”

I glanced at Jon then back at the preacher. “Yes, I’m ready.”

Reverend Henderson placed his hat on the bench beside him and sat up straighter. “Then let’s begin.”

For the next half hour, Jon and I listened silently while the preacher told us the story of Bessie and her grandfather, Joshua. As Mary mentioned, Joshua was renowned for his ability to bring the best colors out of the indigo plant, which caused buyers from as far away as England to seek out the paste he produced.

He worked for the Pinckney family, which was regarded as a feat in itself due to their reputation for being fair to their workers. But it was also rare for a freedman, as former slaves were known in those days, to be elevated to the rank of foreman on a plantation. Joshua’s skill with indigo earned him the title of Indigo Master, and there was no shortage of young men and women anxious to be counted among those lucky enough to work under his tutelage.

“At that time, it was common practice for urine to be mixed into a vat of water that was used to get the dye out of the plants. That practice was discontinued in later years after coal tar was distilled to produce ammonia, making the use of urine unnecessary. But when Joshua worked with the plants, there wasn’t any other way.

“The exportation of indigo from Carolina began to drop-off greatly in the late 1700s when England decided to start turning to India for their supply. That’s when most Carolina planters switched to growing cotton or rice instead. The exception to that was the Pinckney plantation that lay just off-island between Hilton Head and the mainland. You passed by where it used to be when you came over the bridge. The land is being turned into a nature preserve now, but back in those days it was a very successful, working plantation. Despite the lessening popularity of indigo in the rest of the state, the Pinckney family kept right on instructing Joshua to produce it, which he did up to the time of his death in 1945. If you look on any official records, you won’t see indigo listed as a Carolina export. It was mostly produced locally, and used locally.”

He pointed to his pants leg. "You see that color? That's from Carolina indigo. It's faded now, 'cause I've worn the color off. But when they were new, you couldn't find a prettier blue. A lot of soldiers used Carolina indigo, too, and it's even supposed to be the source of the blue on our United States flag. When indigo was in its heyday, a lot of planters around the state were puzzled how Joshua's dye could always produce such an intense blue, but he never shared his secret."

"Do you know what it was?" I asked.

"That's where things get peculiar. I told you that urine was used in those days, but that wasn't uncommon. Some say it was where Joshua got it from that made the difference." He looked down at the floor as if he was considering whether or not to say more.

"And where was that?" I was glad Jon had voiced the question I had been hesitant to ask.

"Pregnant cows. Wouldn't use any other kind. He believed the urine from cows that were carrying calves, contained special ingredients that affected the indigo plants in a way no other urine did."

I remembered something Mary told me. "Mary said a preacher came and blessed the soil where Joshua's indigo plants were growing. She said that was supposed to ward off evil spirits believed to be attracted to the smell of the urine, or something like that. Were you that preacher?"

Reverend Henderson looked at me with surprise and burst out laughing. "I'm not THAT old!" He shook his head. "He was the preacher who used to hold services for the freedmen and their families. Drove over from Charleston to do it. He was well thought of, although nowadays his beliefs and ways of doing things might be considered unusual."

I nodded thoughtfully. "Mary also said some people wondered if the preacher's blessing could have had the opposite effect; if it might have been the cause of Bessie's grandfather becoming sick."

Reverend Henderson nodded slowly. "I've heard rumors about that. But there was no reason why the preacher would have had any cause to wish Joshua harm. He was his nephew, after all."

I looked up in surprise. "His nephew? So, that would have made the preacher Bessie's…cousin?"

"That's right. Her granddaddy's sister was the preacher's mother."

I frowned as the pieces of this story began to fall into place. "Then I would guess Joshua's death must have bothered the preacher as much as it did Bessie. What happened to him after Joshua died?"

"Moved away. Took his family and headed up North. Worked for a small church in Pennsylvania. He had some family there. A sister and her husband and their children. Grandchildren came along later, too."

"Did any of them ever come back to Hilton Head Island?" I asked.

He retrieved his hat and began to twirl it between his hands. "One did." He looked up at me. "I was the only one who ever came back here."

It took a couple of seconds for what he was saying to register. "You? You mean that preacher was your daddy?"

He nodded his head. "I decided to become a minister when I was just a boy. Wanted to follow in his footsteps. Once we moved to Pennsylvania, he helped me get the training I needed." His dark eyes looked into mine. "He was never right again after what happened to my Great Uncle Joshua. It seemed to take the spirit right out of him. I decided to come back here to see if I could right any wrong that may have come of his actions. As far as I could tell, there wasn't anything he did that could have caused Uncle Joshua's death. It was one of those mysteries that never gets explained." He looked at me long and hard. "Until now. Maybe there's some reason why Aunt Bessie has been appearing to you."

I took a deep breath and let it out slowly. "That's a lot to take in." I looked at Jon with a silent plea for help. Luckily, his radar was working, and he stood and held out his hand to the Reverend.

"Reverend Henderson, you have been extremely informative today. Georgia and I are grateful for your candor. I think Georgia could use a little time to process all of it. Would it be okay if we got back in touch with you again? Perhaps before we leave?"

The Reverend got slowly to his feet. "Of course. I'm a little hard to catch by telephone, 'cause I'm usually out and about visiting parishioners, but Henry usually knows how to find me." He waved his hand toward the back of the church. "Here they are now."

I turned to see Mary and Henry walking down the aisle. Mary's face widened into a huge grin. "Sorry! Sorry! Daa'tuh drap een jis' as us leabe home. Try tuh 'splain we hab tuh go but hab sump'n'nurrah on 'e min'. Tek w'ile tuh get 'e said." She shook her head with a smile. "Uh g'em exwice 'cep'm 'e ent pay no min'." She glanced between the three of us. "Look lak de paa'ty done bruk-up."

The sight of our new friends warmed my heart, much like the steady throbbing of the amulet which has not stopped since our arrival at the church. Henry was a sweetheart, pure and simple, and Mary radiated loving kindness. I felt safe with them in a way unmarred by differences imposed by race, generation or geography. It was a rare feeling, made even more special by the unusual circumstances that brought us together.

I smiled at them apologetically. "I'm glad to see you but, unfortunately, Jon and I were just about to leave."

Henry held up a large plastic bag. "Pull dese swimps out de net dis mawnin'. Mary say kin bile dem up out back."

I looked at Jon questioningly. He smiled at Henry but shook his head. "That's very kind of you, but we really have to be going now." He looked back at me. "I'm sure Georgia will be in touch with you soon. The reverend has given her a lot to think about."

Henry looked back and forth between us then nodded understandingly. "'Spect so." He held the bag out to Jon. "Yuh. Tek dishyuh swimps. Mo' weh dey cum f'um."

Jon accepted the bag and held out his hand for Henry to shake. "Thanks, Henry. That's very kind of you. We'll be in touch soon." He nodded to Mary. "I haven't had the pleasure of meeting you before now, Mrs. Palmer. I hope we'll see you again soon."

She smiled, winking at me. "Bofe hansum an' wid mannus. Unh, unh, unh!"

Jon returned her smile and stepped aside so I could pass in front of him. I started to leave then stopped and turned back to the reverend.

"If you don't mind me asking, what was your Daddy's name? The one who put a spell on the ground where Joshua was working."

"Moses. Moses Henderson. His mother was Joshua's sister. She married Thomas Henderson. I was named for him, though most folks jis' call me Tom."

I nodded my thanks and walked past Jon as I headed toward the rear of the church, my steps quickening as I neared the door. I turned the knob and pushed the heavy door open, stepping quickly into the fading light of the late afternoon sun. Once I was outside, I paused to let Jon catch up with me, and to breath in the mixture of pine and sea salt wafting in from the nearby shore.

Jon placed a hand on my shoulder, and I turned to look at him. "Are you okay? That was some pretty heavy stuff."

I nodded and shrugged. "Yes, it was. It's all kind of swirling around in my head."

"Just give it some time and maybe things will become a little clearer."

We turned and walked silently toward our car. There wasn't much else I could say. I had hoped that talking to Reverend Henderson would shed some light on the mystery surrounding Joshua Barnhill's death. All I was left with were more questions as I attempted to bridge the distance between life and death. To the Gullah, a person's spirit was present in both realms, which meant that it could just as easily be sensed in one as the other. I had been taught something similar to that in my Catholic upbringing, but that didn't make it any easier to grasp. To be handed physical evidence in the form of the amulet was mind-boggling and a constant reminder of just how unusual it was that the Spirit of Miss Bessie had appeared to me; a non-member of her people and a virtual stranger. It was baffling, to say the least. But it was also a gift, and one I needed to treasure.

CHAPTER TWENTY-FOUR

The drive back to Nashville was fairly easy, at least it passed more quickly than I was used to from my previous trips to and from Hilton Head. I spent a lot of the drive mulling over what the reverend said about his relationship to the Barnhills, and wondering what that meant in the bigger picture of things.

Even though he was willing for us to see him again before we left the island, I decided against it. I guess you could say I was procrastinating. It was true, I was trying to delay digging deeper into the mystery that Bessie's appearance had stirred up. My mind was already a bubbling cauldron of confusion, and I wasn't sure there was any more room in the pot for additional ingredients.

I had hoped things would be peaceful after we returned to Nashville. After all, I was off work for the summer, and Jon was basically moving into a state of unemployment. I assumed that meant we would have a lot of time to just hang out and relax while we figured out what was next for him. But that's the thing about falling into the trap of assuming something. Almost as soon as we walked in the house, things began to escalate into a flurry of activity, spurred on by Ebie, who purred and mewed until I picked her up and clutched her to my chest. Her head kept bumping against the amulet until she finally began to paw insistently at the place where it lay hidden. Its throbbing increased uncomfortably until I had no choice but to reach into my clothes and unpin it, accidentally dropping it on the floor where Ebie pounced on it excitedly. By the time I retrieved it, she had shifted her interest to Jon, and lay purring on his chest where he lay stretched out on the sofa.

Two messages had been left on our answering machine while we were out of town. The first had been from my boss, Thomas Bookman, informing me that he had received a grant which would enable our Journalism Department at Belmont College to host a workshop during July. Thomas was a staunch proponent of what was called New Journalism, and he had been trying to garner support for its inclusion in the college curricula of journalism programs since before he came to Nashville. Apparently, his steadfast determination had finally reached the right ears. He had been awarded a grant by the Bernhardt Foundation, set up by one of the former reporters for the Washington Post who was notorious for having been instrumental in breaking the story that ended the presidency of Richard Milhous Nixon.

Bernhardt's role in that event garnered him, not only accolades from his peers, but also an impressive amount of financial backing from publishing companies eager to help promote new and innovative journalistic styles. The problem was, according to Thomas' message, there was an expiration date on the funds that required they be spent before September. Thomas, in his infinite inclination toward optimism, had promised he could pull it off, causing him to send out an S.O.S. to the rest of us in the Belmont program in hopes we would rally around him. Never mind what he was proposing was a feat that would require Herculean-like efforts from all of us involved! Thomas was convinced it was an opportunity we just couldn't pass up.

The other message was even more of a surprise. Jon's father had phoned to say he would be arriving on Saturday for a visit, and he wanted us to join him for dinner that night. Since we hadn't gotten the message until late Wednesday afternoon after we returned from Hilton Head, that meant he would be arriving in less than three days. I found it a little odd that he didn't ask if we could meet him for dinner. The tone of the message made it clear that saying "no" was not an option.

I wasn't sure which of the calls alarmed me the most: the idea that my peaceful summer was about to be shot to hell by Thomas' latest undertaking; or that Jon's father, an intimidating man I had only met once when we'd visited D.C. after our wedding, wanted to see us for reasons he didn't bother to reveal.

Jon and I were both too tired Wednesday night to tackle the task of responding to either request, so we decided to sleep on it, so to speak. I can't say for my part that I did much sleeping that night. There was too much churning around in my mind to allow me more than a few hours of sleep. From what I could tell by the flip-flopping movements from Jon's side of the bed, he wasn't any more successful.

When I finally gave up the quest to sleep and stumbled out of bed early the next morning, I decided the best thing I could do to prepare myself to face either event was to enlist the aid of Julie and Harry. They could always be counted on to lend perspective to any situation, and these two unexpected twists in our plans could definitely benefit from their calm assessment. When I mentioned the idea of inviting Julie and Harry over for dinner that night, Jon surprised me by agreeing enthusiastically.

"Yeah, that sounds good. I've been wanting to run something by Harry anyway, so that will give me the perfect opportunity. How about I go buy some steaks and potatoes to toss on the grill? Do you have what you need to make salad?"

Jon was the grill master in our home. The idea of getting within an arm's length of hot smoking charcoal intimidated me. So, on grill nights, Jon always assigned me the salad-fixing duties. I poked my head in the refrigerator and scanned the contents.

"We have plenty of iceberg lettuce and a couple of bell peppers." I turned around and looked at the kitchen table. "And there are some great looking Bradley tomatoes we brought back from Hilton Head. I'll make some Thousand Island dressing to go with the salad. Why don't you pick up a loaf of French bread and some ice cream? That should be enough."

He reached into the cut-glass bowl that we kept at one end of the kitchen counter and fished out his car keys. The bowl had been a wedding gift from Mrs. Hanson and, although I'm sure she had imagined we would find a more suitable use for it, it had proven to be a handy spot to deposit keys and spare change.

"Sure thing. I'll be back in a jiff, and I'll stop by the liquor store, too." He leaned over and kissed me on the forehead as he whistled his way out the door.

"What's gotten into him?" I wondered out loud. He'd barely slept the night before and hosting a visit from his father were hardly the makings for a happy mood. Jon loved his father, and wanted nothing more than to make him happy. But he also had more than a little resentment toward him for basically commandeering his life in the direction he wanted, without giving Jon a chance to have much of a say about it. I shook my head as I put our coffee mugs in the sink. *Don't invite worries*, I reminded myself. Whatever was going on with him must be a good thing, because I rarely saw him so chipper.

At that moment, Ebie sauntered into the hallway from where she had been sleeping in a patch of sunlight and stood looking at me. It had been necessary for us to leave her behind while we were on our trip because the Atlanta hotel didn't look kindly on furry guests. But she had been well cared for by Julie in our absence. I swooped her into my arms and showered her with kisses until she pushed her front paws against my chest and stared at me intently.

"You can't be hungry since I noticed you ate every last morsel of the food I left in your bowl last night." She blinked at me with what I could swear was a smug grin.

I took out a can of cat food, dumping it in her bowl before adding some fresh water to the dish beside it. Ebie walked eagerly to the food bowl and sniffed at the contents before starting to eat.

I reached down and stroked my hand along her spine causing her to arch her back. "Slow down, girl! It's all yours." She looked up at me briefly before resuming her meal. When she finished, she sat on her haunches, lifting one front paw so she could lick it wet before rubbing it over her face.

I collected all of the salad ingredients into a heap on the kitchen counter and gave them a thorough washing in the sink before laying them on a cutting board. By that time, Ebie had finished her post-meal bath and was standing in front of the door to the patio starring at it pointedly. "Ready to go out?" I opened the door and she scurried past me.

The temperature had risen considerably since we arrived home the night before, and I pulled the hair off the back of my neck, twisting it into a ponytail. The morning news said the weather was supposed to be sunny and in the mid-90s, but by the time we were ready for dinner the patio should be nicely shaded by the two large oak trees that stood nearby.

I walked over to the wrought iron table we used for outdoor dining and pushed it a little further to where I suspected the shady spot would be, then placed each of the four matching chairs around it. A clay pot full of petunias sat on one side of the patio. The flowers were looking a little straggly from the heat, and I went back into the kitchen to fill a pitcher of water to douse them. The phone rang as soon as I stepped inside the house.

"Hello?"

"Georgia? It's Thomas."

My stomach sank a little as I remembered the message he left on my phone. "Hey, Thomas. Sorry I haven't called you back. I'm still trying to settle in after our trip to Hilton Head."

"I can only imagine. Well, actually I can't. It's been so long since I took a vacation that Mary Alice is threatening to kidnap me one day and force me to go somewhere. What do you think about the news? Pretty great, huh?"

I paused before answering. "Yeah. It's great. Congratulations on getting the grant."

I could hear him chuckle over the receiver. "Do I sense a little hesitation on your part? I know you were probably looking forward to having the summer off, but I assure you I will make it financially worth your while. I'm figuring I'll only need you for a few hours a day, and not every day at that. I've been able to line up a couple of students to help as well. Between them and the time my secretary and I can put in, things should move along fairly swiftly."

The idea of devoting even the amount of time he was describing was depressing, but I hesitated to let him know that. Since it looked like Jon was going to be out of work soon, we could use the cushion of a little extra income. "Okay. When do you need me to start?"

I could almost see him squirm over the phone. "That's the thing. I need you right away. The workshop is scheduled for the last week in July, and there's a lot to do before then. Can you come in tomorrow? Say, around nine? I figured we could tackle some of the scheduling details over the next few days, then get to work on the actual content."

I considered what he was saying. Jon's father was arriving sometime Saturday. Luckily, he hadn't asked to stay with us, but I still wanted to make sure the house looked presentable in case he decided to stop by.

"Yeah, I can do that. I have some things I need to do around the house because Jon's dad is coming to town on Saturday, but I should be able to take care of them that morning."

"His dad is coming to Nashville? That sounds serious. I don't think I can recall Jon mentioning him visiting before, even when there was all of that mess with the newspapers. He stayed conveniently out of the picture that time and let Jon take the heat. I hope his coming to town isn't a foreboding of something bad happening?"

I started to fill him in on what Jon told me after we'd left Atlanta but decided that was Jon's story to tell, if and when he chose to. "We really don't know why he's coming. He just left a message on the answering machine saying that he'd be here on Saturday, and would like us to meet him for dinner."

"Maybe you shouldn't come to work tomorrow then. I'm sure you have a ton of things to do before he arrives."

I considered his offer. "Actually, working will be a nice distraction. It will help keep me from running through a laundry list of what he may or may not be coming here to stir up. I've only met him once, and he didn't exactly shower me with affection."

"Well, okay. If you're sure, I'll see you tomorrow morning."

After I hung up the phone, I had a momentary panic attack, as the possibilities of what lay in store for me over the next few days began to sink in. I sat on one of the kitchen chairs and let my breath out slowly, unconsciously reaching for a pad of paper and a pencil to jot down one of my endless to-do lists. My therapist, Dr. Blackburn, helped me understand that keeping these lists was an antidote to the anxiety that tended to overcome me anytime I felt things were moving out of my control. I held the pencil over the paper for a moment, then wrote the number one. I glanced around the kitchen before adding the words "make salad" next to it. Something about writing down that simple task made it feel less daunting, and I quickly began to add to the list until I arrived at the number eight.

I placed the pencil on the table and leaned against the chair. "Okay. That's done." I let my eyes scan the page before I stood and headed to the kitchen counter so I could chop the vegetables for the salad. I placed the lettuce and peppers into a bowl and set it in the refrigerator so they would stay crisp, then mixed up the ingredients for the dressing which I also placed in the fridge to chill. Since tomatoes tasted better at room temperature, I decided to wait and slice them just before serving the salad.

I wiped my hands on a dish towel and picked up the pencil so I could make a checkmark next to the number one, immediately feeling a sense of relief that there was one less thing to worry about. Then number two.

"Laundry. This isn't so bad."

I peeked out the window to make sure Ebie was content staying outside, then headed for the bedroom so I could collect our dirty clothes from the trip.

CHAPTER TWENTY-FIVE

By the time Julie and Harry arrived for dinner, I managed to check off three more items from my to-do list. All that was really left was to go to work, tidy up the house on Saturday morning, and get a haircut. Since all of that was perfectly doable in the time I had left, I was able to relax and enjoy the evening with our best friends.

Jon and Harry immediately grabbed a couple of cold drinks and headed for the grill on the patio, which allowed Julie and I a chance to catch up. I poured two glasses of white wine from the bottle chilling in the refrigerator.

"Let's take these into the living room where we can talk without being overheard." I said.

She looked at me curiously as she followed me out of the kitchen. As soon as we sat, she turned to me with an insistent look. "Okay. Spill it."

I rolled my eyes at her over the top of my glass. "How do you do that? No, wait, don't tell me. I'd rather keep it a mystery." I took another sip of wine. "Jon's dad is coming to Nashville on

Saturday and he wants us to meet him for dinner. Plus, Thomas called and I have to go into work tomorrow and several days after that. Plus, Jon found out while we were in Atlanta that his company has been sold, so he's basically unemployed."

Her eyes grew wider with each thing I added to my reply. Finally, she shook her head in disbelief. "Good grief. That's quite a list. Why is his dad coming to town? And why do you have to work over the summer? And what did you say about Jon being unemployed? I don't know what to ask first. Why don't you start with what happened in Atlanta?"

"Jon had a meeting while he was there with some men who informed him that his father sold the family business to them. The first thing they plan to do is to shut down the Nashville office because they said it wasn't cost-effective to keep it open. Jon's been making some phone calls that I assume were related to that, but he's kept them to himself. I don't know if his father's visit has anything to do with the sale, but I have to guess it does. As for the rest, Thomas got a grant to hold a workshop in July, and he asked me to come in to help with the arrangements."

Julie leaned back against the sofa and shook her head as if she was in a daze. "Is that all? Any one of those things by themselves would be enough to have me crawl under the covers and threaten to never come out again. How are you handling it all?"

I realized when she asked the question that I hadn't really allowed myself to consider what I was feeling. "It's funny, but the idea of seeing his dad bothers me the most. For some reason he makes me feel ten years old when I'm around him, although I've only seen him a few times when we took that trip to D.C. after we got married."

"Well, you remember that saying by Eleanor Roosevelt that you told me Ida was always quoting to you."

"Yeah. 'No one can make you feel intimidated without your consent.' It used to piss me off when she said that, although she was always right on target when she did. You think that's what's happening to me with Jon's dad? If so, then that must mean

I'm in control of how I feel." I shook my head in confusion. "I'm not sure I believe that's true, but it's definitely something to think about."

"I didn't mean to imply it would be easy to change how you feel. It just seems, from what you've told me, he's a Class A bully, and bullies gain power when they see they can intimidate their prey. Why do you think he's coming to Nashville? Especially at this particular time."

I had asked myself the same question, and the only answer I could come up with was that he thought he might be able to use the leverage he'd gained from the sale of the business to coerce Jon into returning to D.C. "Jon seems to think his dad has the idea this recent turn of events will be enough to cause Jon to run home to D.C. like a good little boy. Jon doesn't seem inclined to do that. At least, I hope not. I know that's a selfish thing to say, but I really can't imagine living there. We only visited for a few days, but I never felt comfortable the entire time."

Julie waved her hand in an attempt to erase my concern, but her gesture was useless. The notion that I might find myself uprooted and replanted in hostile territory was now firmly planted in my mind, and I could already feel it beginning to grow in magnitude. Julie patted my knee reassuringly. "Let's change the subject. Tell me about the job Thomas has you coming in for tomorrow."

It was a relief to talk about something else. "The workshop is funded by a grant out of D.C. It's pretty impressive that he was awarded it, but it stipulates the funds have to be used before September. Thomas agreed to host the workshop in July, and he needs all of us who work for him to come in right away in order to pull it off. The extra money is a plus since Jon may be out of work for a while, but I really wanted to have the rest of the summer off. Especially since Jon may have a lot of time on his hands. I thought maybe we could take another vacation together. Maybe go back to Hilton Head, or check out some other beach somewhere."

Julie sat up straight and swiveled to face me. "Oh! I forgot to ask! How did things go when you were there? Did you get any closer to figuring out what's going on with the ghost story, at least that's how I've come to think of it?"

I was about to launch into a description of what I learned from Reverend Henderson when Harry appeared at the door to the living room.

"Dinner's almost ready. Jon said to bring out the salad and bread, and I'm going to fix us a refill on our drinks. Should I grab the rest of the wine for you two?" He gestured to our almost empty glasses.

Saved by the bell, I thought. "Thanks, we'll grab a refill before we come out, but you could take that pitcher of ice water from the kitchen counter."

He gave me the OK sign and turned back toward the kitchen.

We all busied ourselves collecting the rest of the dinner things and stepped out onto the patio. I was pleased to see the table had already been set, and the Tiki torches surrounding the patio had been lit. They were supposed to repel mosquitoes and other flying pests, although their effectiveness was suspect. Regardless, they cast a cheery glow to the dimming light and made me think of the Tiki Hut bar Julie and I visited during our last trip to Hilton Head. I wanted to show it to Jon while we were there this past week, but the rain and the shortness of our stay had interfered with my plans.

We all sat at the table as Jon doled out the steaks and potatoes. The smell was incredible! There was really nothing like the smell of grilled meat, and Jon's steaks were as good as any I'd ever had. Julie and I switched to red wine to complement the meat, and I lifted my glass in a toast.

"Here's to good food and better friends. May we always find the time to enjoy both."

Everyone clinked glasses before diving into the food. I looked around the table at the three people who I loved as much as anyone in my life and gave a silent prayer of thanks for their presence. There was still a lot of uncertainty that loomed over my life. Especially for the immediate future. But I felt a twinge of hope everything was going to work out alright.

Later that evening, I was still thinking about something Harry said at dinner when Jon walked into the kitchen and wrapped his arms around me from behind. I leaned back against his firm chest and sank into the embrace, relishing the feeling of closeness between us. It hadn't always been that way. Sometimes it seemed as if our communication was hampered by a thousand little niggling irritations that kept us from relaxing in each other's company. But when things were going well, it was a feeling I treasured.

"What did Harry mean at dinner when he said you had a wild card up your sleeve? I got the feeling he let something slip that he wasn't supposed to."

I could feel his grip loosen around me as he took a half step backwards. "What was that? Oh, you know Harry. He gets an idea into his head, and he's convinced everyone else knows what he's going on about." The heat from his body was replaced by coolness as I felt him move further away from me. "There's a little bit of wine left. Do you want to finish it off?" He held up the almost empty bottle.

I regarded him out of the corner of my eye. It was obvious he was trying to distract me, but I decided to let it pass without comment. "No, thanks. I should go to bed soon. I have to be at work tomorrow morning at nine o'clock."

"I have to be somewhere around that time, too. Want me to drop you off? I can pick you up anytime you're ready, and we can stop somewhere for a bite on the way home."

His behavior was growing even more curious by the moment. Jon rarely suggested that we ride together to work, since he usually liked to keep his schedule free for whatever came up. It was just as unusual for him to suggest we stop somewhere on the way home. Jon was a homebody by nature. He'd much rather sit in his own living room sipping a scotch, or fire up the grill for dinner on the patio, than pay to eat and drink somewhere else. It wasn't that he couldn't afford to do those things, it was just, according to him, he'd spent too many years living in hotels and eating in restaurants to enjoy it anymore.

I decided not to question a gift horse when it trotted by me. "Sure. That'd be great. I don't know what time I'll be finished, but I can give you a call when I know. Will you be at home, or should I call your office?

"Let me call you. That way, you won't have to track me down." He busied himself putting away the rest of the leftovers. "I think I'm going to work in my study for a while." He leaned over and kissed me on the forehead. "Come say goodnight before you go to bed."

I watched him as he walked quickly out of the room.

Ebie moved from where she'd been indulging in a post-meal bath and rubbed against my legs. Jon had pampered her as usual by filling her bowl with scraps of steak from our plates, and she was licking her lips with pleasure. I reached down and picked her up, shifting her weight so I could peer into her eyes. "What do you think he's up to?" She looked back at me innocently then began to purr as she rubbed her head under my chin. I had taken to wearing the amulet closer to the side of my chest than the front so that she was less likely to bump against it and set off its insistent throbbing. "I wish life was as simple for me as it seems to be for you. All you need is something good to eat, someone to pet you, and a comfortable place to sleep, and you're happy." I considered what I just said. "You know what? Maybe I'm making things too complicated, because that's pretty much all I need, too."

I turned off the kitchen light and set off up the stairs with her in my arms.

CHAPTER TWENTY-SIX

The next day proved to be less grueling than I anticipated. Thomas had been hard at work laying out the workshop schedule and lining up presenters for the various topics. Luckily, he had a long list of ready candidates among his professional colleagues who seemed to be just as uninterested as he was in taking an entire summer off from work. The stipends they would be receiving were pretty good too, which I was certain had been a factor in his managing to convince some of them to give up their free time.

By late afternoon, we had completed the scheduling and arranged for the AV equipment that would be needed. There was still the matter of printing out notices about the workshop, generating a mailing list that could reach as many potential participants as possible, then tacking on addresses before dropping them at the post office. And all of that needed to be finished over the next couple of days. The workshop was scheduled to take place in just a little over three weeks, which was a ridiculously short amount of time to pull off a project of this magnitude. Only the formidable efforts of everyone involved could assure that it would not turn out to be a total disaster.

Luckily, Thomas' secretary, Mrs. Stayhill, had been keeping detailed records of every contact Thomas had generated since he had been working at Belmont. Quite a few others she'd been able to ferret out from the scraps of paper he brought with him from his previous job. She also managed to convince an administrative assistant at the *Daily Courier* to turn over a list of names and contact information for every newspaper reporter who worked within a 200-mile radius of Nashville. Since the workshop only needed about 25 bodies to be considered full, it didn't look like finding enough attendees should be a problem. Especially since the grant provided for free attendance, lunch each day, and a catered banquet on the next to last night.

I was just putting the finishing touches on the program announcement, so I could run it by Thomas then hand it off to Mrs. Stayhill for printing and mailing, when I heard a familiar voice behind me.

"This looks like Grand Central Station on a Friday afternoon."

I turned to see Jon leaning nonchalantly against the door frame.

"What are you doing here?" I glanced at my watch. "Oh! It's almost six'o clock. I'm sorry. I thought we'd be finished before now."

He pushed away from the doorframe and walked over to where I was sitting, leaning over my shoulder so he could glance at the program I was working on. "Impressive. It looks like you've made a lot of progress in one day." He lifted the paper from my desk and studied it thoughtfully.

"This looks good. I'll bet I can round up a few folks who might be interested in attending. Including myself."

I looked at him in surprise. "Really? You'd want to attend the workshop?"

He shrugged his reply. "Why not? I seem to have some extra time on my hands. Besides. It might be fun to see what you do over here." He laid the program back on my desk. "Are you about to finish for the day? I forgot to eat lunch and I'm starving."

When he said that, I suddenly realized I hadn't had lunch, either. Skipping a meal wasn't something I made a habit of, but I could sometimes get so wrapped up in what I was doing, stopping to eat never crossed my mind.

"I just need to go over this with Mrs. Stayhill. It shouldn't take more than ten, maybe fifteen minutes at the most."

"Okay." He walked over to where a rickety folding chair sat empty in one corner. "I'll just wait here." After collecting the program and a few other papers from my desk, I headed out the door to find Mrs. Stayhill. When I returned, he was still sitting where I left him, but he was deeply engaged in conversation with Thomas who was leaning against the bookcase. They both looked up when I entered.

"Jon and I were just discussing the workshop. I think I've convinced him to help conduct the session on innovations in newspaper publishing. It should be a piece of cake for him, given all of his experience in that area."

I glanced from one to the other, noticing a shared expression of satisfaction on their faces. "Great! But I'd better run tell Mrs. Stayhill there's a last-minute change to the schedule." I grabbed a spare copy of the draft from my desk. "What time slot are you putting him in?"

Thomas glanced over the program and pointed about midway down the sheet. "On Wednesday, just after the lunch break. He'll be piggybacking with a buddy of mine from the *Chattanooga Times*. Between the two of them, they should be able to keep everybody from dropping off into a post-lunch snooze."

I smiled at the image and hurried down the hall. When I returned, Thomas was gone, and Jon was perched on the edge of my desk, twirling the car keys in his hand. He stood abruptly when he saw me.

"Now can we go? My stomach-clock says it's half-past-starved."

"Me, too." I walked to my desk and retrieved my purse from the drawer.

Jon turned on his heels and strode purposefully to the door, stepping aside so I could pass before shutting it tightly behind him.

I looped my arm in his and gazed up at him. “Where to, Mr. Barnett?”

“Brown’s Diner? I know it’s a little shabby but they make a great cheeseburger.”

My mouth began to water at the mention of the savory, greasy treat that was one of the specialties of the small establishment. It made me think of Julie and the grease stained bag she brought up from the restaurant for our first night in the Sea Crest Motel. I guess, when I was extra hungry, the idea of fried fat was somehow appealing. “Ummm. That, and an order of their fries, sounds great.”

The next morning, I awoke with the feeling that something was off. My stomach felt tight, and I was sweating even though we lowered the temp on the AC the night before to ward off the sweltering heat typical of summertime in Nashville. It was difficult to keep the indoor temperature comfortable since our window air conditioning units only managed to cool a small area close to where they were located. Plus, all the heat from the bottom floor drifted upwards.

I pushed aside the sheet that had twisted around my feet during the night, and walked to the bathroom. A glance in the mirror told me that I looked as bad as I felt. My eyes were puffy, and my hair stood out in all directions. I leaned over the sink and splashed water over my face then used my wet hands to try to flatten out my hair so I could run a brush through it.

I hadn’t noticed whether or not Jon was out of bed when I’d left the room, but when I returned, I found he was nowhere to be seen. He had kissed me distractedly when I went to say goodnight to him in his study, quickly turning his attention back to some papers strewn across the desk. I hadn’t been aware of him the rest of the night, either. Usually, I could sense him next to me even in the dark, but last night I had been so tired after my long work day I had fallen into a deep sleep as soon as my head hit the pillow.

I pulled off the damp t-shirt I slept in and replaced it with a clean camisole and shorts before heading downstairs. Jon was sitting at the kitchen table when I walked in. His head was bent over the morning paper, a half-empty mug of coffee in one hand.

"'Morning. Did you sleep well?" I asked.

When he looked at me, I could see dark circles under his eyes and his hair was as tousled as mine had been.

"I didn't get much sleep. I got engrossed in what I was working on and time just slipped past me. I didn't want to disturb you so I conked out on the sofa for a little while." He stretched and rubbed the small of his back. "That sofa may look nice, but believe me, it leaves a lot to be desired as a bed."

I walked to the coffee pot and filled a mug before sitting at the table across from him. "I know. I've napped on it a few times, and I always end up wishing I had taken the time to go upstairs." I took a sip of the hot coffee then added a healthy dose of milk to cool it slightly. "What were you working on so late?"

He cleared his throat and sat back in his chair. "I was just trying to work out some thoughts so I could get them clearer in my mind. I haven't quite gotten there yet, so I'd rather wait to talk to you about it when I know exactly where I'm headed."

I frowned at his explanation, which made little-to-no sense to me at all. I wasn't sure if he was being intentionally vague, or if my addled brain was just having trouble comprehending anything. "Am I supposed to understand what you just said?"

He smiled. "Not really. I'm sorry for being unclear. I'm just not ready to talk about it yet."

Jon was a perfect example of an analytical mind. He liked to work out the details of any situation before he would discuss it. Since I was the opposite, in the sense that I liked to verbally hash things out from all angles before arriving at a consensus, we tended to regularly butt heads over even the simplest decisions.

I sighed and decided to let the discussion drop. Truth was, I was just too out-of-sorts to get into a verbal tug of war. "I'm not doing very well this morning. My stomach feels weird. Maybe it was all of the grease I ate at dinner."

His look said he understood. "Could it have anything to do with what's happening tonight?"

His question startled me into remembering this was the night we were supposed to meet his dad for dinner. "I'd almost forgotten! Is it possible my subconscious remembered before my conscious mind did?"

He frowned. "That sounds a little too much like something your therapist would say, or I imagine she would, since I've never met her. I just meant; it wouldn't be unusual if you were a little apprehensive about seeing my father again. The two of you didn't exactly hit it off the first time you met."

"That's putting it mildly. I had the feeling he was sizing me up and I fell short on every level. It was almost like he was determined not to like me before we even met."

"That's probably true. He was a big fan of my first wife. He never lets me forget how disappointed he is that I, in his words, 'let the best thing that ever happened to me go wrong', which is pretty crazy given that she cheated on me and practically ruined my life."

"I remember you telling me the marriage was set-up by your father and hers. That doesn't exactly sound like a recipe for success. But I don't understand why he chooses to regard me as part of the problem. Surely he doesn't believe you would have gotten back together with her if I hadn't come along?"

He shook his head emphatically. "There was absolutely no chance of that happening, and he knew it. He just isn't one to ever admit fault, and to be honest, setting us up in the first place was wrong. My father is a clear example of someone who believes it's his way or the highway. I've heard him say more than once that unless I do what he tells me, whether it's in relation to my career or personal life, I'll just have to accept the consequences. I suspect he's behind the decision by the new buyers to close the

Nashville office. It's probably his thinly veiled attempt to corral me into doing what he wants."

"Which is?"

"Move back to D.C. and take over the family business. It's what he planned for me to do my whole life. Moving to Nashville to try to carve out a life for myself has been a huge irritant to him. I don't imagine it's something he's willing to let go of without a fight."

I rested my elbows on the table and leaned my chin on my hands. If what he was saying was true, and I had every reason to believe it was, then it was quite likely his father was coming to town with one purpose in mind; to convince, or coerce Jon into returning to D.C.

I could feel my stomach tighten even further as these thoughts filled my mind. I realized my physical discomfort was most definitely a symptom of my mental and emotional distress over the approaching visit. I looked at Jon to see if I could gauge how he was feeling. His jaw was set in the hard angle that I recognized, meaning he intended to have his way. At times, when the way he wanted was in opposition to what I had in mind, this image was off-putting. But knowing what situation he was likely marshalling his strength against today helped to ease my discomfort.

"What will you do if he tries to insist that you move back?"

He stood abruptly, causing his chair to fall backward. Ebie took off like she'd been shot from a cannon and disappeared down the hallway. Jon looked stunned. He bent and lifted the chair back into place and rubbed his hand through his hair.

"Sorry. I guess I'm more agitated than I realized. Don't worry. I'm not about to let anything happen that wouldn't be good for us. You have my word on that."

I looked at him uncertainly. "Okay. I can't say I feel one-hundred percent certain of what that means, but I'm willing to trust you."

He smiled slightly. “Good. Now what do you say about getting out of here for a while. Why don’t we walk to Hillsboro Village? Maybe have some pancakes at the Pantry?”

My stomach growled in response.

He smiled at me knowingly. “I guess that’s a ‘yes’. Why don’t you run up and change while I make a phone call? I’ll only be a few minutes.”

It seemed to me that he had been making an awful lot of private phone calls the past few days, but I decided not to comment on what he said. If there was one thing I learned in my numerous therapy sessions, there was a time to speak, and a time to remain silent. Or in the words of one of my favorite songs by The Byrds, which was a direct adaptation of part of the Book of Ecclesiastes, ‘To everything – turn, turn, turn. There is a season – turn, turn, turn. And a time to every purpose under heaven’. This was clearly the time to hold my tongue and see what happens.

CHAPTER TWENTY-SEVEN

When we returned from our walk and breakfast at the Pancake Pantry, there was a message on the answering machine from Jon's dad telling us to meet him at seven o'clock that evening at Mario's. Mario's was regarded as one of—if not the—top restaurants in Nashville, and, to go along with that status, one of the most expensive. I shouldn't have been surprised that Jon's dad would have picked it for our dinner, but the realization of where we were going that night meant I had to find something suitable to wear. Given the choices I knew were hanging in my closet, I realized I needed to recruit someone with a keener eye for clothes than my own.

The last time it had been necessary for me to step outside of my comfort zone and wear something dressier than my usual attire, I enlisted Julie's help. That occasion had been a formal dinner held by the *Nashville News* in the ballroom of the Cheekwood Mansion. Although I didn't need something nearly as fancy for the dinner with Jon's dad, I decided to ask her advice.

Julie arrived at our house within thirty minutes of my cry for help, and ten minutes later we had collected a sizable pile of rejected outfits on the floor of my bedroom. I was just about to give up on the idea that we could find anything appropriate when Julie cried out in delight as she turned to me with a dress in her hand.

It was a simple, sleeveless black sheath. I had only worn it once when I attended Ida's funeral, which explained why I had hung it at the very back of my closet where it was both out of sight and out of mind.

"Are you sure that's suitable for dinner with Jon's dad?"

She looked at me like I was crazy. "Absolutely! A little black dress is always appropriate for special occasions. Except weddings, I guess, unless you're trying to send a particular message to the bride and groom." She hung the dress on the closet door and started rummaging through my shoes. "These will do." She held up a pair of black pumps with a two-inch heel. I usually avoided wearing heels because they made me feel off-balance. But on this occasion, I felt the added height might help me feel less insignificant next to his father.

I looked at the outfit and nodded my approval. "Okay. I'm glad that's taken care of. Thanks, Julie."

She tucked her hands into the pockets of her shorts and shrugged. "Glad to help. Now, what are we going to do with your hair?"

I reached up to feel the ponytail that I had been wearing since the weather turned hot. "I suppose I need to wash it and coax it into submission." My hair had a tendency to grow in width when it encountered humidity, which was why I often kept it tied up.

"What time are you meeting him for dinner?"

"I think Jon said seven o'clock. We'll probably leave here around 6:40 pm."

"Great. I'll come over at 5:30 with my curling iron. Just be sure you've washed your hair by then, and wrap it in a towel. I can use the iron to straighten out the kinks. As long as you don't go outside before you leave, it should stay pretty straight until you get to the restaurant."

I looked at her with appreciation. "You're a lifesaver. I never learned to do a lot of these girly things when I was growing up. It's nice to have a sister around to help me."

A flush covered her cheeks as she dipped her head. "I think of you as my sister, too. I'd better be going. Harry and I are supposed to pick up Sunny and Barkster and take them to the park. I'll see you later."

I followed her out of the bedroom and watched as she scurried down the stairs, chuckling to myself as I realized that my simple reference to her as my sister had embarrassed her. Although I'd never said the word out loud before now, I thought of Julie as my sister almost from the first day we met. At least, she embodied what I imagined a great sister would be like; someone I could bounce ideas off without having them immediately negate my feelings, who wouldn't hesitate to tell me when I was wrong, but was just as quick to tell me when I was right. Someone to guide me in ways my mother never had.

I guess that's what it really came down to. I never had the kind of guidance from my mother that helped me grow to become a confident woman. Therapy had helped a lot in that regard, but it couldn't replace the importance of having someone like Julie in my life. Well, not just someone like Julie, but Julie specifically. She was a special person, and I valued her friendship tremendously.

I headed down the stairs to find Jon, and I vowed to myself to find more ways to let her know just how important she was to me.

Jon and I arrived at Mario's restaurant about ten minutes past 7 o'clock. We left home early enough to arrive on time, but an accident we encountered along the way held us up. I could tell by the brooding silence surrounding Jon while we waited for the traffic to clear, that any delay in meeting his father would not be well received, and I could feel my own anxiety begin to grow.

We pulled up to the valet parking counter and handed over the keys to a young man in a red coat who traded them for a ticket that would, hopefully, guarantee that our car would be safely returned to us.

After Jon gave the hostess his father's name, we were led to the far dining room where his father was already sitting at a table. He stood as we approached, offering his hand to Jon to shake and regarding me with a dismissive nod. Once we were seated, he motioned to a waiter who promptly approached to take our drink orders. Jon ordered his usual Scotch and I asked for a gin and tonic. I noticed his dad gestured for his half empty glass to be refilled with some sort of amber colored liquid.

"Bourbon," he announced in reply to my unspoken question. His gaze turned to Jon. "You still haven't learned a good bourbon beats the hell out of that foreign crap you drink, have you?"

Jon gave him a tight-lipped look. "Technically, both Scotch and Bourbon are whiskey. The main difference, other than one originates in Scotland and is labeled as Whiskey, and the other is mostly made in Kentucky, is that Scotch is made with barley and Bourbon with corn. It's simply a matter of taste which one is preferred."

The waiter returned with our drinks at that moment. I noticed Jon seemed to take particular care to swirl the liquid in his glass, sniff the aroma that escaped, and take a satisfied sip. His father, on the other hand, threw back the remainder of his first drink and slammed the glass down on the table, gesturing to the waiter to take it away.

"Well at least you haven't resorted to ordering a sissy drink, like a gin and tonic." He looked at me pointedly.

I could feel myself start to shrink in the intensity of his glare, but I remembered the Eleanor Roosevelt quote and straightened my back, returning his look evenly. "I usually prefer wine with food, but Jon introduced me to the pleasures of a cold gin and tonic before dinner. It's very refreshing, especially in the summer." I lifted my glass to my lips and took a welcome sip.

Thankfully, the waiter returned, preventing the need for any further conversation on that particular topic. He laid a leather-bound menu in front of each of us and recited the specials of the day. I opened the heavy menu and scanned the listings, finding it hard to get past the prices posted beside each item. Everything was priced separately, and priced high, which meant that if we wanted a salad with our entree it would cost almost as much as an entire dinner at most of the restaurants where I was used to eating.

Jon glanced at me discretely and reached under the table so that he could give my knee a reassuring squeeze. "Why don't I order for us?"

I nodded at him gratefully and closed my menu.

His father ordered a wedge salad to start, followed by a porterhouse steak and a loaded baked potato. Jon asked for a cup of tomato bisque soup for me and a Caesar salad for himself, followed by two filet mignons with béarnaise sauce and a side of burgundy mushrooms. "The lady will have a glass of Cabernet with her meal and I'll have another Scotch." He snapped the menu shut with a satisfied look in my direction.

I thought we would probably pass the next several minutes engaging in idle chitchat until our meals arrived, but Jon's father immediately launched into the reason why he had asked us to meet.

"Jon, I know you met with the new owners of the Barnett Corporation while you were in Atlanta. I also know they informed you they would be shutting down the Nashville branch immediately. I have come here to offer you the opportunity to take over the D.C. enterprise. The new owners need someone at the helm who's familiar with the ins and outs of the publishing business, and I suggested you'd be the man for the job. As I mentioned to you previously, I plan to retire at the end of this year, and I have spent my entire life grooming you to take the reins when I'm ready to relinquish them. It's your birthright, and it's what is expected of you."

Jon sat back in his chair with a slight nod. "Thank you, father, but no thanks. I have something else in mind."

His father's face grew red as he sputtered out a reply. "What could you possibly have in mind? You've been riding my coattails your entire life. There's nothing you've ever done that hasn't involved the family business in some way, shape, or form."

Jon smiled slightly, which was really more of a grimace. "You're absolutely right. Which is why I need to change things now. I've been working on a plan that doesn't depend on the family business or even the family name. I'm long overdue to try to fend for myself, and the fact that you chose to sell the family business and effectively shut down my work here has given me the perfect opportunity to do just that. Maybe if you'd thought to discuss the whole issue with me before making a decision to sell, I might have responded differently. But it doesn't matter now. You've made your choice, and now I'm going to make mine."

The waiter placed our soup and salads in front of us and, after offering to grind fresh pepper over anything, discretely turned on his heel and left.

"Are you going to tell me what you're talking about, or do I have to guess? I'll warn you though, there's no turning back if you decide to forego my offer and head off after some cockamamie notion of your own doing."

Jon looked at me apologetically. "Sorry, Georgia. I had hoped to have this conversation privately with you first." He turned back to his father. "I am in the final stages of making an offer on a property on Hilton Head Island. I've been talking to my financial advisor, and he feels the market there is prime for investing at this time and will only grow stronger in the months ahead. My plan is to renovate the property, then resell it for a substantial profit. At that point, I will invest some of the earnings and use the rest to purchase another property. Eventually, I hope to build up a sizable real estate portfolio."

His father dug into his wedge salad, then placed his fork on his plate and regarded Jon with a squint.

"Real estate! You couldn't pick a more volatile investment if you tried. The real estate market is, by nature, a roller coaster ride. Especially when it comes to vacation property.

There's really no way of predicting with certainty which way the wind will blow until it's upon you. I've known a few top-notch investors who've lost their shirts banking on their ability to predict the trends in a particular prime vacation market. What makes you think you'll be any more successful than any number of others who have tried and failed before you?"

Jon glanced down at his salad but left it untouched. "Because I intend to be conservative. I'll save at least half of everything I make and reinvest the rest. I'll also rely on my partner to advise me about the market trend every step of the way."

Suddenly the pieces of this puzzle began to fall together in my mind. This must have been what he was talking to Harry about, which meant Harry could be the partner to which he was referring. But what else did this mean? Was he suggesting we move to Hilton Head and, if so, where did that leave me? Would I need to start a new career, too?

Jon turned to reassure me. "I know this is a surprise to you too, but I promise I'll explain everything later. This could be a really good thing for both of us." He reached across the table to take my hand and squeeze it gently.

I smiled, but I was not pleased he had kept such an important decision secret. "I trust you. I just wish we'd had a chance to talk it over before tonight."

His father shifted in his chair and glared at me. "Hunh. I wouldn't be surprised if you weren't somehow behind this whole thing. You seem to have a way of getting my son to do what you want without any regard for whether or not it's the best thing for him. Like moving to this ridiculous excuse for a town."

I could feel anger rising from my stomach to lodge itself in my throat preventing me from responding to his accusations. I looked from him to Jon as I struggled to collect myself. Jon's eyes were dark, mirroring my own anger and disbelief.

"I wish I could say Georgia had even an inkling of what I have in mind, but I've kept her in the dark about this. I had a notion that if I talked about it before I had all the plans in order, it would jinx it somehow. Now I realize I was just reacting the way I always have. I had to protect myself from having what I wanted taken away from me. I learned that from you. Georgia is an innocent party in all of this."

The waiter came to check if there was anything else we needed. I guess he wondered why both Jon's salad and my soup had been left untouched. Jon looked up at him apologetically. "I'm sorry, but my wife and I are going to have to leave. Would you mind wrapping up these items and the rest of our dinners to go?" The waiter nodded and left with our food on his tray.

His father dropped his fork on his plate with a clink. "You're leaving? What kind of nonsense is that? At least you can show me the courtesy of staying long enough to finish your dinner."

Jon stood and moved to the back of my chair shifting it so I could stand as well. "I'm sorry, father. But this meal is over."

"And so is my support, financial and otherwise. Don't come running back to me once your little fantasy falls apart." He glanced at me. "And little girl, be sure you don't spawn any brats before your husband finds a way to feed them. Unless, that is, you're already cooking one." He looked pointedly at my stomach.

I gasped in shock as Jon took my arm to lead me from the restaurant. I pulled away from him to look directly at his father. "I don't care what you say about me, but you're an awful man who has no idea what a wonderful son you have. He's smart and kind, and a far better person than he has a right to be, given the arrogant bully he has for a father. I just hope you realize it before it's too late."

Jon looked at me with shock and admiration as he took my arm again, stopping to collect our packaged meals from the hostess stand on our way out.

Once we were inside our car and safely maneuvering our way back home, I turned to Jon with barely controlled tears. "He really is awful. How could you have possibly turned out to be such a good person after having grown up around the likes of him?"

His hands gripped the steering wheel tighter. "My mom ran interference when we were at home. You wouldn't think it, to look at the way he was tonight, but he could turn into a pussy cat when she was around. It was only really bad when I was alone with him. He seemed dead set on beating me into submission, and I don't mean just figuratively."

My heart clenched as I realized what he was saying. "You mean he hit you?"

"Sometimes. But only when no one else was around. Once I grew taller and stronger than him, he quit trying, but not before he broke my arm once trying to show me he was the boss. I told my mom I fell off my bike. I don't know if she believed me, but I noticed he slept in the spare room that night, and for several nights afterward."

"Did he ever hit your sister?"

He shook his head. "I would have killed him if he did. I really think I would have. No, she was his little princess, which wasn't as great for her as you might think. He expected her to be perfect, and she never felt she could match up to his expectations. The best thing that ever happened to her was that she got married right out of high school and moved away. Her husband is a great guy, and he wouldn't let my dad get within ten feet of her without him being nearby. My father got the message loud and clear and backed off." He looked at me with a sideways grin. "Sometimes I used to wish I had been born a girl."

Something about his comment broke the tension in the car and we both began to laugh. Finally, I released a sigh and lifted the bag full of to-go containers. "Well, at least we got a good meal out of it. I'm going to enjoy this food a lot more in the comfort of our own home than I would if we had stayed in the restaurant. And I'm sorry for what I said, but it felt really good."

"I agree. Better company and better conversation."

"Speaking of conversation, you'd better tell me everything you and Harry have been talking about while we eat. I don't think I can handle any more surprises for a while."

"You have a deal. And by the way, I really liked that surprise side of you who showed up back at the restaurant. Way to put my father in his place."

I sighed and shrugged my shoulders. “Desperate times call for desperate measures. Why don’t I grab some dishes and set the table on the patio while you make us some drinks? I’ll light the Tiki torches, too. We may as well make this a festive occasion, since we’re all dressed up for it.”

He parked in front of our house and turned to look at me. “Do you know how much I love you?”

“If I didn’t already, you certainly showed me tonight.”

CHAPTER TWENTY-EIGHT

That night we enjoyed our gourmet dinner in the comfort of our home. Jon laid out the plans he and Harry had been working on since before we returned from our last trip to Hilton Head. I couldn't really follow all of the details he was describing, but the gist of it was, at Jon's request, Harry checked the temperature of the real estate market on the island and found it was a buyer's market. As Jon explained it, this meant the supply of houses exceeded the demand, giving buyers an advantage over sellers in price negotiations.

"Harry said there's no way of predicting how long things will stay that way, but there is every indication this trend will continue for at least a few more years. Apparently, Hilton Head experienced a glut of new building in the late 60s and early 70s. Development has slowed down now, which is keeping prices relatively low. Of course, that also means sellers can't expect to get top dollar for their property. Harry and I weighed that against the advantage we'd have on the buyers' side and we still believe things will fall in our favor even though we may then be sellers in the same market later on.

"According to Harry, the real trick is to buy houses in favorable locations but need some work, then make sure any renovations increase their overall appeal. Once I heard all of that, I had Harry call the owners of the house we rented last week and make them an offer. We lowballed it, which means we offered them less than we expected they would ask. To my surprise they accepted the offer."

I took a sip of my wine and considered what he was saying. "Does that mean you plan for us to move there?"

He cut a large chunk out of his filet, speared a mushroom, and dipped both into the béarnaise sauce. He groaned with pleasure as he chewed heartily and washed the whole thing down with wine. "Not right away. In fact, not at all, if we decide we don't want to. It will take some time to complete the renovations I have in mind for the house. We couldn't possibly live there until they're finished, and even then, we may just decide to turn around and sell it once the changes are made."

Although his explanation gave me a sense of relief that nothing drastic had to change in my life, at least not in the near future, I also found myself feeling regret that spending more time on Hilton Head didn't seem to be a definite part of the plan. Plus, I was still bothered that I heard about the plan at the same time he announced it to his father.

Jon had been studying me carefully while he spoke. "I'm trying to figure out what you think about the whole idea. Do you think I'm crazy, or have I made the right decision?"

I laid my hand on his arm and squeezed it gently. "You're definitely crazy. But in this instance, given Harry's expertise about financial matters, if he thinks it's a good idea, then I think it's the right decision. I guess my only concerns are whether this is something you really want to get involved in, and what it means for our future."

He nodded. "It's hard to explain, but once I got the idea in my head, I've been happier than I can remember being in a long time, at least when it comes to my professional life." He smiled. "This feels like something I can sink my teeth into, and more importantly, something I'll enjoy. I've felt like a giddy kid the past few days just thinking about the possibilities." He cut another hunk of steak and repeated the pattern of spearing and dipping.

"I have to admit, I've noticed a change in you, and I've been wondering what it was all about. You've seemed really happy."

"You mean different than I usually am? I guess I didn't realize how bogged down I've been feeling until I started looking into this possibility. It may be the first time in my life I've chosen to pursue something professionally that I wasn't expected to do." He laid down his fork and stared off into the night. I thought I'd lost his attention until he turned his gaze back to me as quickly as he'd drifted away.

"As for the future, I can't really say what will happen, but I feel certain that wherever this leads will only be a good thing. For both of us." He grinned at me mischievously. "You know, we're going to have to spend a lot more time on Hilton Head once the renovations get underway. We'll have to keep an eye on things, and make sure they're done right."

I frowned in confusion. "But I don't see how I can do that. Once the fall semester starts up again, I won't be able to get away very often. I know I'm your wife, but I have a career too and people counting on me. I can't just walk away from all of that without making some careful decisions."

He gave me a measured look. "I've thought about that, too. How would you feel about correspondent work? I took the liberty of contacting the local newspaper while we were on the island. *The Island Times*, as it's called. It was started in 1970 as a weekly publication mainly geared toward local events and social highlights. Over the years, the increase in year-round residents has demanded the paper be published more frequently. It's a daily now.

"The paper receives most of its financial backing from a guy who used to run the Raleigh paper. We crossed paths a few times when we attended the same conferences in D.C. When this idea started brewing in my brain, I gave him a call, and he told me the editor has been looking for someone to write a weekly human-interest column; something that presents people and their lives in a thought-provoking way."

His comments were intriguing, but I couldn't see how what he was describing could apply to me. "But I don't know anything about the people who live on Hilton Head Island," I said.

"He's not looking for someone to write about the locals. He has reporters who can do that. He wants to give the readership a chance to broaden their horizons by learning about people who live all over the world. Celebrities, political figures, and just regular folks with an interesting story to tell. I convinced him you'd be exactly the person for the job. That is, if it's something you'd like to do."

"And we would still live in Nashville?"

"You could write the column from anywhere. Maybe you could even work something out with Thomas so you could maintain some type of part-time involvement with the Belmont program. I don't know exactly what that would look like, but it's something to explore."

My head felt like it was spinning, and I wasn't sure if it was from the wine I had consumed without much food to accompany it, or the pace at which things were starting to change around me. "Right now, I think I need to focus on eating something."

Jon looked at my barely touched meal and nodded emphatically. "Absolutely. This is one of the best meals I've had in a long time, even if it is the result of having to sit through a very unpleasant exchange with my father." He shook his head. "I don't know why I expected anything different. His behavior was predictable. I guess I just reached my limit for tolerating his bullying, especially when he started to turn it on you."

I couldn't help but smile when I remembered the way Jon had jumped to my defense. I wasn't used to someone sticking up for me the way he did, and it was a good feeling. I was also pretty proud of my own burst of self-defense, though it was so out of character for me. I guess all the years of passive acceptance of being a target finally reached a boiling point when the attack threatened to harm someone I love.

I put my hand on Jon's arm. "You're my hero, you know. It took a lot of courage to speak out the way you did."

He shrugged as if he was embarrassed at the complement. "Not really. I just did what any man would do if his wife was being disrespected. Even if it was by his own father, or maybe especially because it was by his father. The real courage came from you. I'll bet he was floored by the way you stood up to him."

I pushed my plate away and reached for his hand. "This meal is delicious but, if you don't mind, I'd like to save the rest for tomorrow."

His expression grew puzzled. "Sure. But I thought you were hungry."

"I am. But I have a different sort of nourishment in mind right now." I gave him what I hoped was a suggestive look, but it probably came off looking silly. Nonetheless, he must have gotten the drift of my intent because he jumped up and started collecting our unfinished meals. "Grab the rest of these things and help me put them away."

We hurriedly placed the remains of our meal in the refrigerator to protect it from bugs and Ebie, then Jon grabbed my hand and headed into the hallway. He paused briefly to look with interest at the sofa in the living room, before shaking his head firmly and heading up the stairs.

CHAPTER TWENTY-NINE

It would be a few weeks before Jon and I had a chance to talk any more about the ideas we had discussed over dinner. My time was tied up helping with the arrangements for the New Journalism workshop, and Jon ended up having to make a couple of trips to D.C. to participate in meetings with the new owners of his family's business. I was anxious to revisit the issues he had mentioned about the possibility of my doing correspondent work for the Hilton Head paper, but he never seemed to be in the right mood for me to discuss it. Every time he returned from one of those trips, he was a little more edgy and distracted than when he left, and I was reluctant to bring up any topic that might add to his distress.

The arrangements for the Belmont workshop went off much better than I expected. As a result, by the time the last week in July rolled around, there was very little left to do except greet the participants and make sure the catering department at the college came through with the food and drink offerings we had instructed them to provide.

We arranged the schedule to include a seated banquet for all of the presenters, participants, and workshop staff on the next to last evening. Mrs. Stayhill and I put our heads together over the menu, which included drinks and finger foods to be passed around while the guests were arriving, followed by a choice of lemon chicken with rice and green beans, or spinach and cheese stuffed flank steak with baked potatoes and broccoli. Either selection was accompanied by a small Caesar salad to start, and followed by a wedge of apple pie topped with vanilla ice cream.

By our count, there would be sixty people in attendance, which included the participants, the spouses who had chosen to join them, the presenters, and the workshop staff. Ten round tables that seated six persons each had been set up for the banquet, with at least two presenters and one of the staff assigned to sit at each in order to facilitate mingling with the attendees. As a result, Jon and I ended up sitting on opposite sides of the room from each other, which was an arrangement that neither of us was keen about, given how little we had seen each other over the past few weeks.

I was seated between a quiet woman who was the guest of one of our presenters, and a very verbose man who headed up the Journalism program at the University of Tennessee in Knoxville. Every time I tried to turn my attention to the lady on my right, the chatty man would jump in and steer the conversation in his direction. Fortunately, just when I was reaching the limit of my patience with the situation, one of the students from the Belmont program approached the man to introduce himself. This gave me the prefect opportunity to shift in my seat so I could address the woman on my right.

She looked at me with relief and leaned in so she could speak to me without being overheard. "Thank goodness. I thought he'd never shut up.

"Me, too. It's hard to know how to disengage from someone who's so determined to monopolize the conversation." I held my hand out to her. "Georgia Barnett. I'm one of the organizers of the workshop." She took my hand.

"Susan Bentley. My husband, Stan, works for the Methodist Publishing House. This isn't usually his area of interest, but he's been trying to find something new to get involved in. The idea behind this New Journalism idea fascinates him. Me, too, for that matter. Changing the style of reporting to give it more of a human-interest slant appeals to me. How did they describe it; writing non-fiction so it reads like fiction. I like the sound of that."

I nodded my agreement. "Thomas, the head of the department and the organizer of this workshop, has been trying to spearhead a movement within the journalism community to embrace that way of writing. Or at least to consider it. His efforts haven't been enthusiastically received. We're all hoping this workshop will prove to be a springboard for incorporating the ideas presented here into actual practice."

"It certainly seems things are off to a good start. I notice you're married. Is your husband a reporter, too?"

I shook my head. "No, but he's in the publishing business, like your husband. Or at least he used to be."

She looked at me curiously. "Georgia Barnett. Are you married to Jon Barnett? I've never met him, but Stan speaks of him admiringly. That's my Stan over there talking to the black-haired man with the blue tie." She nodded to where Jon was sitting.

"That black-haired man is my husband, Jon." We laughed at the coincidence.

I looked at her curiously. "What do you do for a living?"

"I'm a soil microbiologist."

I squinted my eyes as I tried to recall what I knew about microbiology, which was basically nothing. Luckily, she came to my rescue.

"I study microorganisms and how they affect the plants that grow in the soil."

"Microorganisms...do you mean germs?"

She smiled. "Basically, yes. Little things you can't see, except under a microscope, but can cause sickness, either by direct contact with them, or through exposure to the plants that grow in the contaminated soil."

"That sounds interesting. Where do you work?"

"I do most of my field work at the Ellington Agricultural Center, but I'm actually employed by the Ag Department at the University of Tennessee. When Stan got the job offer at the Methodist Publishing House, I thought for sure I'd have to give up what I do, since there isn't a single Agricultural Department at any of the colleges in Nashville. Luckily, U.T. was about to start a special project in conjunction with the Ellington Center, and they hired me to serve as the on-site coordinator. So far, everything has worked out great."

At that moment, we were interrupted by the appearance of our husbands. Jon put a hand on my shoulder and turned to face the man who I now knew was Susan's husband. "Georgia, I'd like you to meet Stan Bentley."

I smiled at Jon and pointed to my right. "And I'd like you to meet Susan Bentley. Isn't it crazy we all ended up sitting next to each other's spouse?"

Jon gestured at Stan. "I was just telling Stan about your work here with the New Journalism program, and he'd like to learn more about it from an inside perspective. I suggested the four of us get together sometime next week."

"That sounds great. Susan and I were discussing her work, and I'd love to learn more about what she does, too." I thought for a moment about what I had planned for the coming week. "I have to spend some time on Monday and Tuesday helping wrap things up from the workshop, but how about Wednesday night? You could come over to our house for dinner. I might even convince Jon to demonstrate his mastery on the grill." I gave him a hopeful look.

"If that's a thinly veiled attempt to flatter me into cooking, I agree. Since my work has slowed down, I'm actually looking forward to firing up the grill more often."

I smiled at the Bentleys. "Great. Does six o'clock work for the two of you? We don't live far from here. I'll write down the directions."

I lifted my handbag and pulled out a scrap of paper, jotting down our address and phone number before handing it to Susan.

"How lovely of you to invite us to your home. Why don't you let us take care of bringing a salad and some type of dessert?"

"It's a deal. And be sure to dress casually, and coolly. We usually eat out on the patio, and it's still pretty warm at that time of the evening."

The banquet was rapidly winding down and several of the guests had already begun to make their way out the door. Susan and I stood so we could join the men as we started our exit. I was happy I would be seeing Susan again. Something she said made me remember the story of how Bessie's grandfather died and I had a few questions I wanted to ask her that might help me do a little more unraveling of that particular maze.

The next few days seemed to fly by. Once Thomas and Mrs. Stayhill had compiled the evaluations from the workshop, it was clear the event had been a huge success. A few of the participants had indicated they would like to arrange to attend some of the seminars we held monthly at the College, in order to continue expanding their understanding of the New Journalism curriculum. Thomas had been approached by the group that funded the workshop who were interested in backing two internship spots at Belmont for graduates of other journalism programs around the United States.

I hadn't had a chance yet to approach Thomas about the possibility of cutting back on my work with him. Since things seemed to be heating up, I was pessimistic that he would be willing to even consider letting me work less hours, but I knew I had to find out for certain.

On Wednesday afternoon, the opportunity finally presented itself. Everything related to the workshop was wrapped up, and Thomas and I had collapsed in his office while we waited for Mrs. Stayhill to return with sandwiches for the three of us. Thomas had been as excited as a little kid, since it had become clear the workshop had turned out so well. He was sitting with his hands jammed into his pockets while his right foot beat out a staccato pattern where it rested on top of his left knee. He grinned at me.

"Did you even know that work could be this much fun?" He asked.

I considered his question carefully. "It was a lot of work for us to do in such a short time, but I have to admit the workshop went off a lot more smoothly than I anticipated. It was fun to be a part of something so cutting edge."

He stood abruptly. "Exactly. It's what I've been dreaming about for a long time." He started pacing back and forth in front of his desk. "Now I have to figure out how to keep the momentum going." He stopped in front of me. "How would you feel about taking a more active role in our public relations efforts? It occurred to me this week; the reason things went so well, was because our attendees had the chance to see and hear first-hand what the New Journalism approach is all about. If we had someone on staff who could carry the message out to other programs around the United States, or at least within the Southeast to begin with, I believe things would take off like a rocket. Would you be willing to get involved in that?"

His question puzzled me. "I'm not sure what that means. Are you asking if I would be willing to write letters or make phone calls?"

He frowned as he considered my question. "I guess I haven't really thought it out that carefully. Phone calls and letters, sure. But Mrs. Stayhill could do a lot of that. I'm thinking more along the lines of personal visits to other campuses. Mrs. Stayhill could make contact first and finalize the arrangements. You would have to show up and talk about what New Journalism is all about.

For example, you could give a presentation to a small group of faculty and students, or sometimes just meet one-on-one with the Dean or Department Chair."

What he was describing sounded like a lot of travel time, and I wasn't sure how that would fit with what Jon and I had discussed. "I was actually planning to ask you how you would feel if I cut back on my hours. I know Jon mentioned to you the Barnett Corporation has come under new management, and he is thinking about taking a totally different career path. After we returned from Hilton Head, he bought a small house that we rented while we were there. He plans to oversee its renovation, then see if he can re-sell it and buy more property. He suggested, if I could reduce my work here, he and I could spend more of our time on the island while he gets things up and running."

Thomas looked surprised. "I see. Well, I'll have to think about that. Most of the programs that I'd probably want you to visit, at least to start with, are either driving distance or a short flight from Nashville. Since most flights have to connect through the Atlanta airport, and Atlanta is about midway between Nashville and Hilton Head, I suppose it wouldn't matter if you started from here or there." He scratched his head and resumed pacing. "I can't foresee you having to visit more than one campus a month. Two, at most. But that would mean you'd be working here less than half-time. Do you think that would be enough for you to make this work?"

"Our plans are so new I don't really know how it will all work out. But I was hoping, when I'm in Nashville, I could still be involved in the day-to-day activities here. Now that I think about it more carefully, I can see how that could be a problem, since I wouldn't be available consistently. Jon suggested I might be able to get some correspondent work on the local Hilton Head paper. Maybe write a human-interest column. So, I suppose between that, and the occasional visits to college campuses that you suggested, I could put together enough work to replace what I will lose here. Or at least come close."

Thomas's face lit up with enthusiasm. "I just had an idea. Maybe we could piggyback the two and make it work on both ends. You do some on-site visits for Belmont and feature certain key individuals in your column who you meet. Call it something like 'On the Campus Trail'. You wouldn't have to write solely about journalists or journalism professors, but you could gear the column toward educators. Make it like a special feature for prospective students and their parents, but also mix it up to include other notable people you meet along the way."

His idea certainly had merit, and I found myself getting excited about the possibilities. "That might work. I haven't even met with the editor-in-chief at the local paper yet. When I do, I'll have a better idea of what direction he has in mind for the column. In the meantime, would you be okay if we just played it by ear, so to speak? I could let you know in advance when I'll need to be away from Belmont, and Mrs. Stayhill could arrange my campus visits around my schedule."

The door to the office opened and Mrs. Stayhill stepped inside. "I'm sorry it took me so long to get back with lunch. There are several parent-student groups touring campus, and they happened to arrive at the cafeteria at the same time I did." She began emptying the contents of two large paper sacks. "I brought ham and cheese and turkey sandwiches, chips, and soft drinks. There are also some chocolate chip cookies."

Thomas leaned in and scooped up a paper plate, filling it with one of each kind of sandwich, a bag of chips, and two cookies. "This looks great, Mrs. Stayhill."

I surveyed the offerings and selected one of the sandwiches. Suddenly my hunger had diminished and I found I had lost interest in eating. I took one half of a turkey sandwich and carefully rewrapped the other half before laying it back on the table. Mrs. Stayhill watched me with interest.

"Aren't you hungry, Georgia? I could go see what else they have if you'll tell me what you'd like."

"Oh, no thanks. This all looks fine. I guess I wasn't as hungry as I thought I was." I took a small bite of the sandwich and reached for a Coke to wash it down.

Thomas finished and looked at me apologetically. "I guess I'm to blame for Georgia's vanishing appetite. I've already given her a lot to chew on." He grinned at his own joke as he looked pointedly at Mrs. Stayhill. "I'll fill you in later. Why don't we just relax and enjoy the rest of our lunch for now."

She looked at me and back at Thomas with a curious expression. I was glad he suggested we table the conversation of that particular topic. My mind was spinning with the possibilities we had discussed, and I needed time to sort things out.

I glanced around the room, finally letting my gaze focus on the clock on the wall. It was a little past one. In less than four hours our guests would be arriving for dinner, and I still needed to tidy up the house and clean off the patio.

I picked up the rest of my partially eaten sandwich and wrapped the paper tightly around it. "If you'll both excuse me, there are some things I need to take care of at home." I looked at Thomas. "I assume we're finished here?"

He waved his hand in the air. "Absolutely. Go. Take some time to think about what we discussed, and we can talk about it more in a few days. Or even next week. There's no big rush."

I headed for the front of the building and pushed open the heavy wooden door, pausing to allow the warmth of the afternoon sun to bathe my face, closing my eyes so I could feel it seep into my skin. It was still hot, which was no surprise since it was the middle of July, but the heat felt good in contrast to the chill of air conditioning for too many days.

I pulled the hem of my blouse out of my skirt and hurried down the steps, my pace quickening as the realization of what my discussion with Thomas meant. My stomach still felt a little funny, but I was beginning to realize that instead of being due to distress it was actually an offshoot of my excitement over the potential options that lay ahead for me. Other than being away too often from my best friend Julie, I was beginning to feel excited about what the future could hold.

The thought occurred to me that maybe Jon wasn't the only one who was about to launch a new career. My fingers moved unconsciously to the amulet under my blouse, and I rubbed my fingers over the slow heat that was building around it. I reached my car just as the words of Bessie Barnhill, or what I guess was the ghost of Bessie Barnhill, came to mind. She told me the amulet would help me know what to do when the time was right. She also said something else about how a dog has four feet but can only walk one road.

Her words were still about as clear as mud, but somehow in remembering them they gave me a sense of hopeful anticipation. I hopped into my trusty VW bug, Tweedledee, for my short drive home.

CHAPTER THIRTY

Dinner with Stan and Susan Bentley couldn't have been more perfect. Jon decided to try his hand at cooking fresh tuna steaks on the grill, which came out surprisingly good for a first try, and earned rave reviews from our dinner guests. Ebie was especially thrilled with the outcome, since she was treated to a bowl of leftovers. I was a little worried she'd never be happy again with the canned offerings from our kitchen cabinet, but even she was entitled to something special now and then.

Stan quizzed me enthusiastically over dinner about the New Journalism program, causing me to finally throw up my hands in surrender when I reached the pinnacle of my knowledge. I promised to arrange a meeting the following week between him and Thomas so he could have the opportunity to get answers to all of his questions.

Susan helped me carry the dinner dishes into the kitchen, and offered to dry them as I washed.

"I don't know about you, but I hate to wake up to a room full of dirty dishes." she explained.

"I'm the same way, although I have to admit, sometimes I just rinse them and leave them in the sink overnight if I'm too tired to deal with them." I handed her a pot and waited while she dried it. "Can I ask you a question about your work?"

She looked at me curiously. "Of course."

"If someone was out digging in the dirt, and some urine had gotten into it, could it make the person sick?"

Her eyebrows rose as she looked at me. "That's an odd question. In general, urine is rather innocuous compared to, say, feces. Some people like to say urine is sterile, but that's only true when it is stored in the bladder of a healthy person. Once it's excreted, it is non-sterile since it contains microbial activity. For example, it's possible to detect bacteria in a person's urine that can be found in their intestines. Still, the amounts we're talking about are infinitesimally low compared to feces."

I wasn't sure if I understood more or less than I had before she answered my question. "Okay. So, let's say there's feces in the soil that the urine is mixed into. Is that more likely to make someone sick enough to die?"

Her eyes narrowed in concentration. "Why don't you tell me what it is you're trying to ask. I have a feeling that there's more to your question than you're letting on."

I hesitated. If I told her exactly what I was trying to get at, I would have to tell her about my encounters with Bessie Barnhill, and I wasn't sure I was ready to talk about that with anyone besides Jon, Julie, the Palmers, and Reverend Henderson. Certainly not with someone I'd just met. "I heard recently that in the old times, when they were growing plants to make indigo dye, they would sometimes add urine to the vats in order to help extract the dye. The water containing the urine would have to periodically be replaced, which meant that it was drained into the soil surrounding the vats. That made me wonder whether someone working around the vats could get sick from exposure to the urine-soaked soil."

She tilted her head in thought. "It's possible, I suppose. Although it's more likely to happen if the urine came from a person or animal that had a urinary tract or bladder infection. In that case, there would be high levels of harmful bacteria in the urine that could mix with soil pathogens. Still, coming into contact with fresh animal feces in soil, which can occur either intentionally when it is used as fertilizer, or unintentionally when animals are allowed to roam freely in areas where plants are grown, is much more likely to be a source of human illness."

I shuddered at the thought of someone digging around in dirt full of animal waste. "What types of illness?"

"Usually intestinal disease. Diarrhea is the most common one, and in some instances it can become life-threatening. There's a parasite called Cryptosporidium that's the source of most cases of feces-transmitted diarrhea. But the most common forms of zoonotic disease—that means the disease is shared between different species, like animals and humans—are caused by bacteria. In fact, my field work involves the study of animal to human disease transmission that occurs through contact with the bacteria Escherichia coli and salmonella."

I was still trying to make sense of what she was saying. "So, if a person was working in dirt that had the parasites and bacteria you mentioned, they could become really sick. Sick enough to die?"

"That's less common these days because the illness is usually treated before it gets that bad. But before we knew as much about zoonotic disease transmission as we do now, a lot of people died. It's still a major problem in less developed countries."

I finished washing the last dish and handed it to her. "You seem to know a lot about all of this."

She smiled and shrugged. "Stan tells me I'm a 'bug nerd', although microorganisms are not really bugs. He thinks he's being funny. I just find it fascinating that little tiny things we can't even see can affect us so dramatically."

"I hope you're not boring Georgia with your latest bug stories!" We turned to see Stan and Jon walk into the kitchen from the patio.

"I'm afraid it's my fault." I said. "I was asking her some questions about her work, and she didn't have any choice but to answer."

Susan gave me a wink. "It doesn't take much to get me going on about my research. Stan is always telling me to rein it in, but I'm afraid I don't know how to do that very well. Once I get started, my enthusiasm just takes over."

Jon leaned against the counter next to where I stood and wrapped his arm around my waist. "This one's the same way. When she gets something in her head, her reporter instinct takes over." He bent slightly so he could plant a kiss on the top of my head.

"He's right. I don't know when to stop sometimes." I said. "Anyone for more coffee?"

Stan and Susan exchanged a look. "Not for me." she said. "Too much caffeine keeps me awake at night."

Stan smiled at his wife. "It doesn't have the same effect on me. I can drink a cup right before I go to bed and sleep like a baby, but I'll pass on any more tonight, thank you. We really should be going."

We walked them to the door and stood watching until they climbed into their car. Jon turned to me with a quizzical look on his face. "What was that all about?"

I locked the door. "Oh nothing. I was just asking Susan about her work, and it occurred to me that she might be able to help me understand what happened to Bessie Barnhill's grandfather."

He looked at me with alarm. "You didn't tell her about your ghost sightings, did you?"

I shook my head. "No, but maybe I should have. I have a feeling she wouldn't have thought it all that strange."

His mouth twisted into a grimace. "Maybe not, but I'm glad you didn't. I like the Bentley's, and I'd like to see more of them. Let's give them a chance to get to know us before you open that particular can of worms."

I'm usually what you would call a "good sleeper". I tend to fall asleep fairly quickly after my head hits the pillow, other than a nightly visit to the bathroom. I stay asleep until something wakes me the next morning, which is usually either my alarm clock, or Ebie nudging me with her whiskers to insist that she be fed. That had been less true in recent weeks, and it definitely wasn't true the night after the Bentley's were over for dinner. I laid awake forever, hashing and rehashing the things Susan told me. Every time I looked at the clock another hour had passed, until I finally got up and went downstairs.

I went into the living room and sat on the sofa, tucking my bare feet under me to ward off the chill of the window air conditioner. The moon must have been pretty full because the room was bathed in light, even without turning on any lamps. When I glanced out the front window, I could see a sprinkling of stars against the dark sky.

I thought back to what Susan said about how tiny "bugs" in soil from animal waste could pass a disease to humans, and I wondered if the soil that surrounded the indigo vats could have possibly been contaminated with any of those bugs. If so, that would mean either the waste was used to fertilize the soil, which seemed unlikely since there shouldn't have been plants growing immediately next to the vats, or some animal or animals had been allowed to roam around the area where the vats were located. That didn't make much sense either, since I was fairly sure the vats would have been well-protected.

I realized the only way I was going to get any answers to my questions would be to return to Hilton Head Island and talk to Mary and Henry again. Mary in particular, seemed to know quite a bit about what happened during the time Bessie's grandfather worked with indigo on the island. I had a hunch she would either have the answers I was looking for, or at least be able to direct me to someone who would.

I yawned and lay back against the sofa cushions, telling myself I would just relax there a while until I was sleepy enough to go upstairs. Ebie found me, demanding a sleepy hug. That was the last thought I remember before I was awakened by a tug on my sleeve. I opened my eyes to find Jon standing over me with a concerned look on his face.

"Hey," I said. "What time is it?" I shifted to my side to make room for him to sit. Ebie stirred from her spot tucked under my chin.

"It's early. I woke up and realized you weren't in bed, so I came down here to find you."

"I couldn't sleep and I didn't want to disturb you. I guess I did anyway."

He reached to push the hair off my face. "I guess you were thinking about your conversation with Susan Bentley."

"She told me some interesting things that might help explain how Bessie Barnhill's grandfather died, but I can't put all the pieces together without talking to Mary and Henry Palmer again."

He looked off into the distance for a minute before turning his attention back to me. "Then let's go to Hilton Head. You're finished working for a while, and I need to finalize some details about purchasing the house there. It seems like a great time for a trip."

My eyes opened wider and I pushed myself up so I could lean against the arm of the sofa. "Really? That would be great! When do you think we can go?"

He chuckled at my excitement. "I just need to talk to Harry and make sure I have everything I need to wrap up the deal. I'll give him a call later this morning. In the meantime, I'll ask Mrs. Hanson if she can contact the seller and see if we can stay in the house while we're there. That shouldn't be a problem, unless they have someone else renting it."

"Yay!" I threw my arms around his neck and squeezed him.

"Ouch! You're stronger than you look, Mrs. Barnett." He smiled and pushed me away. "Why don't you go get dressed while I fix some breakfast. Is coffee and toast okay? I don't have much of an appetite after that huge dinner last night."

"Coffee and toast is great. I'll be down in a minute to help." I pushed up from the sofa and hurried off up the staircase, followed closely by Ebie who must have sensed my excitement and wanted to see what the commotion was all about. "We're going to Hilton Head, Ebie. And this time I'll bet you can go with us."

She leaped up the stairs in front of me, taking them two at a time while I followed along behind her. If I didn't know any better, I'd swear that cat could read minds, or at least, one mind. And that was just fine with me.

CHAPTER THIRTY-ONE

Three days later, Jon, Ebie and I were on our way to Hilton Head Island. Mrs. Hanson had been able to reach the owners, who were more than happy to let us stay in the house, especially since their realtor told them of our pending purchase offer.

This time we arrived without having to deal with a stall on the bridge crossing, a thunderstorm, or even the hordes of tourists that made their way onto the island every weekend. We left Nashville early on the Monday after our dinner with the Bentleys, which allowed us to pull up in front of what would soon be our house a little after 4 p.m.

It was hot on the island in July, but no hotter than it had been in Nashville, and at least there was a sea breeze that kept the heat from feeling oppressive. Jon handed me the key to the front door and I grabbed Ebie's carrier and headed up the front steps. When I pushed open the door, I was greeted by the same musty smell I remembered from our first visit, and I quickly went around the house and opened the windows before returning to the car to help Jon unload our things. There wasn't that much to bring in since we decided not to stop at Henry's store, opting instead to make a quick trip to the Red and White market as soon as we settled in.

I had opened the back door when I first went in, and I hurried to make sure the latch on the screened door that fronted it was securely shut before letting Ebie out of her carrier. She stepped out and quickly made a prancing tour of the place before hopping onto a window ledge that looked out over the back yard. I carried my small suitcase into the bedroom and opened it onto the bed so I could put away my things. I wasn't exactly what some people would call a neatnik, but I found I felt more relaxed when my things were put away. It was what I did to settle into a place, and I could feel the stiffness from the long drive easing out of my body when I hung the last of my clothes in the closet.

I went back out into the living room where I found Jon starring at a corner of the ceiling. "Want me to put your things away for you?" I asked.

He answering without turning around. "Sure. I just noticed this stain on the ceiling. It might mean that the roof has a leak, or water is getting in under the flashing."

I frowned. "That sounds serious."

He shrugged. "It could be. It might just be related to the age of the house, or no one has really taken care of it since it was built. I'll have someone take a look at it before we sign the papers to finalize the purchase."

Once I finished putting his things away, I grabbed my purse and headed for the front door. "I'm going to walk over to the Red and White. Is there anything in particular you want?"

"Whatever looks good. I'm going to call the realtor and see if I can arrange for the house to be inspected in the next day or two."

The Red and White market was located about five blocks from the house. It felt good to stretch my legs after so many hours of sitting, and I strolled along at a comfortable pace. I passed several people riding bikes or walking dogs and each time we greeted one another with a smile and a friendly wave. There was something about being at the beach that brought out camaraderie among strangers. It was almost as if we were privy to membership in a secret club and our smug exchanges were our way of saying, "Isn't this great? Can you believe we're here in this place?"

When I reached the street that ran beside the bakery, I turned to the right and made my way toward another parking lot in front of the Red and White. There were a lot more cars in the lot than I had encountered on each of my previous visits to the market, and I grabbed one of the last remaining shopping carts after entering the store. I glanced to my left at the check-out counters and spotted the same cashier who I had spoken to during my visit with Julie.

We exchanged a wave and I remembered how she asked me when I was going to give in and move here permanently, before giving me a business card of her realtor cousin. I hadn't remembered the card until that moment, and I wondered where I put it.

I collected several things that I thought would cover a few meals until I had time to return with the car for a larger load, and pushed my shopping cart to the check-out counter. The cashier, whose name badge reminded me her name was Jody, smiled and began to ring up my items.

"So, you came back. How long are you here for this time?" she asked.

"I'm not sure. My husband, Jon, and I are thinking about buying a house here, and we came to take another look at it."

She looked at me curiously. "Which one? My cousin has several listed in the neighborhood."

"It's on Dune Street. I can't remember the number off the top of my head, but it's to the left, just after you turn off of Dove."

"She nodded knowingly. "The Thompson place. That's one of my cousin's listings. Did you give him a call?"

I looked at her apologetically. "I'm afraid I forgot I had his card until I walked into the store. My husband sort of surprised me with the whole idea of possibly buying the house. What's your cousin's name? I'll ask Jon if that's who he's been talking to."

"William Oates. Goes by the name of Bill. If your husband's been investigating buying the Thompson house, I'm sure he's been talking to Bill." She finished bagging up my groceries and handed me my change.

"Thanks. I'll ask him." I picked up the sacks and headed for the exit, thinking how odd it would be if her cousin was the person who Jon had been dealing with all this time. I knew Hilton Head was a fairly small place, but the idea that I kept encountering one coincidence after another was still surprising.

When I returned to the house, I found Jon outside, standing at the top of a tall ladder inspecting the roof line on the right side. "Hey, there," I called to him. "What are you up to?

"I'm trying to see if I can find the source of the leak on the ceiling." He started carefully making his way down the ladder. "I phoned the listing agent, and he's supposed to stop by with a contractor in about an hour to take a look at it."

"Oh! The person who checked me out at the Red and White said she thinks her cousin is the listing realtor on this place. Is the man you spoke to named Bill Oates?"

He stepped off the last rung and turned to face me. "Yeah, that's him. You say you talked to his cousin? That's an odd coincidence."

"I thought so too. I guess this place is really just a small town where everybody knows everybody else."

He frowned. "Maybe so. I hope that doesn't work against us."

His comment confused me. "How could it?"

"Well, if everybody knows everybody else's business, they're also likely to know what this place is worth, which could make bargaining for a better price difficult."

"But I thought you said you already made on offer that was accepted by the owners?"

"I did. But it's pending until the house is inspected. If the contractor Bill Oates is bringing by uncovers any problems, then we'll have grounds to re-negotiate an even better purchase price."

I considered what he was saying. "Then it seems to me, if the neighbors are aware the roof leaks, it could help put us in a better bargaining position. We might be able to show the owners hadn't disclosed a preexisting problem before the sale."

He seemed to consider my point. "Maybe so." He wiped his hands on his jeans. "I'm just going to go in and clean up a little before they get here."

I followed him into the house, stopping in the kitchen to put away the groceries and check to make sure Ebie's food and water bowls were full. Ebie heard me come in and was following me around the kitchen, pausing before her bowl with an expectant look.

"You've had plenty to eat today. I gave you half a can of tuna before I went out, and there's still dry food in your bowl."

She remained standing in front of her bowl, staring at me until a knock on the front door sent her scurrying in the opposite direction. I found two men standing outside. One of them lifted the brim of his baseball cap as he regarded me with a smile.

"Good evening. You must be Mrs. Barnett. Your husband is expecting us. I'm Bill Oates, and this is Randall Evans. He's the contractor your husband asked me to bring to take a look at your roof. We're a little early, but we wanted to get here while there's still some daylight left."

The contractor pushed his hand in my direction and I shook it, noticing the rough texture of the skin on the palm of his hand. "How do, ma'am. I noticed a ladder leaning against the side of the house. If you don't mind, I'll just hop up there and see what's going on." He turned on his heel and headed around the side of the house without waiting for a reply.

Mr. Oates smiled apologetically. "He's not very big on small talk, but I assure you, you won't find a better worker on the island. Or one that's more knowledgeable about construction. If there's a problem with your roof, he'll find it."

At that moment I heard Jon walk up behind me, and I turned so he could see Mr. Oates. “Jon, Mr. Oates is here. He brought the contractor to look at the roof. He already went around to where you left the ladder.”

Jon shook Mr. Oates hand. “Thanks for coming so promptly. I was looking at the ceiling in the living room when we arrived and I noticed what appears to be a water stain. I climbed up to look at the roofline, but I couldn’t really see anything.”

Mr. Oates nodded as he walked into the room. “This house was built in the mid-sixties during what was called the ‘boom years’ for Hilton Head. What that really means is, houses were going up fast to try to keep pace with the demand. That was fine in some areas like Sea Pines, where there was plenty of money to pay for top-notch construction, but the quality of building materials, and the buildings themselves, weren’t always so good outside the gated communities.”

He pointed to the ceiling. “That stain you noticed is most likely the result of the flat roof. When they’re done right, they can last a number of years without any problems. But if the roof membrane isn’t installed properly, or if the roof isn’t checked routinely to make sure the rainwater outlets aren’t blocked with leaves and other stuff, then you can have a slow leak that builds up in the space between the ceiling and the roof line. Eventually, that can cause mold and mildew to develop.” He nodded toward the stain on the ceiling. “My guess is that’s what we’re dealing with here.”

My heart sank as I listened to him, and I turned to Jon to try to gauge his reaction. His face was solemn, and I could detect a tightness in his jaw.

“What does that mean in terms of repair?”

Mr. Oates lifted his cap and scratched his head. “It depends on how extensive the damage is. It could be a simple matter of cleaning out the debris and slapping some mold killer on the ceiling. Worst case scenario, the roof will have to be replaced.” He took in the darkening expression on Jon’s face. “The good news is that since we've caught this before the sale is final, any repairs should be covered by the seller."

I let out the breath I had been holding and looked at Jon whose face had relaxed considerably.

"That's a relief, although it could mean an unexpected delay in the rest of the renovations I had in mind," Jon replied.

Mr. Oates shrugged. "It shouldn't take too long. Even if the roof has to be replaced. Construction on the island has slowed down right now, so there are a lot of workers just waiting for something to do. That's why we were able to get by here so quickly today."

The contractor poked his head in the door at that moment. "Roof's going to have to come off. It looks like the gutters have been clogged up for some time, and there's a lot of visible rot." He regarded Jon evenly. "I assume you're the potential buyer?" Jon nodded and the two men shook hands. "I don't know what you have planned for the place, but if it was me, I'd take advantage of a bad situation to make something good come out of it."

Jon shoved his hands in the back pockets of his jeans and looked squarely at Randall Evans. "What are you suggesting?

The contractor stepped into the house and began walking from one side of the living room to the other, allowing his eyes to scan the space in every direction. "The ceiling is kind of low in here, which is what happens when they install a flat roof. Since you have to remove it anyway, why not replace it with a pitched roof? You could build an attic with a drop-down staircase so you have some storage space, or even put in an actual set of stairs and make a spare room up there. That would also allow you to raise the ceiling down here so it feels larger and more airy."

I could feel my excitement grow as I listened to the changes he described. I could see how raising the ceiling would totally change the feeling of the house, and the idea of adding another room upstairs was interesting. I was already beginning to imagine how we could use that space, that is, if we kept the house after it was remodeled. I looked at Jon eagerly. "That sounds exciting, doesn't it, Jon?"

Jon rubbed his chin as he walked slowly around the living room. "Actually, it's not far off from what I had in mind, although I didn't anticipate having to do it so soon." He stopped in front of Randall Evans. "Can you draw up some specs on what you think could be done with this space, and get them back to us in a couple of days?"

Mr. Evans nodded slowly. "Should be able to get them to you by sometime tomorrow. Work's a little slow right now, and I have a team just chomping at the bit to get going on something." He looked at Mr. Oates. "I suspect you'll need to run all of this by the seller."

"Of course. I'm sure they'll be willing to make a deal that includes deducting the cost of the repairs that Randall anticipates having to make. Let me put together some numbers for them to look over. I'll get back to you sometime later today, if that's alright." He looked at Jon then me for confirmation.

"Sure," Jon said. "We may be out part of the day, so why don't I give you a call if I don't hear from you?"

"Sounds like a plan." He nodded to Randall and started for the door. "Randall, why don't you and I head back to my office and talk over a few things before I discuss this with the owners."

The two men left, and Jon sat at the kitchen table. "Are you hungry?" I asked. "I can make a sandwich."

He nodded. "A sandwich would be good. You know, this just might work out to our advantage after all."

"How do you figure that?" I took out the ham, cheese, mayonnaise, mustard, lettuce and bread I purchased at the Red and White.

"I thought about raising the roof so that we could add a room just like Randall suggested, but I figured we might have to wait a while to do that, because there are other repairs to do first. Since Bill Oates said the expenses associated with replacing the roof and repairing the damage caused by the leaks may be covered by the sellers, it will significantly reduce the cost to us for finishing the rest of the renovation." He looked around the kitchen. "There might even be enough money left over to do a little remodeling in here."

I glanced around the room. "Really? You mean like get some newer appliances and replace this worn-out linoleum?"

He picked up the sandwich I placed in front of him. "AND get rid of these countertops and slap a fresh coat of paint on the walls. The bathrooms could use some work, too. I'm going to give Bill a call and tell him to ask the contractor to figure all of that into his estimate. If it turns out to be too much, we can always scale down the plans." Sandwich in hand, he walked to the phone.

I studied my sandwich before taking a bite. Seeing Jon so enthusiastic about a project that did not involve the publishing business was new to me. I found myself still trying to get used to the whole idea of him walking away from that career to start something brand new. I had to admit; I'd never seen him as happy as he had been since he'd made the decision to branch out on his own. Maybe there was something to be said for taking a chance, for risking what you have on something you want.

I was suddenly reminded of an "Ida-ism". Once, when I was faced with making a decision between accepting an assignment at the newspaper which had the potential of blowing the lid off a secret political conspiracy in Nashville, or playing it safe by pursuing a story about the closing of a local department store. Ida listened patiently to my verbal hand-wringing until I guess she couldn't take it anymore. She grabbed me firmly by the shoulders and forced me to look her in the eyes. "How will you know if you've made the right decision, if you never get around to making it? Sometimes you have to just stop being scared and go for it. Either it will work out, or it won't. That's just the way life is."

On that occasion, I decided to go for the more risky but potentially more rewarding story. It didn't turn out perfectly. But then again, life rarely does. There was also something terribly exciting about diving into the deep end of a pool without being able to see very far below the surface. It was terrifying, but it was also exhilarating, and I guessed that must be something similar to what Jon was feeling. Maybe I should start following his example and figure out what I really wanted to do with my life. It was true that journalism had always been my thing. Was that because I chose it whole-heartedly, or just allowed myself to settle into the first thing that came along? I had to admit, my initial enthusiasm for the work had waned over the years, but I always told myself that was a direct result of everything that had transpired since my firing and Ida's death. Maybe I needed to quit making excuses for how I felt, and figure out where my heart was trying to lead me. The sudden throbbing from the amulet confirmed my thoughts.

I looked over my shoulder to one place I knew without a doubt it was leading. Jon finished his phone call and was staring at the kitchen cabinets. "Penny for your thoughts," I said.

His head jerked around in surprise. "I was wondering if we should totally replace these cabinets or just the doors. It might look nice to leave the shelves exposed. Or at least to use glass doors instead of solid wood." He looked at me questioningly.

I tried to envision what he was describing. "I like the idea of glass doors. That way we can see what's inside without letting in dust and bugs. Seeing as how we're at the beach, that seems like something we need to think about."

He leaned against the kitchen counter, his arms crossed in front of him as he regarded me with a smile. "Sounds like I just might have a partner in this remodeling business."

I considered what he was saying and returned his smile. "I believe you just might." And, as I said the words, I realized I liked the idea a lot.

CHAPTER THIRTY-TWO

By the end of that week, a plan had been set in motion that would lead to the significant renovation of the house on Dune Street. The leaky roof and water stained ceiling turned out to be just the tip of the iceberg of damage the house had sustained due to its poor construction and lack of maintenance. There was also extensive damage to the interior ceiling of the main living area and to the paint and plaster on nearby walls. An even greater concern was black mold had spread from the leaky roof to the wood framing, ceiling, walls and floor coverings. What all of that meant was, repairing the damage, and replacing the affected exterior and interior areas would likely take a few weeks. And that was only because work on the island was slow at the moment and the construction crew had extra time on their hands.

After Randall Evans had drawn up the specs that showed what could potentially be done to the place, Bill Oates had been able to work out a deal with the sellers so more than a third of the cost would be subtracted from the sales price. That meant we would have a tidy chunk of change left over from our savings to cover the rest of the renovations we had in mind.

Randall was able to pull together a crew of men within two days of our signing the final papers to purchase the house, and they immediately began tearing into the place. Since living there while the work was going on was clearly impossible, I made a call to Mrs. McKibben at the Sea Crest Motel who offered to rent us a small unit with a kitchenette. It turned out she had been aware of the condition of the house we were buying, and had been campaigning for it to be either torn down or fixed up for some time. When she found out we were buying the house and overseeing its repair and renovation she said she would be more than happy to provide us with a temporary home since, in her words, we would be increasing the value and desirability of the neighborhood. She'd even given us a discount on the usual rate, and agreed to allow us to bring Ebie.

With everything else that had been going on, I hadn't made any effort to get in touch with Henry and Mary. I still wasn't sure what to make of the things I learned from Susan Bentley. I knew I had to approach the Palmers before I was going to figure out how this new information fit into the puzzle of Joshua Barnhill's death. When Jon and Ebie and I were finally settled into the motel, I decided to take the plunge and call Henry. The phone in his store rang six times before I heard his voice.

"'Enry sto'. Dis be 'enry."

"Hi, Henry. It's Georgia. Georgia Barnett."

I could picture his smile as he spoke. "Bin 'spect'n oonuh call. Hea' 'bout de house be buyin'."

His words surprised me even though I should have become used to the small-town nature of the island. "How did you hear about that?"

"Daa'tuh tol' Mary 'bout it. Hea' 'fo' dat eb'n. Man gwine wu'k dere tol' uh."

I shook my head in disbelief. "Word sure travels fast!"

"Dat it do."

"I called because I was wondering if I could talk to you and Mary again sometime soon. I have some questions about Joshua Barnhill's death I think one of you might be able to help with."

There was silence on the line. Just as I was beginning to wonder if my question had been inappropriate, I heard Mary's voice."

"Chile, huccome oonuh not drap een 'fo' now? Uh hear wuz on de i'lun."

"I'm sorry. Jon and I have been really busy working out the purchase of a house and lining up some work that needs to be done. But then, Henry told me you already know about that."

I heard her familiar chuckle. "Long talk moobe fas'. 'Spec' dere 'lot tuh do 'bout dat house."

"Yes, there is, but things are moving along pretty well now. I was hoping I could talk to the two of you. Maybe stop by the store when you'll both be there. I have some thoughts about Joshua Barnhill's death, but there are some missing pieces of the puzzle I'm hoping you'll be able to fill in."

"Why don' oonuh come obuh yuh now? Uh jis' stop by tuh bring 'enry suppuh. Attuhw'ile, uh gwine home, but not tuhreckly."

"I don't want to interrupt his supper."

"Pfft. No bodduh. Us bofe be glad fo see oonuh."

I hung up after arranging to stop by their store in about half an hour. Jon agreed to join me, and we set about getting ready for the short drive there.

I was glad the parking lot was empty when we pulled in, since I didn't relish the idea of having my questions overheard by anyone else. We found Henry sitting in his usual spot on the raised stool behind the counter while Mary was swiping at the shelves with a dust cloth.

"Well! Y'all cum in." Mary's face widened into a huge grin as she hurried in our direction, engulfing me in a warm embrace before turning to Jon. She must have read the hesitation on his face because she stepped back before she reached him, settling instead for a hand-shake.

"Been hopin' tuh see oonuh. Ain't dat right, 'enry?" She looked back over her shoulder at her husband.

Henry slowly stepped down from his stool and made his way over to where we stood. "Always glad fuh see bofe oonuh." His eyes crinkled as his gaze took us in.

"Leh we go out tuh de po'ch. Talk mo' cumfuh'ble dere." Mary shooed us back out the front door where we settled onto four wooden rocking chairs. Mary turned to me. "Say on de phone hab queschun fuh we."

I nodded hesitantly. "You know how you told me Bessie's grandfather was considered an Indigo Master and he used urine from pregnant cows because he believed it worked best at stripping the deepest dye from the plants? Were the cows housed near the vats?"

Mary frowned as she slowly rocked. "Near as uh kin 'membuh, dey kep' een de shed next tuh de big baa'n. De cows een he'lt' kep' 'p'aat f'um tuh odduh wen dey close tuh drap dey calf.

"Were they ever allowed to roam freely around the yard? I'm wondering if it was possible for their…manure…to get into the soil around the indigo vats."

She shook her head slowly. "Can' see how dat could'uh been. Maussuh Pinckney puhtickluh 'bout keepin' 'e faa'm creetuh 'way f'um weh de indigo wu'k. Only 'cajun uh 'membuh dem cows near dey vats was w'en de shed bruk-up." She leaned back in her chair with a broad grin. "Story go 'roun' dat Joshua come out one mawnin' an' fin' two dem een he'lt' cows grazin' in de indigo. Bofe dey mout blue f'um de flower. Say dey look uh sight!"

I tried to imagine the image she described. "Do you know how long they were out there?"

Mary looked at Henry who shrugged his shoulders before replying. "Mus'a been mos' de night. One dem cows cum up sick f'um eatin' summuch. By de time dey put her back een de shed, 'e down on 'e knees. Nebbuh git back up, eeduh."

"Did any of the other cows get sick?"

Henry leaned back and stared up at the sky. "Now tink 'bout it, 'nudduh one come down sick, too. Tek mo' time, so no one pit dem bofe 'longside each odduh. W'en Joshua git bad off, wha' happen tuh de cows didn' seem 'portun'." He leaned forward with his hands on his knees and studied the floorboards. "Don' know why didn' t'ink 'bout 'e 'fo' now, but dem cow's sickness look lukkuh Joshua's. All dem hab dey insides run out."

"You mean they had diarrhea?" I asked.

"T'ings cum out bofe end. 'Ventually, dey start tuh twitchin' an' den go still. D'et' not long behime attuh dat."

"How long was it after the cows got sick that Joshua took ill?"

Mary spoke up. "Reb'ren' come roun' 'bout fo' day attuh dey fix de shed. Joshua fine till two day pas' dat. Luk us tol' oonuh 'fore, folks say how de Reb'ren' mite hab cast uh ebil spell on Joshua 'stead ub de he'p he s'pose tuh gib 'e. Attuhw'ile, talk jis' stop. Noone wan' tuh bad mout' de Reb'ren'."

I looked over at Jon who had remained quiet throughout the entire conversation. His eyes caught mine and he gave me a raised eyebrow, which I interpreted as indicating he thought it was time to go. I got up from my chair and turned to look first at Mary then Henry.

"I appreciate you sharing all of this with me. It's been very helpful."

Mary looked at me curiously. "'E hep oonuh fin' de ansuh bin luk fo'?"

I considered her question carefully. "Maybe. There's just one more piece of the puzzle I need to find." I started to walk away, but then turned once more to Henry. "Do you remember if any of the other cows got sick besides the first two you mentioned?"

He nodded slowly. "Two mo' down wid de same sickness come t'ree day. Attuh aw cows gone, Maussuh Pinckney set duh shed tuh fiah. Say 'e don' wan' no 'memb'unce wha' happ'n tuh Joshua. Say it haant 'e. Pit boddle tree weh shed wuz. Wawn folks don' go 'roun' dere. Dat las' time mek indigo on 'e faa'm."

I nodded my thanks and began walking toward the car. Mary's voice stopped me part way there. "Tek care yo'se'f. Gwine nee' mo' res' soon." I looked over my shoulder at her curiously, but she just nodded and waved in my direction.

Later that evening, I dialed Susan Bentley's number. She told me to feel free to call her if I had any more questions about our discussion, or if I just wanted to talk. I was hesitant to bother her, but I didn't know anyone else who could tell me what I needed to know. Luckily, she answered right away.

"Susan? It's Georgia Barnett. I hope I'm not disturbing you."

"Georgia! How are you? I was just talking to Stan about what a lovely evening we had at your house. You'll have to let us have you over soon."

"That would be great. Actually, we're not in Nashville right now. We drove to Hilton Head Island last Monday. Remember that house we mentioned we were hoping to buy? We finalized the purchase this week, and there's a crew already doing some work on it. We had some things we wanted to do to spruce it up a bit, and we also learned the house needed some pretty major repairs. We moved into a motel so they could get started on what needs to be done."

"That's wonderful! I'm envious of you for having a house at the beach. That's on my wish list."

"Well, when it's finished, perhaps you and Stan can come for a visit. We haven't decided yet whether we're going to keep it for a while or turn around and sell it again, but I'm hoping we'll keep it long enough to enjoy it some." I paused to collect my thoughts. "I'm actually calling you about another matter. Do you remember our conversation about soil-transmitted illness?"

She chuckled. "You mean the 'boring topic' that Stan insisted I never bring up at a dinner party again? Of course, I remember."

"Good. You mentioned something I believe you called 'zoonotic' disease that can be shared between humans and animals. If an animal was sick, and it was walking around in the area where a human was working, could the human get the same sickness as the animal?"

There was a brief silence before she replied. "If the animal defecated in the area where the person was working, then the sickness could certainly be spread. Especially if the human ate any plants growing there, or if they got the soil on their hands and touched their mouth afterwards." She paused before continuing. "Is there someone who you think became sick after working around diseased animals?"

I wasn't sure how honest I should be with her, but I finally decided there was nothing to lose by telling her the whole story. I recounted the details of Joshua Barnhill's death, including the time period when it occurred, and the recent information that Mary and Henry shared about the sick cows, only leaving out the part about Bessie Barnhill's ghost visiting me at the cemetery. When I finished the story, I could hear her release a whoosh of breath on the other end of the line.

"That's quite a story. Unfortunately, at that time, very little was known about zoonotic diseases or how to treat them. If Joshua Barnhill had indeed been infected by contact with the feces-contaminated soil of the diseased cows, then he would have died within a few days without treatment. I wonder what the public records would have listed as the cause of death."

"I doubt there were any public records at that time. At least not the type you and I are used to. The deceased was a black man. What they called a freedman back then, which referred to someone who used to be a slave, but later worked for wages. As I understand it from talking to some people who knew his family and were familiar with part of the story, his death was attributed to hoodoo. Black magic, some people call it. The actual cause of his death has been a source of torment for his family since that time." Both living and dead, I thought, but I left that part out.

"Then sharing this information with them should bring some level of comfort. At least they'll understand more about what happened to cause his death. Will you get a chance to talk with any of the remaining family members while you're there?"

I thought about the Reverend Henderson. I should definitely pay him a visit and share what I'd found. Maybe Mary and Henry could be there too. And there was one more person I needed to talk to.

"Yes, I plan to do just that. Thank you so much, Susan. You'll never know how much help it has been for me to talk with you."

"Anytime, Georgia. Give me a call when you're back in Nashville and we'll get together."

I hung up the phone and walked over to the windows of the motel room to look out at the dunes and the ocean beyond. I couldn't see much in the darkness, but just knowing what was out there just beyond the parking lot made my heart swell with pleasure.

I turned away from the window and walked into the adjacent living/dining/kitchenette to where Jon lay sprawled out on the sofa, reading. I sat in an armchair next to the sofa and waited for him to look up.

"I take it you reached Susan Bentley? Did the conversation go well?" He lay his open book on the floor and turned onto his side so he could face me.

"Very well. In fact, I think I finally have the answers I've been looking for. What are you doing tomorrow? Would you be interested in taking a bike ride with me?"

He squinted, considering my question. "Maybe. I have to meet with the construction crew in the morning, and I told Bill Oates I'd stop by his office in the afternoon. What do you have in mind?"

"I need to go to the cemetery. The one I told you about near Harbour Town. After that, I want to see if I can meet with Mary and Henry, and Reverend Henderson."

Jon propped his head up on his hand. “I can arrange to join you when you see the Reverend and the Palmers if you want, but maybe it would be a good idea for you to go to the cemetery by yourself. Your ‘ghost’ might be less inclined to show up if you have a stranger tagging along.”

“You may be right. I’ll bike there while you meet with the construction crew, then we can go together to talk to the Reverend, Mary, and Henry after you see Bill Oates.” I pushed myself up from the chair. “I’ll call them now to set that up.”

CHAPTER THIRTY-THREE

I arranged to meet the Reverend, Mary, and Henry at the church the next afternoon. With that taken care of, I walked down to the reception area to inquire whether Billy's Bike Shop would be open the next morning. Mrs. McKibben's daughter, Sharon, was at the desk again, and she assured me it would be open. She would personally make sure Billy and his brother had a clean and well-oiled bike waiting for me.

I lay awake most of the night staring at the ceiling or checking the clock to see how much more time I had before the sun would be up. When the illuminated clock face showed three in the morning, I finally gave up on my efforts at sleeping and went out into the kitchen to make a cup of tea.

This waking up in the middle of the night thing was beginning to wear on me. My nerves felt raw, I was exhausted, and I could feel my heart fluttering in my chest. I carried my cup to the sofa and sat, tucking my feet under my legs. Ebie promptly hopped up beside me and began walking over my legs until she was able to burrow herself in my lap. I shifted my cup into my left hand so I could stroke her head and back.

"I wish I knew your secret to happiness."

She looked up at me and blinked her eyes slowly as she began the push-pull pattern of her paws on my lap, which meant she was totally content and preparing for sleep.

I sipped my tea, relishing its warmth, then set the cup aside so that I could stretch my legs straight out on the sofa, adjusting Ebie's body so she could move along with me. I scooted down so I could rest my head against the arm of the sofa, closing my eyes and trying to relax. My mind was spinning with images and words, and I tried to still them by counting backwards from one hundred. I remember making it to fifty-five, and the next thing I knew I was awakened by the sun filling my eyes with light pouring in from the front window.

I pushed up to a sitting position, noticing that Ebie was no longer on my lap. When I heard a familiar crunching sound, I knew she was helping herself to some of the dry food in her bowl. The clock on the kitchen wall indicated it was nearly eight. The bike shop opened at nine, so I decided to fix a slice of peanut butter toast and carry it out to the beach so I could loosen my legs and wake up a bit before picking up the bike. My stomach had been queasy off and on for a week or so, and I found that peanut butter toast helped to settle it.

I peeked in the bedroom and noticed Jon was already up. When I went to the bathroom, I noticed a folded note propped up against the toothbrush holder:

> *Gone to check on the work at the house. Have a good bike ride and I'll see you back here around Noon.*

I dressed quickly, pulling on a pair of khaki shorts and a pale blue t-shirt and sandals.

There were already several people walking on the beach when I arrived. The tide was low, which meant there was a lot of firm sand to walk on between the dunes and the water. I turned to my left and began walking in the opposite direction from the Holiday Inn and the Tiki Hut. The sky was a cloudless blue, marred only by a flight of pelicans flying in a V formation nearly touching the water. Occasionally, one of them lifted slightly from the rest before diving beak first into the ocean. It emerged to rest on top of the water until its catch was safely swallowed, before pushing off again to rejoin the others.

I continued walking for another thirty minutes or so, finishing my peanut butter toast and a cup of coffee I grabbed from the reception area as I was leaving. I turned around to head back to Billy's Bike Shop. True to her word, Sharon had called ahead to make sure the brothers had a bike ready for me. I paid for a two-day rental and hopped on the bike to head down the paved path that led to the Sea Pines entrance. I decided to bike directly up to the gate, stopping to pay the $3 fee required of non-residents who wanted to bike inside the Resort.

The ride to Harbour Town took about twenty-five minutes from the time I passed through the gated entrance. The path took me past lagoons where I could spot partially submerged alligators, long-legged blue herons, snowy white egrets, and an occasional Anhinga with wings outspread to allow its feathers to dry in the sun. My route also took me around the Sea Pines stables where I stopped for a drink from the thermos of water I carried in the basket that hung from the handlebars.

I turned off the path just before reaching Harbour Town so I could loop around past the yacht basin to the cemetery. I leaned my bike against a tree and made my way toward the wooden rocking chair where I first spotted Bessie Barnhill, stepping carefully between the stones that marked the numerous graves located there.

Everything looked the same as the last time I visited with Julie, except the rocking chair was once more upright and facing the nearby grave of Joshua Barnhill. I glanced around the cemetery, unsure of whether I should sit somewhere or remain standing as I hoped for Bessie's arrival. It didn't seem right to sit inside the graveyard, so I walked over to the side and leaned against the wooden fence.

The sun was well up in the sky by the time I arrived, but the nearby buildings blocked the sun from the entire area, giving it a somewhat creepy feeling. I shuddered and wrapped my arms around my body, wondering how long I would have to wait for some sign from Bessie, or if she would even show up. The thought I might not be able to tell her what I learned caused my heart to sink.

After I had been waiting about 15 minutes, I heard a sound like boards creaking from a weight that was laid upon them. I glanced in the direction of the rocking chair and saw its gentle swaying motion. My hand automatically moved to cover the amulet through my shirt. It felt warm and dry in contrast to the clamminess of my sweat-soaked skin.

I kept my eyes fixed on the chair as I noticed the gradual appearance of the wispy image of a woman. As the image became clearer, there was no mistaking it was Bessie. I held my breath until she finally turned to look in my direction.

"Bin wait'n' fuh oonuh. Time don' madduh much on dis side, but seem uh w'ile."

I pushed away from the fence so I could walk a little closer to where she sat. "I've been trying to find some answers about what happened to your grandfather. It took me a while to figure it out."

The light in her eyes seem to grow brighter as she gazed at me with expectation. "Wha' oonuh fin'?"

"I believe your grandfather was poisoned. But not by a person, by the soil he worked in. I was told he used the urine from pregnant cows in the vats of water where he soaked the indigo plants. He believed it would help get the richest color from the dye. The pregnant cows were kept in a shed near the indigo vats. The door to the shed broke open one evening, and the cows ended up grazing on the indigo that grew nearby. It seems that one or more of the cows was sick. They had some kind of bug that messed up their intestines and eventually killed them.

"I met someone who knows a lot about this illness. She said it can be transferred from the sick cows to a human, especially if the person comes in contact with soil that has remnants of the intestinal contents of the animals. Since your grandfather worked in that soil, it's quite likely he was contaminated by the same little bugs. We can't know this for certain, because they didn't keep public health records back in those days. But since the symptoms he had before his death were the same as the ones shown by the cows, it's likely they shared the same disease."

Bessie shook her head slowly. "Unh, unh, unh. Sick f'um de cows? Wha' 'bout dat reb'ren? De one dat pit uh spell on deh groun'. Could'n' de spell mek me grum'pa git de cow's sickness?

I wasn't sure how to answer her question. It was still possible there was something else going on that could have contributed to her grandfathers' illness, but that was outside of my realm of knowledge. All I could do was relay the facts as I understood them. I guess it came down to my reporter's instinct, which said that Bessie's grandfather died because public health care in those days was sorely lacking, especially for slaves and freedmen.

"I don't think so. In particular, because that reverend, whose name I was told was Thomas Henderson, was your grandfather's nephew and your uncle. I met his son recently, whose name is also Tom Henderson, and he told me his daddy felt really bad about what happened to your grandfather. Said he moved north because of it."

She looked off into the distance before nodding her agreement. "'E me farruh's bubbuh. 'E son, Tom junior, play 'roun we house. Sad w'en dey moobe 'way." She shook her head slowly. "Uh fo'git 'bout dat. Reckon grum'pa' de't' twist uh t'ink'n. W'en dey 'bout tuh moobe up nawt', axe'um did wan'go wid dem. Say uh redduh stay yuh. Haffuh fin' ansuh. Din' know how dat gon' happen till see oonuh. Bring uh back tuh de light."

My hand went to the amulet again. Bessie must have noticed, because she looked directly at where I was pressing.

"Oonuh hab' dat sack? Wha' 'e do?"

"It's growing hotter. Before we started speaking it was barely warm."

"Humph. Dat cha'm tell if wha' b'leebe tru', be de trute. If 'e de't' be debblement or Gawd doin'."

I suddenly remembered what she told me about the amulet when she gave it to me. "You said it would help me know what to do when the time was right. I thought you were talking about my boyfriend who, by the way, is my husband now."

Her face lit up with a grin. "Dat rite? Uh glad fuh oonuh. De cha'm tell 'bout lot ub t'ings. Lub, wu'k, weh lib." She paused and seemed to look deep into my eyes. "Uh t'ink you fin' de ansuh. Not jis' 'bout uh grum'pa, 'bout mo' t'ings den dat. Got tuh 'cide w'ich way tuh go. Can' be walkin' mo' dan one paat' at uh time. Dishyuh uh debble uh t'ing, but now uh know wuz acksident, won' agguhnize obuh 'e no mo'. Kin res' um bones now." She nodded in the direction of her grandfather's grave. "Bofe we kin res'."

She rocked slowly as she stared at her grandfather's gravestone, finally looking up at me with what appeared to be tears glistening in her eyes. "Uh 'preciate wha' oonuh dun' fo' we."

We continued looking at each other for a long moment as she gradually began to fade from sight. Just as her image was about to disappear, I shouted at her to stop.

"Wait, Miss Bessie! I need to know one last thing before you go."

Her image began to fill in again as her eyes turned to mine. "Wha' oonuh needin', chile?"

"I want to understand why you choose to appear to me? I didn't know your family. I'm not from around here, and I'm not even familiar with the Gullah beliefs. What made you think I might be able to help?"

She smiled softly as she stared at the sky and began to rock slowly in the chair. "Fus' time oonuh cum' 'roun, uh know. Don' hab de same lan'widge but uh shum de trute een oonuh haa't.

Knew oonuh was boun' tuh fin' de ansa an' won' gib up 'til 'e foun'.

"Odduh folks kum' 'roun. Some same fambly wid we. Don' mean dey kin hep. Eb'ry frog praise 'e ownt pond on top, but tek mo' tuh fin' de boddum. B'leebe oonuh wan' tuh fin' de boddum dis story."

Her words touched me deeply. They implied that she looked deep inside of me and found me worthy of her trust. "I don't know what to say. I'm flattered that you believed I could help, but more importantly, I'm so happy I could."

"'E be alrigh' now. Jis' trus' de haa't. An keep dat cha'm clo'tu oonah. Hab' mo trute fo oonah dat hep 'cide oonah pat'."

Her image began to fade again. I watched it until I couldn't see her anymore, then walked over to the rocking chair and caressed the wooden slats that had supported her back. They were smooth to the touch but bore no warmth, unlike the person who I had understood her to be.

I smiled at the memory of our first meeting, and the two times that followed. Who would have thought I would have found a friend in such an unusual way?

I stood for a long time in that graveyard, waiting to see if Bessie would return. Hoping to get one more chance to talk to her. Her last words kept echoing in my mind, like a favorite song that keeps spinning on the turntable. Jis' trus' de haa't. Jis' trus' de haa't.

As I turned to walk toward my bicycle, I could feel a lightness in my steps I hadn't felt for some time.

CHAPTER THIRTY-FOUR

That afternoon, Jon and I drove to the First African Church where we arranged to meet Mary, Henry, and the Reverend Tom Henderson. The building felt familiar to me now, like a welcoming lamp that shone through the darkness to guide my journey.

When Jon and I stepped through the front door of the church, the others were already inside waiting. I looked at each of their faces. Mary's glowed with warmth while Henry's looked peaceful and kind. It was clear that they took comfort from the two worlds they straddled: their Christian faith, which enriched their daily lives, and their African Gullah heritage, which kept them firmly rooted to the past in sometimes supernatural ways. The Reverend's face was harder to read. He looked as though he was uncertain how to act as he shifted from one foot to the other and flipped his straw hat between his hands.

Mary walked briskly toward us and gave me a hug. "How oonuh be, chile?"

Her sudden, but not totally unexpected gesture caused my throat to fill with emotion so I could only nod in her direction.

Jon smiled at her and went to shake the hands of the two men. "Let's sit. Georgia has a lot to share with all of you."

The men moved five of the wooden chairs from the back of the church and placed them in the middle of the space between the two rows of pews. After taking a deep breath, I proceeded to tell them all I had learned. About the illness that was likely passed between the sick cows and Joshua. About my odd encounters with Bessie at the cemetery and our most recent exchange. About how she told me she felt at peace now with her grandfather's death, just before she faded from sight.

I also took out the amulet she had given me and held it in the palm of my hand for them to see.

"Bessie gave me this the first time I met her. She told me it would help me know what to do when the time was right. Ever since then, I've worn it under my clothes near my heart, and I've noticed it grows warm—hot even—whenever I reach the right decision regarding something I've been struggling with."

I turned to look directly at Jon. "It was scorching hot the day you asked me to marry you. That's how I knew in my heart it was right, even though my mind wasn't so sure." I shifted so I could look at Henry and Mary. "It throbbed every time I saw either of you, even though you scared me sometimes with your kindness and honesty." Finally, I looked at Reverend Tom. "And it started heating up the minute you told me that Joshua was your great uncle, and explained how your uncle Moses felt heartbroken at Joshua's death.

"I don't believe Joshua's death had anything to do with witchcraft or whatever you want to call it. I think it was just the result of a series of unfortunate events, and I think what Bessie would want us to do, and what HE would want us to do, is to put it to rest and let his memory live on in peace."

The reverend looked at Mary and Henry, who looked at each other. For a moment, I thought I had said the wrong thing, but luckily the reverend stood and put my mind at ease. "I think you're right, Miss Georgia. Nothing good ever came of holding on to a worry just because we've been living with it for a long while." He turned so he could glance at Mary and Henry, both of whom nodded their agreement. He turned back to me. "I'm grateful to you. To both of you." He looked at Jon, who shook his head from side to side.

"It was all Georgia. I've just been a silent observer in all of this. She's the one with the courage and the tenacity to see it through." He took my hand in his. "She's something else."

His words moved me deeply. I wasn't sure I agreed with his depiction of himself as a silent observer. Jon had a way of saying a lot, even when he said very little. Just knowing I could follow my hunches without worrying about what he would think of me, gave me strength.

Mary took my hand in hers. "'E special. Knowed 'e fus' time uh see huh. Hab uh good haa't, 'n brains tuh match. Seek dey trute til' fin' 'e. Don' let nutt'n' stop huh 'fo' 'e know wha' right." She squeezed my hand before releasing it so she could clap her hands together. "Well! 'Spect us all hongry aftuh all dis bidness. 'Enry an' me eenbite oonuh kum tuh suppuh. Got swimp ready tuh bile an' taters een de oben. Ripe maters, and watuhmelyun fo' attuh." She gave Jon a smug look, then playfully reached out to take his arm and started for the door. "Eben pick up some uh dat drink 'enry say oonuh lukkuh."

Jon laid his hand over Mary's. "You had me at shrimp, Mary, but I could sure use a drink about now."

We made arrangements to meet up again at Mary and Henry's in half an hour, which would give them enough time to get there before us and do whatever they needed to do to get ready for our arrival. Reverend Tom declined the invitation explaining he was scheduled to give an evening service at a church in Charleston, so we said our goodbyes to him and stepped outside together.

I took a deep breath of the salt scented air and smiled with relief at the two men who stood on either side of me. Jon returned my smile with a wink, and the Reverend nodded as he pulled his hat firmly onto his head. He reached into the front pocket of his shirt and handed me a black and white photograph. It was a picture of two men, two women, and a young boy standing in a field covered in flower-filled plants. He pointed to each of the people in turn. "This was my great-uncle Joshua, my father, Aunt Bessie, my mother, and me. You can't tell from the picture, but those plants were full of bright, blue flowers."

I studied the photograph carefully. "Indigo." I looked at him for confirmation.

He nodded with a smile. "Yes. This was taken right before great-uncle Joshua made up his first batch of dye." He shook his head slowly. "I never would have thought that such pretty things could bring such misery."

I rested my hand on his arm and nodded, knowing there was nothing more I could say that would help.

Reverend Henderson touched the brim of his straw hat in a farewell gesture saying, "May God's peace go with you," before walking in the direction of the parking lot.

Jon and I stood where we were for a few minutes, enjoying the late afternoon sunlight and allowing the gentle sea breeze flowing from the nearby shore to drift over us.

I linked my arm through Jon's and he turned to me. "I forgot to ask how your meeting with Bill Oates went," I said.

He reached into the back pocket of his jeans and pulled out a folded paper which he shook open and held in front of me. "We are now proud owners of a house on the beach."

My eyes grew wide as I stared at the piece of paper. I had been expecting that everything would go well with the purchase, but somehow seeing it in print caught me off guard.

"So, it's a done deal? The house is ours?"

"Yep. As soon as the renovations are complete, we can move in. Or at least we can figure out how much of the old furnishings we want to keep and what to replace. I thought that was something you and Julie might find enjoyable."

My face lit up with pleasure. "I saw a couple of stores on the island, the last time Julie and I were here, that sell used household goods. Furniture, glassware, rugs, pretty much everything that someone might need for a new house. Maybe I can get her to come back for a visit and see what we can find."

He grinned at my excitement. "I don't see why not. I could use Harry's opinion on how to go about continuing to build on what we've started here anyway. Once the house is finished, there'll be plenty of room for all of us."

I looked at him hesitantly. "I might have mentioned something to Susan Bentley too, about coming for a visit."

He shook his head in disbelief. "I guess you've already started to find reasons why we can't sell the house right away."

When I started to protest, he waved his hand in dismissal. "Don't worry about it. Frankly, I'm in no hurry to get rid of it either. Why don't we just take our time and figure out our next move?"

His words were a great relief. "That sounds great. There's so much to figure out anyway, what with the change in your job and the possibility of me working on PR for Thomas' program. I haven't even spoken to the guy at the local paper about the column you mentioned either. I think taking things a step at a time is a good plan."

Jon agreed. Or at least he didn't disagree. It was more like a silent truce where no words were needed to express what we felt. That was a rarity between Jon and me, but I was beginning to realize there were a lot of things I had come to assume about my husband that were not necessarily correct.

I looked at him with new appreciation. "Ready for dinner?" I asked.

"Ready for a drink," he replied.

Well, I guess some things hadn't changed after all…

GULLAH-ENGLISH DICTIONARY

A list of Gullah words used in this book with their English translation beside them.

Gullah Word	English Word
aa'my	army
Acksident	accident
Aff'iky	Africa
aftuh	after
agguhnize	agonize
ah'mee	army
alltime	always
alltwo	both
an'	and
ansuh	answer
ankyhall	alcohol
attuh	after
attuh dat	after that
attuh'e gwin	after she was gone
attuhw'ile	after awhile
ax	ask
ax'um	ask him/her/it/them
baa'n	barn
ba'tis'	baptist
bawn	born
Beaufor'	Beaufort
bed child	infant/toddler
behime	behind
bes'	best
bettuh	better
bex tek'um	anger overcame her/him
b'fo'	before
bidness	business
bile	boil
bin	been/was
binnuh	was a
bis'tor	visitor
bittle	food
bizzit	visit
blan-b'long	used to belong
b'leebe	believe
candl'light'n'	dusk
cawd	called
'cide	decide
'citin'	exciting
clearin'	clearing
col'	cold
contraban'	contraband
cooluh	cooler
cos'	cost
co'se	of course
could'uh	could have
coundee	county
crack 'e teet	speak/say anything
creetuh	creatures

crick creek
cum come
cumfuh'ble comfortable
cump'ny company
cumpuhsayshun conversation
cuz'n cousin
cya' carry
cyas cast
daa'k dark
daa'tuh daughter
dan than
dat that

dat beat me time! (expression of surprise)
dayclean sunrise
de the
debble devil
debblement devilment
deestrus' distressed
dem them
demse'f themselves
den then
dere there
dese these
de't death
dey they
din' didn't
dinnuh dinner
dis this
dishyuh this here
'do though
do' door
'do' although
doctuh doctor
do'um do it
don' don't
drap drop
dun' done
'e he/she/it
'ead head
eben even
ebenin' evening
ebil evil
eb'n even
eb'ry ever
eb'ryt'ing everything
een in
eeduh either
eenbite invite
ef if
'enry Henry
enty isn't she
'ese'f himself
exwice advice
eye duh leak cry
faa'm farm
fambly family
farruh father
fav'rite favorite
fetch get/bring
fiah fire
fibe five
fin' find
firs' first
fi'teen fifteen
fo' for
'fo' before
fo'eber forever
fo'git forget
foun' found

freedmun freedmen
fren(s) friend(s)
fuh for
fuhgit forget
fuhr'um for
him/her/it/them
f'um from
fun'real funeral
fus' first
Gawd God
gedduh gather
gedduh tuhgedduhgather
together
g'em gave
her/him/it/them
'gen again/against
Gen'rl General
gib give
git get
gi'we gave us
gone-'cross died (gone
across)
grabe grave
grebe grieve
grum'pa
grandfather/grandpa
gubmunt government
gwine going
gun-shoot war
haa'buh harbor
haa'd hard
haa'dly hardly
haant haunt
haants ghosts
haa't heart
hab have
habin' having
haffuh have to
hangry hungry
happ'n happen
happ'n long drop
in/visit unexpectedly
hawspittle hospital
hea' hear
hebby heavy

hebby belly great
appetite
he'lt health
hep help
his own him own
hisself himself
hol' hold
hongry hungry
huccome how come
hun'ud hundred
i'lun' island
jis' just
jisso just so
'joy enjoy
Juntlemun husband
ketch catch
kep' kept
kin can
laa'n l earn(ing)/teach(ing)
lan'widge language
las' last
lawfully lady wife
leabe leave
leetle little
leh let

le'm'lone let him/her/it/them alone
lib live
libben living
light out leave hurriedly
'lone alone
lonesum' lonely
'long along
longside connect the two
long talk gossip
los' lost
'lot alot
'low allow(ed)
'low'um allow me
lub love
luk/lukkuh like
maa'k mark
maa'sh marsh
maamy mother
madduh matter
'magine imagine

mainlan' mainland
mannus manners
maters tomatoes
mawnin' morning
med'sin medicine
meetin' meeting
mek make
mek'ace make haste
'membuh remember
'memb'unce remembrance
migh' might
min' mind/mine
mo' more
mo' nuh more than
moobe move
'morrow tomorrow
mos' most
'mos' almost
mout' mouth
munt month
murruh mother
mus'e must be
navuh neighbor
nawt' north
nebbuh never
needin' needing
needuh neither
nemmin' never mind
'nuf enough
numbuh number
'nurruh another
nuss nurse
nutt'n nothing
nyuse used
obuh over
odduh other
odduh'res' the others/the rest
offuh offer
okffuhr'um offer he/she/it/them
onduhstan' understand
oshtuh oyster
ooman woman
oonuh you
ownt own
pa father
paa't part(s)

paat' path
paa'ty party
pastuh pastor
'paw'tun' important
'pear appear
pi'chuh pitcher
playin' playing
pledjuh pleasure
po' poor
po'ch porch
'portun' important
'preciate appreciate
Puhtekshun protection
puhtickluh particular
'quaintun' acquainted
queschun question
rebil' rebuilt
Reb'ren' Reverend
redduh rather
remin' remind
repeah appear(ed)
res' rest
resplain explain
'roun' around
rite right
rockuh cheer rocking chair
'roun around
Sabannah Savannah
san' sand
seben seven
seddown sit down
se'f self
shet shut
sho' sure
sho'ent sure don't
shuguh sugar
shum see/saw
slabes slaves
sol' sold
'spect expect
'spect'n expecting
spen' spend

sperrit spirit
'speshly especially
'splain explain
'spose' supposed
staa't start
'stablish establish
stan' appears to be
star' start
stet state
stillyet still/yet
sto' store
strengk strength
sty'foam Styrofoam
sum some
summuch so much
summuh summer
sump'n' something
sump'n'nurruh something or another
sum'time sometime
sun-lean sundown/dus
swimp shrimp
tas'e taste
taters potatoes
tek take
tem'chuh temperature
'ten' attend
ten' tent

‘tention attention
tetch touch/small amount
timbuh timber
t’ink think
t’ing(s) thing(s)
t’ird third
t’irty thirty
todduh the other
tol’ told
‘trac’ attract
tran’po’tation transportation
truk truck
trus’ trust
tru’ true
trute truth

tuh to
tuh’day today
tuhgedduh together
tuhreckly directly
tummuch too much
twelb twelve
‘tween between
ub of
uh I
uhhead’uh way up ahead a way
um them
ustuh used to
‘ventually eventually
wait’n’ waiting
wan’ want
warruh what I
watuh water
wawn warn
‘way away
wedduh weather
weh where
w’en when
wha’ what
wid with
w’ile while
windo’ window
wintuh winter
wiskey whiskey
Wi’um William
wuh what
wu’k work
wurry worry
wuss’ worst
wusshup worship
wuz was
yalluh yellow
yeah year
yeddy hear
yeddy’um hear them
yent am/did/do not
yez ear(s)
yez tuh yez grin broadly
yuh here
‘zackly exactly
‘zammine examine

A FEW GULLAH PROVERBS/SAYINGS USED IN THIS NOVEL

Dog got four feet but can't walk but one road. (No matter how many things you'd like to do, you can only do one thing at a time.)

Every frog praise e ownt pond. (It is expected that one will speak favorably of one's self or one's kin folk disregarding the accuracy of the statement.)

Leetle pitcher got big ears. (Be careful what you say around little children, they may be able to understand more than you think they can.)

De sun lean fuh down. (The sun is beginning to set.)

Een he'lt' cows. (Refers to pregnant cows)

ANNELL ST. CHARLES

Following a long career in the medical profession, Annell St. Charles turned her attention to writing fiction and producing photography. Her first two novels, "The Things Left Unsaid" and "The Choices We Make", were published in 2016. She also has two books of photography, "Sunrise On Hilton Head Island: Coligny Beach" and "Island Life", and a book of poetry, "The Clam Shell", also published in 2016. She has been a member of the self-proclaimed "Greater Nashville Book and Wine Club" for around 20 years (who she describes as her toughest critics and greatest friends), and holds a certificate in digital photography from the Shaw Institute. She is an avid walker and can usually be found roaming the streets and beaches around her homes in Nashville, Tennessee and Hilton Head Island with her camera slung over one shoulder while she ponders her next work of fiction. She is married to Constantine Tsinakis, and borrows her friends "Ebie-like cats every chance she gets.